DEATH OF A MYSTERY GUEST

Also by Alex Coombs

The Old Forge Café Mysteries

Murder on the Menu

Death in Nonna's Kitchen

A Knife in the Back

The Hanlon PI Series

Silenced for Good

Missing for Good

Buried for Good

The DCI Hanlon Series

The Stolen Child

The Innocent Girl

The Missing Husband

The Silent Victims

DEATH OF A MYSTERY GUEST

ALEX COOMBS

NO EXIT PRESS

First published in the UK in 2025 by No Exit Press,
an imprint of Bedford Square Publishers Ltd,
London, UK

noexit.co.uk
@noexitpress

A CIP catalogue record for this book is available from
the British Library.

This is a work of fiction. Names, characters, places, and incidents
either are the product of the author's imagination or are used fictitiously,
and any resemblance to actual persons, living or dead, businesses,
companies, events or locales is entirely coincidental.

ISBN
978-1-83501-117-1 (Paperback)
978-1-83501-118-8 (eBook)

2 4 6 8 10 9 7 5 3 1

Typeset by Palimpsest Book Production Limited, Falkirk, Stirlingshire

Printed in Great Britain by CPI Group (UK) Ltd, Croydon CR0 4YY

The manufacturer's authorised representative in the EU for product safety
is Easy Access System Europe, Mustamäe tee 50, 10621 Tallinn, Estonia

gpsr.requests@easproject.com

For Chef Kevin Hay,
thanks for the cookery lessons

Chapter One

Moray Place, in Edinburgh's New Town, is large and circular in shape, fed by four cobbled roads at the cardinal points and a funereal, residents only, garden in the centre behind sensible black railings. It's a place of Apollonian order and unostentatious wealth.

The buildings are classically Georgian in style, semi-circles of four storey grandeur. It is beautifully proportioned. The stone of the houses is a very pale honey colour, mottled and streaked with a darker patina from years of pollution. Windows are long and narrow, here they run floor to ceiling and the doors to the townhouses are huge. But as I arrived in the black cab at the Moray Place Hotel on that dark winter afternoon, it wasn't the architecture that drew my eye, it was the ambulance.

The one and only time I saw my new head chef, although I didn't know it at the time, was his shiny black work boots, as the stretcher on which he lay slid into the waiting vehicle and the paramedics banged the doors shut behind him.

Then the blue light came on and the ambulance sped away into the gloomy grey afternoon.

I got out of the taxi and went up to a small group of people, shell-shocked in their kitchen whites, assembled by the side of the road.

'Hello everybody,' I said brightly, 'my name's Charlie Hunter, I'm your new chef.'

Chapter Two

A week before this dramatic start to a new job, I had no inkling I would be in Edinburgh at all.

It was the last week of October and I was in my local pub discussing Christmas menus with Graeme Strickland, Michelin starred chef in the restaurant up the road and close personal friend.

I had just finalised my Christmas menu which would run 25 November to 25 December. I was open Christmas Day. I'd give everyone else the day off and do it myself, Jess had volunteered to come in and work from twelve until three. Christmas lunch at her house was served for some reason at 4 o'clock.

My menu was straightforward but good. I was pleased with it. Starters: salmon gravadlax, homemade rye bread; celeriac and apple soup, garlic and parmesan croutons; ham hock terrine with cranberries.

Mains: turkey with all the trimmings; roast cod on a bed of roast seasonal veg, beurre blanc; goat's cheese, walnut and vegetable tart.

Desserts: Christmas pudding, crème anglaise; sticky toffee pudding; selection of local cheeses.

I would also say that like many chefs, I cannot stand cooking turkey and Brussels sprouts every day for a month. Let's just say you can go off things.

I pulled a face at the thought of Christmas, had a swig of red wine and pulled another face. God it was awful. You didn't have to be a connoisseur to know that. Every so often I have a drink of the Three Bells red wine just to confirm it was as bad as I remembered. I was never disappointed.

'Christmas, eh,' Strickland said, smiling, 'only time I ever overcook veg. Have you ever tried serving sprouts al dente at Christmas?'

'Only once,' I said, shuddering at the memory. I'd sent them out still with a bit of bite to them. It had been a disaster; people don't want their Brussels sprouts perfectly cooked, they want them soggy. As I soon found out from the first customers to order the Christmas menu, the Thursday Group, a collection of old age pensioners. Jesus, the row from the restaurant! 'These are raw!' 'Ugh, disgusting.' 'What are you trying to do? Poison us?' And those were some of the milder comments.

'So why did you want to see me?' I asked, pushing the memory aside. Strickland had called me the night before wanting to meet up after service. This was unusual. He was a busy guy, he wouldn't have called for simply a chat.

'Do you remember your first head chef?' he asked. He was a small, neat, good-looking man, about my age. An air of steely efficiency enveloped him at all times; he was immensely self-assured. Maybe that comes with being so successful, it's far from easy to get a star.

The question surprised me. 'Yeah, of course… why?'

'Mine was called Dave Holland, big bloke, kind of over-weight, great cook, traditional French cuisine.'

'Nice…' I said.

'Yeah, he's a great bloke, we've always kept in touch, he's probably my oldest friend.'

I was wondering where was all this leading. Strickland wasn't one for cosy reminiscence. Things had to have a definite purpose in his universe and fond memories did not make the cut.

'Yeah, he part owns a hotel in Edinburgh. He runs the kitchen there, his sous has left suddenly and he was asking if I knew anyone who could do a bit of temping while he sorts a replacement.'

I shrugged. What was this to do with me?

Strickland leaned forward over the table, his brown eyes boring into mine, his next question taking me by surprise. 'You know how you've always wanted to go to Scotland?'

I blinked in surprise, this was news to me. Although, now he had suggested it, I wouldn't mind. But I was pretty sure I had never raised it as a thing.

'Do I?' I asked. Perplexed, wondering what he was on about. Then I realised what he was suggesting.

'No Graeme,' I shook my head firmly, 'I don't want to go and work for your mate up in Edinburgh.'

'Yes, of course you do,' he said in exasperation, pulling a kind of 'Doh!' face. 'He's a great chef and a good guy to be around. He's one of those larger than life people… likes a laugh, great bants, never loses his temper...' So not like you, Graeme, I thought. 'Not like me,' he added. Well, I had to hand it to him, he wasn't blind to his faults. 'Really good with his other chefs, trainees love him.' He smiled reminiscently. 'Obsessed with mushrooms. I learnt a lot from him and so will you. It'll take your cooking to another level and give you new ideas.' He sat back, looking at me expectantly. One of the traits that made Strickland so successful was his incredible certainty about things. Even when he was totally wrong, like now.

'And you think I should go there, do you?' God knows why I was asking him, I knew I had no particular desire to go.

'Of course you should.' His confidence undented. 'You're always saying you never get to go anywhere and that you could do with getting out of the village for a bit.'

'Well, yes...' That was certainly true, but I had meant somewhere hot and sunny... Barbados maybe. Certainly not Scotland in November. And most certainly not being a sous in a fine-dining restaurant. Presumably Strickland thought that either I would benefit from some cookery lessons from his former mentor, or that it would be work that I could do without too much thinking, leaving my mind free to marvel at what I could be seeing of Scotland's capital city if I wasn't chained to a stove. Neither seemed overly appealing.

'Edinburgh's very scenic, you'll see.'

'Oh will I?' I said sarcastically.

'Yes, you will, Charlie. I'll arrange cover for you for a fortnight.' He smiled winningly. 'A break from the norm is exactly what you need.' He nodded approvingly at his wisdom. 'It'll reinvigorate you; a change is as good as a rest.'

'In Edinburgh?' I said incredulously.

'Yes, in Edinburgh. That's the place you need to be.'

'Graeme,' I said, 'I'm not going to Scotland.'

Then, with the air and the flourish of a man laying a trump card, he said, 'It'll take your mind off Christmas.'

And so, of course, I did.

Chapter Three

I arrived at the Moray Place Hotel in time to see the ambulance that would take Dave Holland, Strickland's oldest friend, off to hospital.

I got out of the taxi with my suitcase and knife box. Assembled on the pavement in front of the steps of the discreetly signposted hotel were what I assumed was the kitchen brigade. There was a burly, overweight elderly guy in a T-shirt and jeans and an apron who I assumed was the kp, the kitchen-porter or washer-upper. There was a skinny blond man, with extremely blond, practically white hair, like Julian Assange, whom he resembled slightly, and another chef, a young, dark-haired girl who looked like a teenager. I guessed she was the apprentice. The three of them looked stupefied.

I walked over to them, greeted them and then I said politely, 'I'm looking for the head chef.'

'You've just missed him, hen,' said pot-wash guy, 'he's awa' in the ambulance.'

'Oh God, no,' I said with alarm. 'Nothing too serious?'

'Heart,' said the blond guy. Decisively. He looked around him, chin lifted as if expecting dissent.

'We dinnae know that yet, Euan,' pot-wash guy said. Euan frowned and opened his mouth to speak. It looked like an argument was brewing. Just then the front door of the hotel opened and a woman walked out. She was about my age I guessed, very elegant in a short black skirt and jacket. She glared down at us from the top of the stairs.

'Show's over,' she said, in a voice like a whip-crack. 'Back to the kitchen.'

Obediently, the group shuffled away. She looked down at me, standing alone on the pavement with my cases.

'Can I help you?' she said, looking down at me, icily polite. I heard my dead father's voice in my head: 'Lady Muck.'

'I'm Charlie Hunter,' I said, staring up at her, 'I'm expected.'

'Oh,' she said, looking momentarily nonplussed, 'I thought you were a man.'

'Well, I'm not,' I said, helpfully.

'Do come in,' she said, somewhat put-out by being wrong-footed. I started to walk up the steps towards the entrance flanked by two high Doric columns, so it was like entering a temple or a church. She opened the door and held it open for me and shouted, 'Donald!'

A silver-haired guy in a dark suit, medium height, slim build, appeared. He looked very neat, very well-groomed. His hair had a ruler-straight side parting and a slight flick to it at the front.

'Come and take this lady's suitcase, please.'

'Certainly.' His black brogues glinted in the dying afternoon light. I shivered; it was very cold and a breeze was getting up.

'Thank you,' I said as he took my bag and we walked up the last few broad steps together, me admiring his gleaming footwear. I appreciate a man who takes care of his shoes.

'My pleasure,' he replied with a slight head tilt and a hint of a wink, a conspiratorial gesture, as if the whole thing was some kind of game we were playing to humour the woman at the top of the stairs.

As we drew level to her she held her hand out. 'I'm Lorna Farson. I'm the manager here.'

She was slim and good-looking, wearing black killer heels and dark tights, the kind that you just know are extremely expensive. She was wearing a gold necklace that contrasted well with the crisp white blouse. I bet it had been ironed within an inch of its life. She had a broad, generous mouth, the kind that rich women pay a fortune to surgeons to get and never do.

'So.' Brisk tone. 'You're Charlie,' she said, 'I do apologise for my mistake, Dave never said... do come in.'

We went inside through the tall, imposing doors of the hotel into the lobby and I got my first proper look at the Moray Place Hotel. The inside of the hotel was classic, old-school luxury. Dull gold wallpaper, heavy gilt-framed pictures of Scottish scenery and architectural drawings from yesteryears of plans and designs for Edinburgh New Town. The ceilings were very high, with an elaborate moulding picked out in gold surrounding, the mounting for a huge, glittering chandelier, and the carpet was very thick. There was a smell of pot-pourri and moneyed calm. The inevitable stag's head on the wall looked down on us with its glassy eyes. A young guy, maybe about twenty, in a dark suit sat behind the desk, pale, with mousy hair and androgynous features. He smiled at me nervously.

'This is Craig,' Lorna said then introduced me. Craig murmured something about being pleased to meet me. He looked painfully shy and had a very soft voice, almost feminine. His handshake was soft and delicate.

Lorna led me past a bar, Donald was bringing up the rear with my case. I glanced inside; wood-panelling, high ceilings, leather chesterfields, more stags' heads on the wall, stuffed birds and animals in cases, and I could see a sign pointing upstairs to the restaurant. That caught my attention. Lorna noticed this.

'The restaurant is upstairs on the first floor,' she informed me, 'that way the best tables get a view over the square and the others benefit from the natural light. It's quite sizeable.'

'How many does it take?' I asked.

'Forty. We'll go and look at it later... now, let's go in my office. Donald will take your bags to your room.'

'Thanks, Donald,' I said.

'No problem, Chef.' He smiled at me warmly. 'It'll be nice having you around.'

I returned his smile. 'Call me Charlie.' He bowed his head in acknowledgement and turned away. I liked Donald, he looked friendly without being obsequious, and capable. Just the combination you need in a front-desk person.

12

We walked down the corridor, past the bar and a door leading to the toilets. There was another door at the end marked 'Private'. Next to it, another door marked 'Staff Only'. Indicating it, Lorna said, 'That will take you down to the kitchen.'

'That's in the basement then?'

'Yes.' Seeing my slight confusion she explained. 'We have a lift to send the food up to the restaurant.'

'Oh, I see.'

She unlocked the door marked 'Private' and ushered me inside. The office was as uncluttered as I expected. It matched its owner. Sleek, tidy, well-organised, not a hair out of place. We sat down opposite each other. An open laptop on her desk connected to a couple of screens, a black filing cabinet and a bookshelf with neatly arranged papers and a couple of awards prominently displayed. Last year she had been awarded Hotel Manager of the Year by some association I had never heard of.

'So what's happening with the chef?' I asked. 'Someone mentioned a heart attack.'

'We don't know. It only happened half an hour ago. But it wouldn't surprise me at all.' Lorna sighed. 'Dave was overweight, never exercised, drank too much… hopefully it's nothing too serious.'

'So, who's running the kitchen?' I asked. It was kind of a stupid question really.

She looked me in the eye.

'As of now, you are.'

Chapter Four

We left her office, my mind still processing the implications of what she had just said. It was very unwelcome news. I had been expecting a moderately hard time in Edinburgh but not the enormous task of running a strange kitchen with no real guidance.

Lorna wanted me to see the kitchen and meet the brigade before they went home. She had already explained that there was no Sunday evening food and that Room Service for food was within kitchen hours. The kitchen was closed on a Monday except for breakfast. There was a separate bar menu, most of which was taken from the main menu, but simplified.

We opened the door marked 'Staff Only' next to her office and descended the stairs into the basement kitchen. The door at the bottom was controlled by a keypad. 'I'll text you the number,' Lorna said as she pushed the door open and ushered me inside.

The kitchen occupied the entire basement in one gigantic room. As we emerged into it and stood blinking in the harsh, bright light, I looked around at what would be my

15

kingdom for the next couple of weeks, inventorying my workspace.

I could see in the far corner what looked like a walk-in fridge. There were a couple of other fridges, big uprights next to it, and a small walk-in freezer, about the size of a large wardrobe. There was a large range and chargrill, a dual unit deep-fat fryer, steel prep tables and sinks. By the door with its chain fly screens, I could see the large industrial dishwasher and a big double washing up sink.

Near the pass I could see two large hatches in the wall. 'What are they?' I asked.

'Dumb-waiters,' Lorna explained. 'One up and one down. Obviously they both go up and down, but the left hand one we use for sending the food up, the other one is where the waiting staff in the restaurant send down the used dishes. That way in busy times there's no log-jam, no having to wait down here for the lift while it's being loaded upstairs.'

That made sense. I'd worked in basement kitchens before with a dumb-waiter and they can be problematic. I'd also worked in a prestigious hotel with a basement kitchen and no dumb-waiter, and the waiting staff had to leg it up an incredibly steep flight of stairs to the dining room above. I guess it kept them fit.

By way of demonstration she opened the door of one of them. It was capacious, and surprisingly high, you could have fitted a sizeable suitcase inside the metal compartment.

'Any more questions for now?' Lorna asked.

'Chef's office?' I asked.

'That glass cubicle over there.'

I nodded. I hoped I wouldn't be there long enough to

need to use it that much. Maybe Dave Holland wouldn't be away more than a day or so.

'Ordering?'

'We have online accounts with the main suppliers, veg, fish, meat, game, cheese and deli and dry stores,' she said. 'I'll email you the links; it's very straightforward, just adding the numbers to the listed items. I'll also give you budgetary guidelines so you don't blow your allowance on caviar as a special.'

I gave her a tight, sarcastic smile.

'That's fine, then,' I said. 'I'll have a look tonight… you've got the passwords?'

She nodded. 'I'll send them to you within the hour. Anything else?'

The kitchen staff on the other side of the pass were staring at us with unconcealed curiosity. I smiled and waved. No one waved back. Lorna glared at them and they went back to whatever they had been doing.

'Where do people change their clothes for work?' I asked.

'Come on and I'll show you…'

She clicked across the industrial lino floor in her heels followed by me. I was feeling a bit sheepish because these were outdoor shoes and shouldn't be worn in the kitchen for hygiene reasons. But who was going to question Lorna? I glanced back. I could see the quizzical looks on the faces of the other chefs, wondering was I any good and what was I going to be like to work with.

I had been right when I had guessed the old boy was the pot-wash guy; I knew that for sure now because he was standing by the sink.

'This is Ali,' Lorna said, with a somewhat patronising air, 'he's been with us forever.'

Ali had a time-worn, craggy face, and his grey hair was cut short. He was probably in his sixties. He smiled at me warmly.

'Nice tae see yez again,' he said. 'So you're the new chef?'

'Yes, I am.'

I had already told him that but he was probably one of those people who like to have things confirmed so there's no mistake later on. It's very much a kitchen thing, when a waiter gives you an order you repeat it back verbatim; a misunderstanding can be very costly.

'Aye,' he nodded. 'Davie telt me ye'd be here. Charlie isn't it?'

I nodded. 'That's me.' I noticed that the other kitchen staff, the girl and the blond man were staring at me with renewed interest. They were probably wondering what else Dave Holland had told him about me. Well, they'd find out in due course.

'Hi, everyone,' I said, addressing them, 'I'm Charlie Hunter, temporary cover…'

'And Acting Head Chef,' Lorna's voice was steely. 'As of now, she runs the kitchen, I hope that's understood.'

The young girl, pretty, innocent looking, with a pleasant, roundish face, smiled at me. 'I'm Innes,' she said, 'pleased tae meet you, Chef.'

'Likewise,' I said.

'I'm Euan,' said the blond guy, sulkily. He turned away in a kind of disrespectful manner signalling discontent. Oh dear, trouble ahead.

Lorna's eyes narrowed and her lips pursed as she glared at his back. It kind of confirmed my worst suspicions. She shook her head and then turned to me. 'This way, Charlie.'

The kitchen door led out into a yard at the back of the building. We went outside. The ground must have fallen away or been levelled during construction, then I remembered that I had gone up a flight of steps from the street to the ground floor. It was nearly dark now, startling after the brilliantly lit kitchen. A bitter wind was blowing. Edinburgh felt very cold all of a sudden. Lights were on in the rear rooms of the tenements, five or six storeys in height, that backed onto the hotel, I shivered as I looked around. There was a row of wheelie bins on one side of the yard. Opposite us was a high stone wall with a large gate set in it and behind that the tenement blocks rising high above us into the blackness of the night.

'Where does that lead to?' I asked, pointing at the gate.

'An access passage for the bin men,' she said, 'comes out in a kind of little alleyway behind us.'

She indicated a small outhouse to the right of the kitchen door.

'That's the toilet,' she said, then she pointed to a kind of cabin brightly lit in the darkness, 'and that's the changing area. Come and see.' She led me across the flagstones and we went inside. It was surprisingly nice inside. I'd been expecting a frowsty old place with a locker-room smell. There was a couple of toilet stalls and opposite them were wash basins with mirrors and half a dozen metal lockers with padlocks, and a couple of benches. Everything was remarkably clean. The sinks gleamed, there was even a vase with flowers on the window ledge. I commented on this.

'That's down to Ali,' said Lorna. 'We pay him overtime for keeping the external areas clean.'

'Money well spent,' I said approvingly. I had seen staff changing areas that would shame a pigsty.

'Seen enough?' she asked.

'Yeah, I guess.'

'Good. Let's go back up to my office.'

We walked back through the kitchen. Ali gave me an ironic salute, the teenager smiled shyly, Euan's back radiated displeasure. Someone's got the hump, I thought.

Chapter Five

'Well, what do you think?' Lorna asked.

I made a few comments then asked, 'Who else is in the kitchen team?'

'Just Martin, the breakfast chef. You can meet him tomorrow morning, he does six until ten in the morning. Erik, the sous, has left, as you know. He was the one you were supposed to replace so you'll be a man down, I'm afraid.'

There was no mention of getting a temp in. I wasn't expecting one. Kitchens run on very fine margins and it costs a lot to bring in an agency chef, plus, by the time you've trained them up, it's time for them to go. You just have to work twelve hour days and kiss goodbye to your day off.

She sighed. 'Dave, of course, is at the Royal Infirmary.' She paused. 'Oh, I nearly forgot, and there's Rosa, she's our part time pastry chef. She just works two days a week, usually a Tuesday and a Friday. She makes the desserts, she's very good.'

I digested this; I was thinking in terms of work-loads. It

seemed okay, apart from one potential problem area. I was glad we had a bespoke pastry chef. I love making desserts but they are time consuming. Time would be something I would be very short of from now on. Mentally I cursed myself for allowing Strickland to persuade me to come here. I might have known something like this would happen. Things rarely run smoothly in the catering trade.

'Tell me about Euan,' I said, thinking of the sulky blond guy.

'Oh, Christ,' Lorna shook her head. 'He came about twelve years ago and has never left. He was a junior sous then…'

'And he's still a junior sous!' I said incredulously.

The sous chef is the number two in a kitchen. He or she can also deputise for the head chef on their days off or holidays. After a while, they normally leave to become a head chef somewhere else. Sometimes they stay on, but generally only because they really like where they are, for whatever reason. The junior sous reports to the sous and is a step down the ladder. But to be a 'junior' after twelve years – more than a decade of being continually passed over for promotion, that was kind of alarming.

'Yes,' she said. Flatly. No love lost, obviously.

'What's going on there then?' I wondered aloud.

'Being a dick is a spectrum,' Lorna said, grimly and somewhat unexpectedly. 'In my experience, a lot of people are a bit of a dick, some people are dicks most of the time, but that man' – she shook her head angrily – 'is a Dick with a capital "d", no, wait, strike that, he is a DICK, full caps. All of the time.'

'Why's he still here then?'

'We can't really get rid of him.' She sighed. 'His work is seemingly not awful, just not good.' I had been wondering about that, if he was as poor a chef or as a human being. 'And to say he lacks imagination, flair or leadership skills' – her hands moved in an expressive gesture – 'goes without saying. But it's not like the old days when you could just fire someone.' There was a wistful tone in her voice. 'Everyone's got "rights".' She spat the word out.

Well, I'd find out soon enough what his cooking skills were like.

'So what's his problem with me then? Doesn't he like women chefs in particular, or is he just an old-school mis-ogynist and doesn't like women at all?' Always useful to know, just in case there was some danger of him running amok. Strange things can happen in kitchens.

Lorna shook her head. 'I doubt if he gets on with anyone, quite frankly. When Erik left he thought he was going to get the job. Dave told him he wasn't, he'd get the job "over his dead body" and that he'd got temporary cover from, and I quote, "someone who knows what they're doing" and that he'd be interviewing after Christmas. Euan came whining to me, said he was being discriminated against. I said, "You're a straight, white male, how are we discriminating against you? You're just not up to the job."' She grinned. 'Then I said, "You know where the door is." He didn't like that.'

So, mystery solved. Resentment. Well, I only had to put up with him for two weeks.

'So, we're closed tomorrow, on a Monday?' Just for confirmation.

'That's right, closed on Mondays. That'll give you a day to get acclimatised. Ready for Tuesday service.'

'And there's a chef called Martin who covers the breakfast shift?'

'That's right, he gets in at six, leaves at ten.' Lorna smiled. 'He's ultra-reliable.'

'Well,' I said, thinking, Thank God for that, 'I'll meet him tomorrow. I'll get up early, give him a hand so I can get a feel of the kitchen.'

There was a knock on the door and Donald stuck his head round. 'Your room's ready, Charlie.'

'I'll see you on Tuesday,' Lorna said. 'I'm off tomorrow. I'll send you those numbers and codes. Call me any time if there's something I can help you with, but I'm afraid I know next to nothing about the kitchen, that's Dave's kingdom.' She frowned. 'You know, everyone says how easy-going Dave is, but I warn you now, Charlie, he's stubborn as a mule when it comes to change and he will not listen to criticism.' She ran her eyes over me in an evaluating way, 'And he has an eye for attractive women… just saying.'

'Okay,' I said – what else could I say – 'I'll see you then.'

'If you'd like to follow me,' Donald said and led me out of Lorna's office into the old-fashioned opulence of the hotel.

Chapter Six

I couldn't fault my room. In a word, it was luxurious. It had a massive bed. The ceilings were very high; there were equally tall windows, more or less floor to ceiling, over-looking Moray Place. I stood a while looking out from my room, admiring the faultless, graceful Georgian proportions of the sweeping terraces, their stone dark and slick with rain, the Circus lit with yellow street lights. It looked like a scene from a Victorian melodrama. An austere backdrop for foul deeds. I remembered Jess reading an old novel, *Confessions of a Justified Sinner*, that she'd told me was set in Edinburgh way back then. Glancing out of the window at a scene more or less unchanged in a couple of hundred years apart from the cars, it was easy to imagine Moray Place as a scene for dark misdeeds, the devil disguised in a frock coat and top hat as a mysterious stranger, standing by those mottled sandstone walls.

I kicked my trainers off and lay on the bed, my fingers laced behind my head as I stared at the ceiling far above with its elaborate cornices and moulding.

I was in a strange hotel in an unknown city. The menu

which I'd looked at during my train journey was a mystery. What was Cullen Skink? Ditto Cranachan. Petits fours including Tablet and Shortbread. Well, shortbread I knew, although I think I've only made it once in my life, but what was tablet? The head chef who should have been explaining the menu was somewhere in intensive care; the junior sous chef, currently acting sous, was not only incompetent, he hated my guts. I could just see him being a great help…

Given all that, what else could possibly go wrong?

I slept for an hour or so and then went out to grab a burger from Five Guys, which wasn't far away. I got my first proper glimpse of the Scottish capital, an impressionistic blur of freezing rain and wind, dark streets, Georgian tenements and gardens behind railings.

Later that night, after ten, end of service at his place (The King's Head was open Sunday evening), I called Strickland and told him the news about Dave Holland.

'Oh my God, I hope he's okay… fat bastard.' He sounded alarmed. 'Have you been to the hospital?'

'No I have not, Graeme.' I was a little testy. 'I haven't had time and as of now, I'm the bloody head chef here, thanks to you… cooking a menu I don't know in a strange kitchen, with a sous chef who resents me…'

'You'll be fine, Charlie,' he reassured me. 'I have every faith. You're a good chef, otherwise I wouldn't have recommended you.'

Irritated as I was, I was kind of flattered by his high opinion of me. Strickland didn't give out praise lightly.

'Have you met the manageress?'

'Lorna? Yes.'

'What's she like?'

'Steely.'

'What does that mean?'

'She strikes me as tough and durable with no soft edges. What do you think it means?'

He went on to ask me a slew of questions I hadn't been expecting about the state of the hotel, the kitchen, my feeling about it.

'What is it with all these bloody questions, Graeme?' I didn't really mind; face it, he was the only person I was going to speak to that evening and I was feeling kind of lonely, stuck in my room.

'Just making conversation, Charlie,' he said, huffily. 'I'll go now and I'll be in touch to find out how Dave's getting on.'

'Okay, speak tomorrow.'

I ended the call, showered and crawled into bed.

What had I let myself in for?

Chapter Seven

My alarm woke me at six. For a confused moment I lay there wondering where I was before I realised I was in a hotel room in central Edinburgh. At home I sleep with my curtains open, I'm not overlooked where I live, and I had done the same here, although the windows had big, old-fashioned wooden shutters, which I rather liked. The room was softly lit by the orange light of the streetlamp outside. I got out of bed and walked over to the huge, rectangular sash window.

My usual view is over the grass common in the village where I live in South Bucks. Today I was looking over the silent Georgian buildings in their graceful curve, secretive in the darkness with the garden in the centre. It could hardly be more different. I was looking at a cityscape unchanged in a couple of centuries, history come to life.

I was suddenly elated by the novelty of my urban surrounding, so different from the Chilterns countryside, and I was desperate to explore. I pulled on my running clothes and padded down the broad carpeted stairs to reception. Nobody was visible at this early hour, not even at reception. I guessed either Donald or Craig would be asleep in their office behind the front desk.

I opened the huge front door, let myself out and started running along the street-lamp lit roads in a cold, light drizzle.

I was following a five kilometre loop that I'd set on one of my running apps on my phone and saved. The only noise as I tracked the blue triangle on my phone along its trail of blue dots, apart from a distant rumble of traffic, was of my shoes slapping on the wet pavements. The silence of the dark, empty streets was thrilling. The air was cold, damp, kind of industrial, with a hint of dank vegetation. There was nobody around, just the very occasional car. I descended a steep, narrow street; there were side streets that had obviously been mews back in the day where the carriages were stored. The roads were cobbled and there were occasional antique black-painted metal posts, waist height, which added a quaint, otherworldly air to the place, as if I was in some sort of dream.

My run took me through a boho kind of neighbourhood by a narrow, shallow river, fast flowing and tumbling over boulders and stones. I later learned it was called the Water of Leith. I leaned over the parapet and looked at the water foaming and rushing over the rocks. I shivered; it looked icy cold. I ran on down the street past the shuttered shops and closed restaurants and cafés.

I was in Stockbridge according to the screen of my phone. Always good to orient yourself. Past a church and a park. I ran by a fancy-looking school, the kind of place Harry Potter might have gone to, but this was the school, I learnt later, where a former Labour leader had been educated, and it wasn't called Hogwarts but Fettes College. I went out on a limb and guessed it wasn't where Murdo, the current sous chef in my restaurant, who was from Edinburgh, had been schooled. If so, his parents had really wasted their money.

I ran round a second side of the park and through a more normal-looking part of Edinburgh, that is, somewhere that did not look stratospherically expensive (Moray Place) or quite expensive (Stockbridge).

I ran up a hill. I could see that the road would take me to Princes Street where the castle dominated the city, but halfway up I turned and ran back home.

When I got back to the hotel, I ran past it and found the alley that led to the gate I had seen in the wall of the kitchen yard. I tried the handle, but it was locked.

Of course it would be. The hotel would not want thieves breaking in the back door in the small hours, stealing hundreds of pounds worth of meat and fish from the fridges. Or maybe street drunks or drug users stumbling in looking for somewhere to drink or use. I was there because I wanted to see the breakfast chef incognito. Lorna had praised him, but I wanted to see him in action myself. It's one thing watching someone at work when they know they are being evaluated, quite another if you can spy on them unobserved. Wandering around in the darkness, using the torch on my phone, I found someone's wheelie bin that they hadn't taken in and pushed it against the wall. I clambered on top of this, hoisted myself on the wall and dropped down into the shadows of the kitchen yard below.

It was just before seven now, it wouldn't be light for another half hour I guessed. I quietly crossed the empty space, the cabin that was the changing room waiting patiently for the arrival of the chefs, slipped by the dark shape of the toilet building and peered in through the kitchen window at the brightly lit interior to see what was going on.

Chapter Eight

Breakfast chefs can be a strange bunch. Sometimes they're chefs who just aren't particularly good but who have found a comfortable niche doing that one meal. That's not to throw shade on the skill of a good breakfast chef. Like everything, there's an art to it, particularly with the eggs, but you're working with a very limited palette of colours. You really are doing the same thing over and over again. Occasionally it's true you get outliers, Smashed Avocado, Patatas Bravas, but generally, people are very conservative at breakfast. It's not the place for innovation.

Sometimes you get retired chefs who need the money and not the grief. There's certainly very little in the way of mise en place to worry about, no 'Oh my God! I forgot to make the pâté' moment. You crack eggs, open packets of bacon or sausage and tins of beans, occasionally slice mushrooms or tomatoes.

Personally, whenever I've worked in hotels I've tended to avoid the breakfast shift, which often runs from six in the morning until middday, plus or minus. That's not because I mind getting up early but because customers would get arsey about breakfast in a way that doesn't happen at lunch or dinner. Porridge, a particular nightmare. Some like it salted, some like it sweet. Different porridge brands have different cooking times. I never know if I've done it right or not, I can't stand the stuff. You get complaints. 'Oh, it's not like I do it at home,' or 'Oh, it's not done the way my mum used to do it…' that kind of criticism. They're not going to say that about your Sole Meunèire or White Chocolate Parfait paired with Dark Chocolate Mousse.

So, I pressed my nose up against the cold window like a Lycra-clad peeping Tom.

This is what I saw.

A muscular looking elderly man with a bald head and a drooping white moustache moving purposefully and somehow gracefully across the kitchen, carrying a large frying pan in one hand. Those old ones can weigh a ton, he held it as if it were as light as a side plate. He approached the pass and carefully and efficiently slid a couple of eggs onto a plate that had fried mushrooms and several rashers of bacon on it. He briefly inspected it, nodded to himself with satisfaction and then carried it over to the dumb-waiter, put it inside, closed the door and pressed a button.

I could see the ticket machine on the pass that sent orders down from the dining room above to the kitchen spit out another couple of breakfast cheques. I watched as he cooked these. He was obviously very good and I particularly liked the way he was attentive and present, honouring the food as well as cooking it. No swearing, no waste, no faff. He was deft, graceful, economic with his movements, and fast. I liked what I saw.

I rapped on the kitchen door. His reaction was interesting. If it had been me, I would have jumped out of my skin. Who could be in the kitchen yard at that hour of the morning?

But this guy simply turned, raised a questioning eyebrow and walked over to the kitchen door which he opened. He stood for a moment, looking at me questioningly.

'Hello,' I said brightly, 'I'm Charlie Hunter, I'm the temporary acting head chef.'

'Do come in Charlie Hunter,' he said. He had a soft Scottish accent, a soft voice in general. 'I'm Martin Blair, I'm the breakfast chef.' He grinned. 'As you may have gathered by my cooking breakfasts.'

I took my trail shoes off at the door, I didn't want to be tracking mud and dirt through the kitchen. The ticket machine whirred and printed out another couple of cheques; he tore them off and went into action.

Between seven and eight Martin was fairly busy as he did about twenty more breakfasts. He'd done the usual thing of pre-cooking the sausages and grilled tomatoes and keeping them warm under the lights. Bacon he had par-cooked and just flashed through under the salamander as we call the eye high grill in the trade.

We chatted as he worked. He'd refused my offer of help. 'There's only thirty people staying in the hotel, Chef, I think I can cope…'

He did more than cope, it was like a master class in breakfast cooking. The kitchen phone rang. 'Un hunh, aye, I can do that.'

He hung up. 'Customers eh? There's about twenty to

thirty things in total on that menu and they want to know can I do them eggs Benedict?'

I watched as he quickly made a hollandaise sauce. Eggs Benedict is poached eggs with a hollandaise sauce. That's basically melted butter whisked into egg yolks.

It was a pleasure watching him work. Hollandaise can be a pig to make. If the egg yolks get too hot they'll start to cook through rather than thicken and you'll end up with scrambled eggs.

While he was doing this he cooked a piece of brown toast, poached two eggs and then effortlessly slid the eggs onto the toast, dressed them with the Hollandaise, garnished them with a sprig of parsley and said to me, 'If you wouldn't mind sending those up for me, Chef.'

I carried the plate over to the dumb-waiter and sent it upstairs. While I was at it I opened the other hatch and carried the dirty plates and cutlery over to the kp area to be washed up by... what was his name... Ali, that was it, to do later.

'Thank you, Chef.'

'Call me Charlie, Martin,' I said. 'It's a bit early for formalities... I can see you've done this before...'

He smiled. 'I have indeed. I used to be a chef full-time and then a while ago I worked with David Holland for a couple of years, I was his chef de partie, then his sous. Then I got out of cheffing.'

'What brought you back again?' I asked. 'Nostalgia?'

He laughed. 'Hardly. No, this is a sideline. I teach Tai Chi, meditation and yoga these days, much more calming than cooking. But it can be irregular, the work, and, like cooking, it's not fantastically paid.' He smiled. 'I needed extra money, and I think I'm a wee bit auld to be a TikTok influencer, so...' he shrugged and indicated the kitchen. 'But it's nice to see David again... and to work with him.'

'So he's good to work with?' I asked.

'Oh, aye. He's got the gift of patience, he's no prima donna, and he is unflappable. I've never seen him panicking, or close to it, which is after all someone panicking but trying to hide it. I think you'll get on with him.'

That was a relief to know. For some reason I found myself trusting Martin's judgements more than might be expected after such a short time.

'Do you know how he's doing?' I asked.

He shook his head. 'I went to the hospital, he's no' on a ward yet which isnae a guid sign, he's still in ICU. I hope he pulls through, he's a lovely guy, although Herself wouldnae agree.' He rolled his eyes towards the ceiling. I guessed he meant Lorna.

'Do you mean Lorna?'

'Aye.' He nodded.

'What's the issue there?' I asked, curious to learn about the internal politics of a place like this. I guessed Strickland would want to know too.

Martin opened his hands and made a kind of all-encompassing gesture. 'This,' he said simply, 'the hotel and its future.'

'How do you mean?'

The ticket machine suddenly spat out four breakfast cheques. He frowned at them.

'Could you come and do some eggs for me?'

'I'd be delighted.'

He handed me a jacket and an apron that were hanging near the door. I pulled them on and hurriedly twisted my hair up and rammed a cap over it. I have very nice hair, reddish brown, shoulder length – but nice as it is, nobody wants bits of it in their food. For the next ten minutes I cooked eggs to order while he attended to the rest of the breakfasts. It was quite enjoyable, I didn't have to do anything except listen to Martin's calm instructions: 'three fried eggs please', 'two poached eggs', 'two portions scrambled eggs with smoked salmon', 'one mushroom omelette'. The universe contracted to just me and the eggs.

Finally the orders dried up and when we were finished I carried on with our conversation.

'You were saying,' I said, 'about her plans for this place.'

'Lorna wants the hotel to become a chic, trendy, up to the minute members' club,' he explained, 'a wee bit like Soho House.'

'And David?'

'Ach, he likes it just fine the way it is.'

'How do you mean?'

'You'll have noticed, Charlie, it's very traditional here. Do you see smashed avocado on toast on the breakfast menu?' I smiled at the reference, the thought I'd had earlier. 'Salsa verde baked eggs? Most of the punters have been coming here year after year. The lunch and dinner food is very trad too, classic French. It's done very well, but it's not going to be Instagrammed. There's hasselback potatoes on the menu, but they're not loaded hasselback potatoes with Guanciale lardons, neither is there cheese and black garlic served with chargrilled hispi cabbage.' He smiled. 'I done a lot of that three years ago in a restaurant down in Leith, it was very popular.' He looked at me meaningfully. 'You maybe wouldnae know but Leith has changed an awful lot in the past few years.'

I didn't, but I guessed he meant gentrification. He went on to explain that the hotel was an independent, not part of a chain. Lorna had a twenty per cent share in the hotel, David Holland thirty-five per cent and the other forty-five per cent belonged to a property investment group.

'She wants to modernise, he doesn't. And the other shareholders will go with him, they're risk averse. Probably woman averse too, I gather there's a lot of that about. But until he goes she'll just have to suck it up, he just blocks all her suggestions, must be very frustrating for her.'

'I can imagine…'

I thought of the following day, and the other days to come. I needed help and I'm not too proud to ask. I did so now. I liked him a lot.

'Look, Martin, I've got to cook David's menu tomorrow, he should have been here to show me how things are plated.' I found and glanced at the Moray Place Hotel menu I had on my phone. 'For example, this wine-poached Loch Duart salmon, hasselback potatoes' – I smiled – 'like you just mentioned, with crushed peas. I can poach a bit of fish, make hasselbacks and crush peas, but my way of doing things won't be the same as his… do you know he's got a recipe file anywhere? Or spec sheets so I can at least see a photo of what it's supposed to look like?'

He nodded. 'Aye, I know where the recipe sheets are

kept, there's no pictures, but I know what the dishes look like fine enough. Would you like me to stay for a couple of hours after my shift to talk it through with you?'

'God, yes,' I said fervently, thinking, You are such an angel!

'They'll have to pay me,' he said warningly.

'They'll pay you double time,' I promised immediately, probably exceeding my authority.

'Lorna won't like that.' He shook his head. 'She doesn't like spending money on kitchen staff.'

'If Lorna doesn't, I'll just get on the next train home. She'll pay.' I added confidently, 'If not, Euan can cook.'

He laughed. 'She'll pay.'

It was two hours later when we were discussing the venison fillet with a wild mushroom pithivier, that we got the news.

David Holland had died at 8 o'clock that morning.

Chapter Nine

'Morning, Chef,' Euan said morosely on Tuesday morning as he arrived.

'Good morning,' I said. I'd been in the kitchen since eight that morning, two hours previously. I'd checked the walk-in fridge to see how the food was stored and if it had been correctly labelled and day-dotted. I like day-dotting. Day dots are circular coloured adhesive stickers that indicate when a food item has reached its use by date. Three days is the rule of thumb for cooked goods and then it either goes in the bin or goes to the staff for food.

Everything was in order. Well, that was one worry off my mind. I'd asked Martin about it, he'd told me that Euan did it, he was obsessively tidy and orderly.

'Well that's something positive,' I said.

'Maybe tae a fault,' Martin had mused. So, maybe not.

Euan was the third chef that I'd spoken to that morning. Martin, the breakfast chef, had been hard at it when I had started work. I'd made him a coffee and we'd chatted while he cooked and, this second time I had met him, he told me more about his yoga and meditation business and his past in catering. Like Murdo in my kitchen, he'd done stints on cruise ships, saving his money until he'd made enough to go on a six month training course for yoga teachers in India. He'd shown me some of his poses. He was impressively flexible. I did yoga myself, I'd started attending a new class back in Hampden Green. Martin offered to give me a bit of extra coaching. I declined. I thought it would be hard to maintain my dignity wobbling around on one leg as I did Warrior 3.

At half nine, Rosa had arrived. She was a cheery Italian woman, thirty-something I guessed, with brown hair tied back, a Roman nose and an enormous bust. Startlingly so. She was very friendly, knew exactly what she was doing and started work immediately on the week's desserts: white chocolate parfait with hazelnuts, crème brûlées, an orange cake with a whisky sauce and (my suggestion) a tiramisu.

'Tiramisu?' She stared at me like I was mad.

'Tiramisu,' I said firmly. 'People like it, and we can say it's authentically Italian.' I'd instruct the waitresses to tell the customers. 'Oh, and could you make a dozen panna cottas, I've got some double cream I'm keen to use up, vanilla ones, there's some vanilla pods I found in the dry store that are getting a bit elderly.'

'Chef wouldn't have liked that,' she said, 'not tiramisu!' and then burst into tears. I put my arms around her and patted her back while her body heaved with sobs. She was obviously very fond of him.

'I'm sorry… dispiace… it's just that he was so… he was so good to me…' While I held her I wondered what's wrong with bloody tiramisu, Dave Holland. Not French enough

I suppose. We were not, after all, a French restaurant. Since I was now the head chef we'd be doing things my way and if that meant adding touches from wherever I fancied, so be it.

Later, when she recovered, at my prompting as we were working in close proximity, she told me about herself. Indeed it was hard to shut her up. Euan scowled at her from across the kitchen. He was such a dog in the manger; if he couldn't be nice, nobody else could be either. Fortunately, the kitchen had obviously decided long ago to ignore him whenever possible.

She was very talkative. I learnt that she'd come over here with her husband. 'A chef?' I'd asked. 'No, a software developer, computer games', and he'd dumped her, run off with a colleague, and left her with two kids in a flat just down the road.

Now I was speaking to Euan. We'd got off to a bad start, but I would win him round with charm.

'Did you have a nice day off?' I asked, as he put his apron on and carefully tied the strings behind his back.

He thought for a moment and just then Ali arrived, as did Innes. They both greeted us cheerily. Ali started work on the backlog of dishes and pans from the breakfast shift.

Innes joined us, her innocent girl's face pink and scrubbed, devoid of makeup. She looked incredibly young to my eyes.

'No,' Euan said. Finally.

'Why? What happened?' I asked. With mild concern, just in case.

'Well,' Euan said, huffily, 'where to begin? I mean when

Din' – Who? I thought – 'wants someone to help him explore Mandalore, he gets the IG-11 repaired…' he shook his head sadly. 'Unbelievable.'

This wasn't the way I had expected the conversation to go.

'Um, I'm sorry, Euan, you've lost me?' All of this was gibberish to me.

'He's talking about the Mandalorian,' Innes explained from her workstation across the way. 'He was going to spend the Monday catching up on series three.'

I didn't have time to explain that I had absolutely no idea as to who or what the Mandalorian was. Euan carried on irritably, squatting to inspect a fridge.

'The IG-11 was completely blown up in season one,' he looked up accusingly at me, as if it were my fault, 'completely! And yet we're expected to believe its top half survived, unscathed.' Dramatic pause. 'Unscathed!'

'So, maybe the bomb wisnae very guid?' Innes suggested, helpfully.

'There was nothing wrong with the bomb,' Euan said, crossly, 'and it was strapped to his chest!' He looked around at us as if any of us was going to query this. He carried on.

'I was really looking forward to catching up on series three, I missed it stuck in here… but now… I'm not so sure.'

With a sinking heart I suspected I was going to hear a lot more about the Mandalorian in the next few days.

I got Euan to show me how to prep the venison Wellingtons. It was more or less as I expected. We made a duxelles of mushrooms, that was mushrooms, shallots and herbs whizzed to almost breadcrumb texture in a blender and then gently sautéed. We seared off 160 gram cuts of venison fillet per portion and then when everything was cool, covered them in the mushroom paste and then puff pastry.

I would then cook them to order for about twenty-five minutes in the oven. There was more to it than that, but that gives the general picture.

For the fish dishes, there was salmon with a lovage sauce, seabass with a salsa verde, smoked trout with a mango and lime coulis.

All of that was fairly straightforward, the garnishes were too – except for the pickled ceps, a kind of mushroom. That went with the terrine. Mushrooms were obviously a thing here at the Moray Place Hotel. We had 'champignons de couche à la tomate', which were served on bruschetta as one of the amuse-bouches and there was a tagliatelle with wild mushrooms as the vegetarian option. If we added the duxelles to the list we were getting through a fair amount of funghi.

I put this to Innes as we were making a bordelaise sauce for the steaks. While she was fine-dicing shallots I asked her, 'What's it with the mushrooms?' Then as soon as I'd asked the question I remembered that Strickland had mentioned Dave Holland was a mushroom fan. I'd broken the news to Strickland the night before. He was less upset than I'd imagined he would be, if anything he seemed rather cross that Dave Holland had died, but I guess grief takes you in different ways.

'Chef…' her eyes filled with tears as she thought about him. He really was liked by his brigade, I thought. Particularly the women. 'Chef loved mushrooms and that restaurant in France that had the Michelin star, the Trompette Sauvage, where he had trained, that specialised in them.'

I nodded. A trompette is a kind of wild mushroom. One of my few words of French. That and 'ça marche', which I think means something like, 'it goes' in the sense of 'let's go', which old-school chefs use to announce a new cheque. Innes continued, with a break in her voice, 'He loved eating mushrooms, it's what he'd eat just before service. Every day, it was like a ritual. It was part of my job to cook him mushrooms on toast at quarter to twelve.'

'Really?' That was disciplined of David Holland to have a healthy snack before the lunch service. Mostly chefs just graze, eating odds and sods that they come across. Sausages left over from breakfast, chips, scraps of ham and cheese, a steak that inadvertently got cooked too long (a rare treat).

'Yeah,' Innes said, blowing her nose, 'he had his own little tub of them in the walk-in. They were special, he used to go into the woods outside Edinburgh and pick his own, and he'd supplement them with ones from a specialist supplier. You weren't allowed near his mushrooms on pain of death.'

'Show me,' I told her, for no very good reason other than curiosity.

She led me into the walk-in fridge and, sure enough, on the steel racking where the veg was stored was a small plastic tub labelled, 'Chef's Property, paws off, DO NOT USE.'

I opened it: there was a collection of various mushrooms,

brown, reddish, beige and black. There were even some of the ones called morels. They look a bit like a loofah to my eyes. All of them were a bit creepy to me. I like mushrooms, but only ones I feel comfortable with, boring old chestnut or closed cup, maybe a Portobello, they're the big ones that unimaginative places give out as the vegetarian option, dolloping a spoon of whatever, chopped fried veg mixed with breadcrumbs and cheese on top – Stuffed Portobello Mushroom. One of those dishes that really annoys me. Lazy and dull in my opinion.

'He was a connoisseur!' Innes said, proud of her dead ex-boss. What touching loyalty, I thought.

'What do you want to do with them?' she asked.

'Chuck 'em,' I said, maybe a tad callously. 'We can't use them.'

She looked upset. God, I thought, we can't hang on to them in his memory.

'You have them if you want,' I said, half-jokingly.

'Can I?' her face brightened.

'Sure.'

Euan wouldn't shut up about sci-fi and the bloody Mandalorian again.

'Don't get me started about the initiation ceremony with the Armourer and the boy…'

'I won't,' I promised. 'Euan, what do we use for grating the truffle on the tagliatelle?'

'This.' He opened a drawer I hadn't noticed and produced a small, wooden handled piece of steel with an angled slit in it, not unlike a pencil sharpener. He handed it to me and carried on about, I think, the Mandalorian.

'That thing like a crocodile, why didn't they use their jet-packs earlier... that was what they would have done... they're trained warriors.'

'Oh, I see... where do you live in Edinburgh, Euan?'

That was a question that could not possibly involve sci-fi. Anything to change the subject.

'Granton.'

'Oh, is that nice?'

He scowled at me. 'No.' Just the monosyllable.

I persevered. 'My sous chef back home is from Pilton.'

He glared at me. 'That's a dump too.' Then he turned his back on me and went on with his work, tuning me out.

Ali caught my eye and rolled his sympathetically. I grinned and gave him a thumbs up sign. It was cheering to know he was on my side. As was Innes. Two out of three ain't bad.

I watched as Euan produced a spider, a kind of sieve-like spoon, and started straining the jus I had made on Monday. That's a job Ali could have done. There were plenty of other more complex things on the MEP list that needed doing. I was going to say something but I held my tongue. I didn't want to hear any more about Din Djarin aka The Mandalorian. At least I had learned something, maybe it would come in handy in a pub quiz.

The morning wore on. We had about fifteen booked in for lunch, a small number. I was used to doing about twenty to thirty by myself on a Tuesday, but that was my menu, I knew it intimately. I knew the timings of everything, I was aware of the vagaries of my oven. How ovens can vary so much in temperature from one side to another or front to back, is a complete mystery to me, but they do and the Moray Place oven, although larger, swankier and more complex than mine, would almost certainly be as idiosyncratic.

I was looking forward to the challenge. I was aware of a current of interested expectation in the kitchen from my three colleagues. Could this unknown female who'd mysteriously appeared in their midst cut the mustard? Well, I was more than up for the challenge. This was my milieu. I'd spent nearly thirty years (Jesus, three decades, where did the time go) in kitchens from the best restaurants (doing agency work) to places where I wouldn't let a dog eat. Bring it on, I thought to myself.

At half eleven Rosa came up to me.

'The crème brûlées are made, they're cooling down over there. The tiramisu is in the fridge setting, the orange cake is in the oven – I've set a timer, should be ready about twelve – do a skewer test before you take it out. Remember that you've got some desserts that I made late last week in the fridge, they'll be okay until tomorrow.'

'Parfait?' I asked.

'There's still most of one in the freezer. I guess it's not so popular in the winter. I'll be off now if that's okay with you, I'll be in on Friday. If there's an emergency, Lorna's got my number.'

'Thanks Rosa.'

'Ciao, Charlie, have a good week.'

Just as she left, the kitchen phone rang. I picked it up. 'Kitchen.'

It was Lorna's voice at the other end of the line.

'Would you mind coming up to my office please, Charlie.'

Well, yes I very much would. I was still getting things ready; as well as that, this unexpected summons had jarred my concentration, you don't interrupt a chef just before service for some trivial meeting.

I looked around the kitchen. Euan was checking his fridges again, in case he'd forgotten anything. I will say this for him, he was incredibly thorough. I could see Innes outside vaping. Dave Holland's mushroom tub was on her workstation together with a couple of slices of bread. I guessed as a tribute to her departed idol she was going to have a mournful farewell lunch. Quasi-religious, subsuming the essence of the dead head chef via the sacrament of mushrooms on toast: 'Take and eat this in memory of me.'

I frowned at the phone. It also felt odd to be holding a receiver like that. It had been a while since I'd used a landline.

'I'm a bit busy now, can't it wait?' I said, irritably.

'No,' Lorna snapped. 'My office. Now.' She hung up.

Cow!

'Hold the fort, Euan,' I called, 'back in a minute.'

I ran upstairs and along the corridor to her office. I rapped on the door and opened it without being asked. There were two men in there, sitting in front of her desk. One quite young in a cheap suit and polyester tie, taller than his colleague, with boyish good looks. The other was much better dressed, slightly haggard looking, and older. They both had an indefinably official look about them. Everyone looked very serious.

'This is Charlie Hunter,' Lorna said, 'our acting head

chef. This is Detective Sergeant Bain and DC Carmichael; they would like a word.'

The DS spoke, his voice quiet and precise. My sensitive nose could smell a strong odour of peppermint from him when he opened his mouth, mouthwash, I thought. I wondered if he'd been out on the town the night before, his eyes had serious bags under them.

'As I was explaining to your colleague, we are awaiting the full results of the autopsy on Mr Holland, but we have discovered something that may be of importance, particularly from a public health point of view.'

If he hadn't had my attention before, he did now. The words 'public health' trigger alarm bells in the mind of every chef.

I looked at him anxiously. 'Do go on.'

'When Mr Holland was admitted to the hospital we weren't sure,' he hesitated, 'we're still not a hundred per cent sure, what the exact problem was. But his bloods were done at the time and they were found to contain toxins derived from mushrooms.'

Oh my God!

That menu was full of sodding mushrooms. They were in the venison Wellington, the tagliatelle, the garnish for the terrine, that French thing whatever it was called that went out on bruschetta.

'What about today's menu?' Lorna asked. 'Just in case we had a bad batch delivered the other day with a rogue poisonous one inside?'

'That should all be fine,' I replied. 'Everything has been prepped from yesterday's delivery.'

'That's a relief,' Lorna said.

'So we don't need to worry about any further incidents coming from this kitchen?' Carmichael asked me. The look he gave me was sympathetic.

'No, you don't,' Lorna answered for me.

'Have there been any other cases similar to Dave's in the hospital? Or in the Lothian area in general?' I asked the two policemen.

Bain shook his head. 'Not that I'm aware of.'

'Okay,' I said. 'It doesn't look like it came from us then, that is, not our food.'

'Thank God,' Lorna said, echoing her earlier comment.

'Do you have any ideas as to how it could have happened?' Carmichael asked. He smiled at me encouragingly.

'Dave Holland liked to forage his own mushrooms,' I said.

'Aha,' DS Bain perked up at this. 'Now we're getting somewhere; that's the most likely explanation. I guess we'll have to go round to his house and have a look in his fridge.'

'No need,' I said, 'we've still got some of his here… Don't worry,' I reassured Lorna who suddenly looked anguished, 'they're his personal property, they're in their own tub, they're not in general circulation.'

'Thank you Ms Hunter,' Carmichael said.

'Charlie, please.' We smiled at each other. Bain darted his colleague an irritated look.

My mind had drifted to the mushrooms on the steel racking in the walk-in fridge. Then my conversation with Innes, the tub on her workstation, I glanced at the time on the clock on the wall, nearly twelve.

'JESUS!'

I was on my feet and out of the door as fast as I could, no time for explanations. She was going to eat them, wasn't she! In memory of Chef. I could remember my thought:

'… take and eat this in memory of me…'

Would I be in time?

Visions of Innes suddenly collapsing at her workstation in my head, two dead, poisoned. I hurtled down the stairs, footsteps pounding behind me, one of the police, I guessed. Lorna wouldn't be running anywhere in her heels.

I burst into the kitchen, the door crashing into the wall, two faces staring at me in astonishment, one bent over her workstation, fork in hand, head bent. Euan had his back to us. As bloody usual, I remember thinking.

But it was Innes who held my attention.

The fork with its poisonous load in front of her open mouth.

'NOOOO INNES!' I screamed. 'NOOOO!'

Chapter Ten

Innes froze, as indeed did Euan and Ali. The entire kitchen was like a paused film, everyone as still as statues.

'Put the fork down!' I shouted, adding, 'move away from the plate.' I must have been watching too many cop shows on late night TV.

Innes dropped it, looking terrified, and retreated from the workstation. She even put her hands up. I strode across the kitchen and looked down. It was as I had thought. A piece of toast, the mushrooms on top. She had neatly cut the toast into four along the diagonal. I looked hard, no bite marks.

'Have you eaten any of this?' I demanded. She stared at me and then at the two policemen behind me who were looking around the kitchen, trying to look in control of things. They probably had no idea of what was going on. Euan had turned to look at what was happening, strangely incuriously, as if a screaming head chef accompanied by two strange men bursting into the kitchen was a fairly normal occurrence. Maybe it was on planet Mandalore. I noticed him give a kind of shrug and then return to what he was doing.

'No, Chef,' she wailed.

A wave of relief swept through me so strongly I thought my legs might buckle.

'Thank God!' I exclaimed.

'Is there a problem?' she asked, worried. 'Chef always said I could eat any of the veg in the fridge. I didn't know I was stealing.' She looked about to cry.

'That's from the fridge?' I demanded. She nodded mutely.

'They're not David Holland mushrooms?'

'No.' She looked at me as if I'd gone crazy.

'Well,' I said, feeling both exasperated and a bit foolish, 'where are they then?'

'In my bag, outside, in the changing room.' She looked nervously at me and the two cops. 'I hope that's all right.'

I nodded reassuringly. 'Everything's fine, Innes.' The two police moved closer to me in what looked like an attempt to stamp their authority on the situation.

I indicated my companions. 'These gentlemen are policemen, Innes. Can you take them outside and give them the tub, they'll want to take them away. Chef might have died from eating a poisonous mushroom, they'll want to have a look.'

The three of them disappeared through the kitchen door. I sat down heavily on the metal of the pass.

'Jesus Christ,' I breathed in and out heavily a couple of times to restore my equilibrium.

'Well,' observed Ali from the kitchen sink area, 'that's a novel start to the week.'

Euan, his back still turned to me, was in a world of his own, or possibly mentally in a galaxy far, far away, checking on something on the stove. He was absolutely maddening. What kind of weirdo would carry on as if nothing out of the ordinary was happening in a situation that was deafeningly dramatic.

At this moment, the ticket machine whirred into life printing off the first of the lunch orders. I took it just as Innes reappeared with the DC. Bain was outside talking to Lorna.

Carmichael gave me a card with his name and mobile number on it.

'If you think of anything, or something crops up that may be of any use, Charlie, please call.'

'I will DC Carmichael.'

'Thank you.'

He rejoined his colleague outside. I glanced at the ticket and called it out before putting it on the cheque grabber above the pass.

'Cheque on; two fillet steaks, medium, one bordelaise, one bearnaise sauce, one salmon and one tagliatelle – no starters.'

And so my first day cooking began.

The show must go on, no matter what.

After service at 3 o'clock, during my break – I was on a split and back at six – I discussed the lunch with Lorna. I sat in the chair in her office opposite her. The sweat had dried on my face but my whites were clammy and cold, the heavy cotton clinging to my skin.

'I'm very pleased, Charlie,' she said, 'lots of compliments, the food looked great. Well done.'

'Thank you,' I said and I meant it. Lorna was not the kind of person to dish out praise just for the sake of it. It had been a hard lunch, mainly because of the novelty of the new menu. As well as Martin's invaluable input, Innes had been extremely helpful with how things should be presented on the plate; Euan, sullen, borderline useless. There was no mystery here, he wanted me to fail.

'How were the kitchen team?' she asked. 'Euan in particular?'

'He was okay,' I said neutrally. That wasn't true of course but there was nothing Lorna could do about it. Euan was my problem now. The weird thing was that periodically he would seem to forget that he didn't like me and start chatty conversations all about his sci-fi interests, which were ridiculously obsessive.

He had seriously annoyed me when I was plating a venison Wellington and he kept wittering on about the bloody Mandalorian again. I could feel my temper rising. Seemingly 'they', I was uncertain as to who 'they' were, could have known that the atmosphere on Mandalore was breathable any time by just sending a drone down. Why, of course! We'd all been asking ourselves that question, hadn't we?

'They would not have had a woman running things,' he said, pointedly, 'they're a warrior race. Bo-Katan would never become their leader in the real world.'

I took this as a dig at me. I held my tongue.

A while later, more unwanted opinions from Euan, interspersed with unimpressive cooking.

'I wonder when the police will get around to finding

Chef's real murderer,' he said at one point. 'We all know it's a woman, but they won't be interested, they'll just pin it on a man as usual…' He banged a pan down on the stove angrily. 'Whereas we all know it'll be some femoid who did it.'

'Give it a rest, Euan,' Ali said, wearily.

'Yeah, that's right Ali,' Euan jeered, 'keep taking the Blue Pill. Wake up and smell the coffee why don't you, the world's being run by feminazis.'

Innes looked close to tears. This was the final straw. I don't like conspiracy theorists at the best of times, the very words 'sheeple', 'QAnon' or any form of anti-vax propaganda makes my blood pressure soar.

As does Matrix references and anti-women sentiments.

I had stopped work for a second. I was hot, sweaty and irritable; I'd been up since six, it had been a stressful morning, to say the least of it. What with the police, and the momentary worry that we, that is the hotel, might have poisoned a fair few of Edinburgh's wealthier inhabitants. Then thinking that maybe Innes had eaten the deadly mushrooms. It hadn't been easy. In addition, I was dealing with an unfamiliar menu in an unfamiliar kitchen, and now I had to listen to Euan either droning on about some sci-fi programme I had never seen or now some bat-shit crazy conspiracy theory offensive to women in general and me in particular.

'Innes, pass me a rolling pin,' I ordered. She looked surprised, put the finishing touches to a starter, sent it upstairs and on her way back, opened a drawer and took out a long, heavy plastic rolling pin. She handed it to me.

'Rolling pin, Chef,' she said, mystified.

'Thank you... Euan.'

'Yes?' He didn't look up from what he was doing, searing duck breasts.

I slammed the rolling pin down hard on a metal work-station. The crash was deafening. It drowned out everything in the kitchen. That made him look up, startled.

'Now I've got your attention,' I snarled. I'd been nice to him, it had got me nowhere. Time for a change of tactics. I advanced towards him menacingly with the rolling pin.

'Do you see this rolling pin?' I tapped it threateningly in the palm of my hand.

He looked at it, mystified. 'Yes, Chef.'

I moved very close to him, invading his body space. 'Any more from you about the sodding Mandalorian or how awful women are and I'm going to shove this where the sun don't shine, are we clear on that?'

He looked alarmed, took a step back, looked at me to see if I was joking. I poked him hard in the ribs with the rolling pin.

'Got that!'

'Yes, Chef,' he said, chastened. I may have confirmed his feminazi views but I didn't care.

'Spoken like Bo-Katan,' called out Ali from the sink. I shook my head. Sometimes you just couldn't win.

'Euan's been fine,' I said to Lorna.

That evening and the following day were uneventful. I got to know my staff and the menu a bit better. Euan had mercifully shut up about TV sci-fi series and sexual politics. He was sulking. He flounced about the kitchen but at least he was doing it silently. Innes regarded me with open-mouthed admiration and Ali, the pot-washer, with amused respect. At least I had established who was in charge.

On Thursday morning Lorna called me into her office again.

'DS Bain has been on the phone,' she said with a smile on her face. 'Those mushrooms in that tub contained a few Amanita virosa,' she pulled a face, a pantomime face of ignorance.

'Me neither,' I said shrugging. 'What does that mean exactly?'

'They are poisonous. They can grow around here and seemingly they're very similar in looks to a field mushroom which is edible,' she explained. 'So it was just a genuine mistake on Dave Holland's part.'

'So there's no further implications for the hotel? No health and safety implications, no need to worry?'

'Exactly.' She stretched in her chair as if freeing herself from tension. 'So, nothing sinister and the hotel is in the clear, no repercussions.'

Well, I guess that was good, although I did feel a little sorry for the departed David Holland that his colleague didn't seem remotely sorry he was gone, just pleased that it wouldn't affect business.

'Is that what killed him then?' I asked.

She shook her head. 'No, well, not directly, seemingly. The doctors said he had an underlying heart condition and the mushrooms together with that finished him off.'

'Oh my God!' I said. 'Poor guy. Did you know about his heart?'

'No,' she said emphatically. 'But it comes as no surprise. He should have taken more care of himself, but he didn't.'

'A terrible shame,' I said. Then I thought about Graeme Strickland.

'Do we know anything about the funeral? I know someone who would like to go.'

'Not yet.' She shook her sleek head. 'I'll let everyone know when I know. His brother will probably be organising it, he often spoke about him, they were close.'

'Thanks.'

Lorna shrugged. 'The main thing is, there will be no police investigation; this is going down as an accidental death, well, that's what DS Bain thinks. It'll be up to the Procurator Fiscal to decide of course, but if the police are satisfied, they should be too.'

'Oh well,' I said, 'so business as normal.'

'Indeed. I'd be grateful if you could let the kitchen know.'

'I will.'

After service that night, Euan had left, as had Innes, and I was having a drink outside with Ali the kp. He had gone out for a cigarette and I joined him. It was cold in the yard, according to my phone about eight degrees colder than Hampden Green, but at least here at the back of the hotel we were sheltered from the worst of the biting wind, which seemed such a feature of Edinburgh.

The yard was in darkness but illuminated faintly by the lights from the tenements that rose beyond its high wall. Ali had been reminiscing about his time with Dave Holland, who'd been a bit of a good-time hellraiser by the sound of things.

'So, the polis think it wis an accident?' he sounded deeply sceptical.

'That's right, Ali. They said it was his heart that gave out because of the additional overload of the toxins. I gather he was a tad overweight.'

'Aye, he wis a great big bear of a man,' he said affectionately, 'he wis certainly heavy. I mind him telling me once aboot his bathroom scales, aboot how when he got on them they'd go' – he waved his arms to indicate the drama – 'PING! Cuz they only went up tae twenty-one stone. He had tae go to a mate in another restaurant who had industrial ones tae weigh himself...' He chuckled at the memory.

'But seriously, Charlie' – he looked at me keenly – 'the idea that this was some kind of accident, well that's a load of pish.' He spat contemptuously on the cobbles of the yard. He drew on his cigarette and the tip glowed in the darkness.

'Why do you say that?' I was faintly alarmed now. He wasn't going to say he had been poisoned, was he?

'Dave knew a lot aboot mushrooms. He wouldnae make a mistake like that. Someone spiked his container wi' poison ones.' He stubbed his cigarette out 'That'll be the way of it.'

'Oh, surely not.' This was an avenue I didn't want to go down. Like one of Euan's conspiracy theories. 'Who would want to do that?' Big Funghi maybe, the mushroom equivalent of Big Pharma?

'It could be Euan.' Once again he spat eloquently on the tiles of the yard.

'Euan!' I was incredulous. That moronic windbag. 'Why Euan?'

'Yon laddie is one great big mass of grievance,' Ali said seriously.

That kind of jolted me. I had thought that he was just useless and annoying, not dangerous.

Ali continued, 'When Dave brought you in to replace Erik he was gutted. He still hopes he'll be made head chef when you go, he hasnae a clue what is going on.' More spitting 'He lives in a bloody dreamworld. All this science-fiction shite has addled what few brains he was born with. He hasnae any originality, not one single drop. If Lorna put him in charge we'd be cooking this menu unchanged until he died or retired.'

I considered this. I could see it was true. Then he added, 'And he was jealous of Chef's way with the ladies; lassies couldnae get enough of him. Unlike Euan. So I wouldn't put it past him to have just made a wee addition tae Dave's tub of mushrooms.'

That was an unexpected take on Dave Holland, the fact that he was a ladies' man, or had been.

'Anyone else?' I asked.

He thought. 'Could be Rosa.'

'Rosa!' She reminded me of a cheery Labrador in human form. I couldn't imagine her hurting a fly.

'Aye. Dave had a wee affair with her a couple of years ago. She's Italian, you know what they're like,' he added darkly.

I did indeed. My ex, Andrea, was Italian. He was my ex because of my own bad behaviour. Not his. Even with the greatest provocation, finding me in bed with another man, Andrea had behaved impeccably. It was infuriating how civilised and reasonable he had been. He hadn't flown into a rage. Well, I wasn't going to bring this up with Ali to counter his racial stereotyping. That was my business.

I considered this. 'Well,' I said, 'you may be right, but it'll be for the Procurator Fiscal I gather to decide if anything is going to be done, not you or I.' I stood up and stretched, it really wasn't my problem.

Then he said something that got me thinking.

'Then there's Lorna,' Ali said. 'She couldnae stand him.'

I thought about this for a moment. No need to ask about motive there, Martin had given me the information on how much she stood to gain through his departure.

'But even if you were right,' I said, doubtfully, 'they would only have made him quite sick if he hadn't had a weak heart, and she didn't know that.'

'What! You're havering, woman,' he snorted. 'Of course she knew he had a bad heart, he was off last year to have a stent put in.'

That silenced me and I thought, you lied to me, Lorna.

Chapter Eleven

After the evening service, I went up to my room. I showered, changed into some jeans and a Scandi-style sweater and looked at my phone. Quarter past ten. Time to ring Strickland.

I called him rather than texting or messaging and he answered immediately. I told him about the police and what they'd said. Accidental death.

'I HAVE NEVER HEARD SUCH BULLSHIT!' he shouted down the phone.

Strickland was legendary for his temper which, fortunately, not working for him, I had never seen. Even a saint might get a tad grumpy working Strickland's hours and he was no saint.

'Calm down, Graeme,' I said. 'What do you mean?'

'Dave would never make a mistake with a mushroom,' he barked, 'no matter how much a poisonous one might look like an edible variety.' He carried on with absolute surety, 'He was insanely knowledgeable about them; someone must have killed him.'

'That's more or less what the kp said,' I, maybe unwisely,

offered. How he'd come to eat a poisoned mushroom was not my problem though.

'What's his name?' he asked.

'Ali, why?'

'Well, Ali's right.'

I wasn't going to disagree with him. 'Well, I'm sure the police will get to the bottom of it,' I said placatingly.

'No they won't,' Strickland's voice, again full of certainty. He was a stranger to self-doubt. 'They've got a woeful clean-up rate. They'll sanitise all this, get it written down as an accident and that'll give them more time to go off on residential "training courses" and get pissed at our expense.'

'I'm sure that's not the case,' I said. 'DS Bain seemed…'

'I don't give a toss how the DS seemed,' he said. 'There's obviously only one thing for it, Charlie, you'll have to stay there and find out who did it.'

What! No way.

'I can't do that, Graeme, what about my restaurant?'

'It's in excellent hands,' he reassured me. 'Patrick and Murdo are doing a great job; I ate there the other day, and that waitress who's stepped in full-time for Jess while she's at uni…'

'Katie.'

'That's her, she is good too. So you can relax up there and devote yourself to finding a murderer. I'll fund Patrick as long as it takes… where are you now?'

'In my room.'

'Well, I'll go now. Get in touch with me when you've learnt something. Night Charlie, thanks for agreeing to do this, you're a legend.'

He ended the call.

I stared at my phone. I hadn't agreed to anything, but that was Strickland all over for you. He'd bulldozed me into coming up here in the first place, now he was committing me to acting as his personal private detective. I marvelled at the audacity of the man, but you had to admire him for it. At least I did.

I sighed. I wasn't going to commit to anything right now. I'd think about it when I was running in the morning. That's when I do my thinking.

I sat for a moment and decided to go to the bar for a drink.

I went downstairs, my feet sinking into the expensive carpeting of the corridor and stairs. Down at reception Craig was on duty. He smiled shyly. Although I liked him, I had been hoping it would be Donald on duty. After what Ali had told me about the hidden undercurrents in the hotel I wanted more detail. Donald, I suspected, would be the man to oblige. He certainly had the air of someone who enjoyed a good gossip. Above all, I wanted to find out some more about Lorna. I couldn't work out if I liked her, admired her, or disliked her. She was a bit of an enigma to me. I had been looking forward to a productive chat with Donald. I didn't think Craig would be forthcoming.

'Hello, Charlie, how are you?' he said in his soft, gentle voice, smiling shyly at me.

'I'm very well, thank you, and you Craig?'

He blushed slightly. 'I'm good, I'm good.'

'I'm just going to the bar,' I said brightly.

'Oh well, if you're going to the bar, I can recommend the cocktails. Annie's a very good mixologist.'

I walked away from reception and into the bar. Annie the barmaid, a pleasant woman in late middle-age, motherly, smiled at me as I ordered. A Merlot; I didn't feel like a cocktail, I wasn't in a frivolous mood.

'Oh, Charlie, there's someone I want you to meet... Katriona!' Annie called to a girl in a white blouse and black trousers collecting glasses from an empty table.

The waitress came over to the bar. She had long dark hair and a pouty, slightly sulky face. Her sleeves were rolled up and her forearms were a riotous mass of colour from her tattoos. I have a very sensitive nose and I could smell a very faint aroma of weed on her. She looked questioningly at Annie.

'This is Charlie, she's filling in for Dave, now he's gone.'

'Temporarily,' I said, emphasising my non-dom status. 'I'm a stop-gap measure.'

Katriona nodded, she didn't seem particularly interested. 'And Charlie, this is Katriona, she's our Restaurant Manager, but she's helping out in the bar at the moment.'

'Pleased to meet you,' she said, although she didn't look particularly delighted. I hoped that she was more efficient than she looked.

'It's strange having the dining room at a different level from the kitchen,' I said to her, by way of a conversational opening, 'I never get to see the waitresses, or the manager, come to that.' It was true. Usually they're in and out of the kitchen carrying plates or when we're prepping, coming in for a chat. None of that happened here. We were hermetically sealed in our respective worlds, the only communication the dumb-waiter, which as its name implies, is no communication at all.

She nodded. 'Oh aye.' She obviously wasn't remotely interested in my opinions or, for that matter, in meeting me.

'Well, nice to have met you,' I said brightly and I went and sat down by myself at a table in the corner. What a bitch, I thought.

Then, slightly to my surprise, Lorna came in. It was gone half ten now; I thought she would have left long ago. Heads turned; she commanded attention. With Lorna around you knew who was in charge.

I had mentioned to Strickland that I thought her steely. It was true. There was something slightly inhuman about her, as if the empathy gene had been removed. She looked like a killer android, I suddenly thought: the Lorna 2000 version, slim and attractive, her sleek black hair framing a striking face and glacially cold eyes. Ali, one of the few people who seemed to like me here, had told me about her work ethic. She was up at five, started work at six and usually only had one day off a week. She was an attractive working machine, more machine than woman, I thought. Like a female Darth Vader. Immediately followed by the worry that Euan's sci-fi tropes were getting addictive.

She came over to me.

'Mind if I join you?' She smiled, but her eyes were cold.

It wasn't really a question. She sat down opposite me. I could smell her perfume; it was quite heady, not what I had expected. Those hard eyes bored into me.

'It's been quite the week, Charlie,' she said.

'I can imagine.' Behind her, the bar was reasonably busy, half-full of well-heeled, affluent Scots for whom the Moray Place Hotel was probably like a home away from home when business or pleasure brought them to Edinburgh. The demographic was middle-aged to elderly. Katriona moved among them; she looked efficient, if unsmiling, taking orders, delivering drinks and cleaning tables. Maybe she was good in the restaurant after all. Lorna carried on talking. 'I started the week without a sous chef, suddenly I'm a head chef down, and now I find out we've got a mystery guest coming. It's quite stressful.'

'I'm sure it is.' She didn't look very stressed. The last part of her sentence had certainly caught my attention. I was now curious. 'Mystery guest?'

She nodded. 'You know Brook-Schlager?'

'Yes.' Who didn't? They were a bit like the Michelin Guide for exclusive hotels. A rival to Forbes Travel Guide. They catered for the rich and powerful, particularly the business community. A favourable entry in their guide, online and app form as well as print, could lead to an uptick of about twenty-five per cent in bookings. If you had an upmarket hotel, you might not chew your arm off for a good review but you'd probably gnaw off a couple of fingers. It was a very big deal, no wonder she was nervous.

She carried on. 'Well, they come and stay as Brook-Schlager, so naturally you pull out all the stops. That went okay. Then, at a later date, they return, but this time they send a mystery guest who stays incognito and reports back.'

'Okay.' I was familiar with the concept.

'Well,' she took a deep breath, 'I've been reliably tipped off that he's on the way, could be tomorrow or it could be a fortnight, my source wasn't sure, and now I haven't got anyone I can trust down in the kitchen. Not now that Dave's gone.'

'That's a shame,' I said. I had an idea where this might be heading.

'Charlie,' Lorna said in a wheedling kind of way, 'how would you feel about staying here a little longer?'

'Absolutely not.' I shook my head. First Strickland, now her. I was getting slightly annoyed that people should imagine I had nothing better to do than run their kitchens for them. 'I have a restaurant of my own to run.'

Lorna frowned. 'But presumably it's getting on all right without you. You have to learn to delegate, otherwise you're chained to the bloody place. Here,' she gestured with her head, an imperious motion, surprisingly graceful but obviously proprietorial, 'at the Moray Place you're expanding your horizons, networking…' I smiled. So far I had made friends with a breakfast chef and the man who washed up.

'Look, I intend to go places, Charlie,' Lorna said in a confiding tone. I didn't doubt her sincerity. 'I don't let things stand in my way.' I nodded politely. I had met lots of people in the course of my life who had said similar things. Some did, the majority didn't. Planning and determination can only get you so far. In my experience the old joke, 'How do you make God laugh?… Tell him your plans', seemed fairly accurate.

'I'll pay you double what you're getting now,' she said, leaning forward to emphasise her offer. 'Plus bed and board.'

Now she had my attention. That was money that could be banked. And, to tell the truth, despite Euan, I was enjoying being in Edinburgh. I was enjoying it a lot. On the one hand, it was cold and grey and dark, quite grotty, and Princes Street, like Oxford Street in London was a horror story, the area round the uni mega shabby but the castle on its rock dominating the town was lovely. Wherever you went, it seemed to be there, and it iconically emphasised, signified, how old the city was. I was living in history come to life. Plus I'd decided I really liked the New Town with its distinctive, beautiful Georgian architecture. I also liked the way Edinburgh seemed a secretive sort of place, mysterious. Especially the New Town with its little mews streets, or the old grey tenements with their closes and the little alleyways under the enveloping greyness of Edinburgh's skies. I liked the sound of car tyres on cobbles, a kind of distinctive rumbling noise; I liked the quality of the light in the day, well – what little I had seen of it, a harsh, grey northern light, subtly different from down south. And I liked (with one exception) my colleagues.

I lived in a village where life was open, everything was visible; here, it was the reverse. And I was also enjoying being in a city again, the excitement of it, having shops and bars you could walk to. Not that I'd had the chance to do these things, this was only my fifth day here, but the fact that it was possible was enough. And the running was so different, pavements instead of mud and seeing places and streets I'd never seen before. In short, it was exciting.

'It's not that simple, Lorna,' I sighed. 'You're paying for my work here but Dave's mate down south, Graeme

Strickland, is paying for the cover in my restaurant. Well, to be precise, he's providing a replacement chef, which amounts to the same thing, but now Dave's gone that is obviously going to stop.'

She frowned and stood up. She reminded me in that way of Strickland. She'd said what she wanted to, why waste time chatting any more.

'I won't deny I'm disappointed, Charlie, but if you change your mind, be sure to let me know.' She stalked away, effortlessly elegant on her killer heels.

Chapter Twelve

The following day I was up at six and ran in a big loop from the New Town to Leith, which I gather had at one time been quite a rough dock area but, as often happens these days, had been changed into 'Marina Style Living' as the brochures would have it. There were plenty of bars and restaurants down there but at this time of the morning hardly anyone was around.

I mulled over Strickland's suggestion, well, more of an order really, to stay longer and find out what had happened to Dave Holland. The plus side was strong, I was enjoying Edinburgh. I liked the place, it was so different from village life in Hampden Green. I had no desire to live in a city again, but it was fun being in one temporarily.

I was also enjoying cooking someone else's menu. I was free of responsibility. If we had no customers at all from now until I went home that wasn't my problem. That being said, did I really want to play the detective and try and find out who had killed Dave Holland? The choice to say no lay with me.

Of course, it was entirely possible, that, like the police

thought, it was just a tragic accident. It was all very well Strickland saying, 'Oh he was an expert, he wouldn't make a mistake like that'. Really? I consider myself quite an expert cook, but I still burn or cut myself occasionally, or cock things up. Not often. But it happens. And ingesting a poisonous mushroom is one of those things that you normally get to do but the once. Anyone can make a mistake.

Deep down, I suspected that this was what had happened.

I was very much in two minds when I got back to the hotel in the chilly darkness of the November morning. I even had that old Clash song, 'Should I Stay or Should I Go?' running around in my head.

I decided to go and speak to Martin, the breakfast chef. I liked him a lot and respected his opinion on things. Talking about it would clarify my thinking. I showered, changed into my whites and went down to the kitchen.

I found him with his backside sticking up in the air, doing Downward Dog. Not what you normally encounter in a breakfast kitchen. The sleeves of his jacket had risen and I noticed that his muscular forearms were covered in tattoos. Old-school ones, not like Katriona's more contemporary designs.

He stepped up, placed his two palms either side of his right leg and pivoting forward, stuck his left leg out behind him and executed a perfect Warrior 3. Wow, I thought, he's really good. I watched entranced as he carried on with his Sun Salute variations and then he came to a graceful halt in the proceedings when the ticket machine printed out a couple of breakfast tickets.

He noticed me standing by the pass looking at him and smiled.

'Guid, eh!' he said. 'Not bad for an auld man. What do you think?'

'Sick,' I said, an expression my staff use all the time.

I watched as he cooked a couple of breakfasts with panache and I carried the plates over to the dumb-waiter, put them in and pressed the button to send them up.

I walked round and joined him in the kitchen proper. I took down the clipboard where I'd made an MEP list the night before, all the things that I needed to do before service started at twelve.

I began by making jus. With Martin's help I lifted the heavy stock pan off the stove where the beef bones and the vegetables had been simmering gently overnight. We carried it the length of the kitchen to the pot-wash area and I started the business of removing all the meat and the other things from the stock and binning them. I'd reduce this down later to an almost syrupy state we call demi-glace.

I decided that if I was going to investigate Dave Holland's death I needed an ally. Someone I could trust, otherwise it would be an intolerable job, working alone and friendless in a strange environment in a strange city. I would take Martin into my full confidence. You know how it is with people, sometimes they just click into place as if they were a piece of jigsaw that could only go into that particular shaped hole. And my Zen style breakfast chef was the perfect fit.

So I got straight to the point and told him about Lorna's

offer and also what Strickland had said to me. I was interested in what Martin had to say. He obviously knew Dave Holland well, but there was more to it than that. He was one of those rare individuals that you occasionally meet who seems to know what's going on at some deeper level than most people. In short, he was spiritually insightful.

'I think you should do what he suggests,' he said, firmly. Well, no ambiguity there then. 'Why?'

Another cheque came, he glanced at it and started frying a couple of eggs before taking up the conversation again.

'If it was an accident, fine...' He slid the eggs onto a plate where their whites nestled against some crisp thick bacon. 'You told me you're enjoying yourself here. You won't often get the chance to stay for free in a luxury Edinburgh hotel; make the most of it, even if it is a busman's holiday. If not,' he said with a smile, 'let justice be done. It's not good to have murderers wandering around. And, more selfishly, well, you'll have avenged both my and your friend's friend.' He gestured with the fish-slice in his hand. 'It seems a win-win situation.'

I mulled this over. Another ticket, another breakfast. I watched as he plated some poached eggs, adding some rashers of bacon, half a grilled tomato and some mushrooms to each plate. The bacon was insanely good; I told him so as I carried the plates over to the dumb-waiter to be sent upstairs to the dining room.

'Aye, it's fae a pig farm in Fife,' he informed me, 'free-range, locally slaughtered and smoked. That was one of the many wee bones of contention between Dave and Lorna.'

'In what respect?' I asked.

'Cost. Quality doesnae come cheap as I'm sure you've noticed. He refused to compromise and she had to back down. Personally I think he was right and she was wrong. It's partly why we get such good reviews and repeat custom.' He took another ticket from the machine. 'People notice quality.' He glanced at the ticket, took a large frying pan from the stack and handed it to me.

'Fill that with hot water, will you.'

'Sure.' I put the pan on the stove, walked over to the sink and came back with a jug of water. I wasn't going to make the mistake of carrying the pan to the tap and slosh water over the floor. He turned the heat on under it.

'It's for a kipper,' he said. 'I poach them for five minutes. Could you go in the walk-in and get me one?'

'Yes, Chef,' I said, grinning at him. I returned with the fish and he slid it into the boiling water, turned the heat off and covered the pan.

'Five minutes, that should do it,' he said. 'Now, where was I, oh aye, quality ingredients. It's the same story with the Lorne sausage and the black pudding; they're from a local butcher in Stockbridge.' He sighed. 'Well, she'll get her own way now.' He laughed. 'She'll have to find a new breakfast chef too.'

'You're going to leave?' I was surprised.

He raised his eyebrows and shrugged in a 'what can I do?' kind of way. 'Probably. I'm no' casting my pearls before any old swine. Dave was the main reason I was here... all of which makes me think you should do what yon friend of yours suggests and find out who killed him.'

'But I don't really want to…'

Another cheque from the machine. He tore it off and glanced at it, sighed and said, 'So what? I don't particularly want to be cooking eggs, yet here I am.' His back was to me as he faced the stove.

'Your happiness and your suffering depend on your actions, Charlie.' He started scrambling some eggs this time and then turned to me. His good humour had gone, he was serious. You could tell he meant what he was saying.

'Not doing something is as much an action as doing something. If you find out the truth behind Dave's death we'll all be grateful. If you don't, whoever killed him will be grateful. It's your choice, but it is a choice.'

'So you *do* think he was murdered!' I said over the noise of the fans. He thought for a while, and then as he was putting the scrambled eggs onto a plate together with a piece of Lorne sausage and some fried potatoes (God, the breakfasts here were good!) and I carried that over to be sent upstairs to the dining room, he replied, 'What I think doesn't matter.' He looked me in the eye and I could see he was deadly serious. 'The ball has landed in your court, nae mine. But remember, if you do nothing you'll have to live with that decision for the rest of your days.' He smiled, his good humour returning. 'It's up to you.'

'Thank you for your input, Martin,' I said. I was feeling a bit stunned by all of that; I'd been expecting a yes, no or whatever.

'Thank you, Chef,' he said ironically and turned back to the stove.

Carrying my muddy running shoes in one hand, I walked up the stairs to shower. I knew what I had to do now. Back in my room I texted Strickland.

'Okay. Deal.'

Chapter Thirteen

Lorna was delighted when I said that I'd be staying. I gave her the news first thing in her office. As usual, despite her staffing troubles and the looming threat of the mystery guest, there was not a hair out of place and her makeup might have been done professionally. I noticed again how attractive she was – those full sensual lips at odds with the cold eyes.

'There are provisos…' I warned. 'I'll need to have two days off a fortnight, Sundays and Mondays, so I can fly home and check on my own place. And I'll need to be reimbursed for that.'

'That's fine,' Lorna said, hurriedly. She was obviously delighted to have a competent head chef in place while she tried to fill the vacancy. I continued.

'My finish day will be 1st January. That gives you nearly two months to find a suitable chef and sous chef. And that should cover the period of your mystery guest visiting too.'

'Thank you so much, Charlie.' She let out a long sigh. 'That's such a load off my shoulders.' She gave me a sharp look. 'What about the Christmas menu? That needs sorting out very quickly.'

'We'll use mine.' I ran the menu that I'd discussed a while ago with Strickland in the bar of the Three Bells past her – how long ago that seemed!

'That sounds okay,' she said, satisfied.

'And I would like to be paid weekly,' I stipulated. I'd been shafted before by unscrupulous employers. I wouldn't say that I mistrusted her but Lorna had struck me as the kind of woman whose heart was about as warm as an Edinburgh winter and who might well decide that economies might need to be made – starting with the quality of the bacon and moving on to include not paying me.

I added another proviso then, triggered by that thought, 'And, so long as I'm here, we won't be changing suppliers, I don't want to upset Martin.'

I didn't want to use the word 'lose'. That would be between the two of them.

'Really?' The tone was that of incredulity. I doubled down on my request.

'Martin is the key to the whole thing working, Lorna,' I insisted. 'We – that is, you, very much need him, he'll be stepping up a gear in the kitchen.'

'I see,' she pressed her lips together irritably. 'Anything else, Charlie? Any more conditions?'

'If I think of any I'll be sure to let you know.'

'Okay.' She adjusted the position of a thin gold bracelet on an elegant wrist. 'Can you put a new vegetarian dish on the menu please. The mushroom risotto is not a great seller, never has been. And it looks horrible too.'

Well, here she was taking an exploratory swing of the axe to Holland's menu. I didn't mind, I didn't like the mushroom risotto either.

'Aubergine vegetable timbale with goats cheese and freekeh salad, as a main for the lunch menu,' I said, off the top of my head. I like freekeh, it's a kind of roasted wheat, which you boil for about quarter of an hour. It tastes nice, it's good for you and it intrigues customers, all good things. 'The salad can go on the à la carte evening menu as a starter too. For the evenings we'll have gnocchi Genovese, that's gnocchi with a pesto sauce with an Italian tomato salad. That do?'

She looked somewhat taken aback, 'nonplussed', Jess would have said. Maybe it was another Italian dish on the menu that wouldn't have been there if Dave Holland had still been about. But she raised no objections.

'Um, that's fine.' I don't think she expected it to be so easy for me to come up with satisfactory alternatives.

'We're not busy tomorrow,' I said. 'I'll make it for you for lunch. You have the final say.'

'Thank you, Charlie, that all sounds perfect. Okay,' she said briskly, 'I'll draw you up a new contract with a revised salary and the other points, travel et cetera included. It'll be ready by this evening.'

She smiled again, this time with genuine feeling, and shook my hand.

'Thank you again and welcome on board.'

After a busy lunch the following day, despite my own predictions, a couple of sizeable non-bookings had turned up, I went up to my room to relax. In my imagination the stuffed stag's head on the wall by the stairs seemed to look on me in a friendly way, now that I was a member of staff. I'd grown quite fond of Staggie as I had, with great originality, decided to call him. I was tired. It was Saturday and we were fully booked that evening. I lay on my back on my bed and stared at the ceiling, high above me. I loved the proportions of these Georgian houses with their massive windows and tall ceilings. Obviously you'd pay for that in your heating bills and in today's energy conscious world they were far from ideal, but this wasn't my problem. Not the ecological aspect, I mean – we're all in that together – I meant I wasn't paying the heating bills.

I idly ran through the list of suspects in my mind who might have poisoned David Holland. There were two main ones:

Euan, continually passed over for promotion, only still employed because he was too difficult to get rid of; Lorna, because she could modernise the hotel as she saw fit, now that Dave was no longer around to veto her suggestions.

There was also Rosa, his ex side-piece. That's if Ali was to be believed. Could it be Ali himself, I wondered. He was said to be devoted to Dave but love can very quickly turn to hate. I doubt if many people have been murdered by indifferent people.

It was half past three now and I didn't have to start work until six. I decided that I would go for a quick run. I hadn't gone out in the morning; it had been pouring with rain and that biting Edinburgh wind would have whipped the rain painfully into my face and eyes. I looked out of the window; the skies were leaden but there was no sign of the earlier downpour.

I changed and left the hotel, running up a hill and then along a wide road with cars parked in the middle that ran parallel to Princes Street, the main street beneath the rock surmounted by the castle that so dominates the skyline. George Street was, I gathered, the main street for the financial services and banks in the city. It looked it; it was all very imposing. I was coming up to an expensive gentlemen's outfitters opposite an equally expensive-looking hotel when, to my surprise, Lorna emerged from the shop, arm in arm with a man. She was carrying a couple of large bags with the shop's name on and they paused and kissed. This was no peck on the cheek. Their mouths meant business. I hung back and hid behind a parked delivery van. I knew Lorna would be furious if she were spotted by a member of staff in a passionate embrace.

When I peeked around the corner of the van they had moved further down the street, heading in the direction of the St James Quarter a new shopping plaza at the far end of Princes Street near Leith Walk. That, I knew, was a wide, broad thoroughfare containing more of the new controversial tramlines that led down from the end of Princes Street by some lovely old buildings, including an enormous Gothic hotel, the Balmoral, down to the now chi-chi Leith harbour area with its new developments.

That was the direction I wanted to run in. I wondered what to do. I didn't want to run past them, I felt it would have been awkward, so I walked a distance behind them. I was wearing a kind of runner's ski mask and a beanie hat against the freezing wind, so only my eyes and nose were visible. Lorna glanced behind her and crossed the road to my side but although I'd been in her line of vision she obviously didn't recognise me.

I followed them into a wide square that had a large central grassy area behind railings bisected by paths, and a statue of some guy on top of a pillar. The stone column seemed inordinately tall, dominating the skyline like an admonishing finger. Behind it was the unlovely shape of the St James Quarter. You looked around you at the beautiful old buildings and then the shopping mall and thought, 'Really? Is that the best you can do?'

Lorna and the man disappeared into a hotel, Number Three St Andrew Square, it was called.

I looked more closely at Number Three. It was an old building, not a tenement like the Moray Place but a big, Victorian edifice, maybe a former bank. As I watched, a post-hipster couple, achingly smart, trotted up the steps where the door was opened for them by a concierge who was about six foot six, with a jet black Mohican, the sides of his head shaven, wearing a kind of faux-Edwardian steampunk-style suit. I thought of Donald and Craig; they seemed so dowdy in comparison. And so old-fashioned.

I was intrigued now. I wanted to know more about Lorna and her beau. What kind of man would she go out with? I studied my reflection in the window of an adjacent shop. My shoes were an expensive brand of running gear, suitably logoed. They weren't muddy for a change. I'd been running on city streets and pavements so they looked pretty good. My Lycra running tights had a kind of crazy Day-Glo pattern on them, and, though I say it myself, I have great legs: long, slim, toned. I pulled my hi-viz running jacket off and folded it up so I was just wearing a hoodie, removed my beanie hat and ski mask, shook my hair free. I now looked pretty good.

I strode arrogantly up the steps of the hotel. Mohican guy gave me a warm smile as he opened the door for me. I was right, I thought, confidence is all.

I walked into the lobby and looked around, trying not to gawp. It was spectacular.

It was funky with ultra-modern vibes. Lots of coloured glass and lights, a couple of disco balls on the ceiling. Ambient jazz, with a tinge of Slowdive, drifted from hidden speakers. There were two people behind the reception desk, one male, one female. The man had a shaved head, and the lights from the ceiling bounced off it like a prototype of the disco balls overhead. He was wearing discreet makeup, eyeliner, and he'd had his nails done in black with silver filigree. He was good-looking in a kind of Austin Butler in *Dune* type way, but better humoured and with nice eyebrows.

I saw Lorna and the man walk around the corner of the reception desk and through a door marked 'Manager'. I was now intrigued.

'Can I help you?' Austin Butler/Feyd-Rautha asked. He'd done a good job with the eyeliner, it had to be said. He was even better-looking up close, with a kind of 'look at me' arrogance, which I kind of liked. He had a name tag on his lapel, he was wearing a two piece suit with a plain white T-shirt. The name on the tag said Gav Schmidt.

I pointed at the door. 'Was that Patrick Svenson I saw going in there?'

'I'm sorry?' Austin was puzzled.

'He's the GM at the Radisson,' I said, lying fluently.

He shook his head, smiling now he understood the question. 'No, that's Ollie McDougall, Director of F & B for the hotel chain.'

I shook my head, giving my embarrassed woman laugh – not a sound I make very often. 'Oh, silly me… well thanks for clearing that up.'

'The Radisson… ?' he mused, then suddenly asked, 'Are you in the trade?'

'Yeah,' I said. There's quite a strong camaraderie in the hospitality trade, we can bond easily. I decided I wanted to bond with Gav, for a variety of reasons. 'I'm a chef. You said chain?'

'Oh, aye,' he said, he smiled deprecatingly, 'a small chain. Not many links yet, we're growing. We've got a place in Glasgow but we're looking to expand here in Edinburgh.'

'Really? Whereabouts?'

'Well, we've got an eye on a place in the New Town,' he smiled, 'we'll need a new kitchen team.'

It sounded a bit like a job offer, one that Gav was in no position to make, in my view. Then, if only you knew, Gav.

'A new team all round,' he continued.

'A new broom?' I suggested helpfully.

'Aye, sweep away all the auld, dead wood. Anyway,' he said briskly, 'we're much nicer than the Radisson.'

I looked around. 'You're certainly more original. Thank you… nice nails.'

He inspected his fingers. 'We do try,' he said, 'I'm Gav by the way…'

I resisted the urge to say I know.

'Charlie, pleased to meet you.'

We shook hands and I walked off to the bar. I could feel Gav's gaze fixed on my backside as I walked away. Maybe he was evaluating my assets as a potential employee, or maybe he had something else on his mind, despite appearances. Or maybe he just had a kink thing about women's running tights. Something told me I'd be seeing him again; maybe I would ask him.

The bar at Number Three was great. It was so unlike the traditional, but, let's face it, boring bar of the Moray Place. It was sizeable and had little natural light but they had turned this into an advantage by making it mysterious. The colour scheme was mainly brown, dark varnished wooden floor, a long bar with three backlit, copper-lined alcoves behind it, artistic neon lighting. The front of the bar was a kind of intricate latticed woodwork. The tables were low and wooden, some with inlaid marquetry, subdued Art Deco lighting and the odd piece of statuary in bronze. Other things to look at were a couple of dazzling light-installations, sculptures of twisted neon in moody purples, pinks and red. It was sumptuous and slightly decadent. Think 1930s Singapore colonial style meets cyberpunk.

I looked at the cocktail menu and wished I wasn't working in less than a couple of hours. I settled for a tonic water from the barista who had entered into the Art Deco vibe with her hair a jet black, geometrically cut bob, her mouth a slash of brilliant red lipstick, 1930s-style pegged trousers and a white blouse, along with a dark green jade necklace. She served me wordlessly with a slight scowl and a major hint of condescension.

Lose the attitude, sweetie, I thought, you're a barmaid.

I sat in a corner and mulled over my talk with Gav. I thought it highly likely that the new hotel he had mentioned was intended to be the Moray Place Hotel. Ali had told me how Lorna wanted to steer it more upmarket, vibier, brighter and on point, more va va voom. And here she was – having an affair with the Food & Beverage director of this jazzy place. I was now thinking, she wants to totally control the hotel and Ollie will provide the finance to buy the others out.

There was a bar menu on the table in front of me. I idly looked at it: chicken katsu sandwich (was that even a good idea?), truffled French toast, crispy salmon sushi, popcorn pork. I thought of the Moray Place bar snack menu: sausage roll, prawn vol au vents, grilled steak baguette and fries. All good, all beautifully done and well-presented but not on point like these. We had a charcuterie platter, they had panko-fried pickles with garlic and chilli mayo.

Well, here was food for thought. Loyal as I was to the old guard as represented by David and his classic menu, if I was out for a fancy cocktail or out to impress a date, I'd rather be eating their food than his, and I had to confess I'd rather be cooking it too.

Of course, the fifty-to-eighty-year-olds and well-heeled businessmen who made up the clientele who stayed in the hotel where I was working would not necessarily want innovation, their tastes in food would be well-fixed by now. Lorna would need a revolution, a total change in customers – but if anyone was going to be a Robespierre to lead a blood-soaked insurrection it would be her, ruthlessly crushing dissent under her killer heels. Currently the Moray Place Hotel had gone as far as it possibly could, and she wanted more than that. And I didn't blame her. Hotels have to modernise or die, unless they have the cachet of the Ritz or Claridge's.

Donald would be out, his gentle face would not fit. Neither would Annie, the competent sixty-something lady behind the bar. Lorna would want someone more like the girl behind the bar here, Gen Z with attitude. Craig might be okay, he was young enough, but he wasn't pure vibes like the staff at Number Three. I strongly suspected that they'd be led away to the knacker's yard for humane slaughter. That would be Lorna's way, it wouldn't be mine. Old and new can co-exist and enhance each other. As Martin would doubtless say, we should be more Tao about this. However, unless something dramatic happened, that would not be in my hands.

I drank up my tonic water, gave an ironic toast to the Ancien Régime of the Moray Place Hotel who were soon going to be all hauled off to the guillotine and left the bar.

Chapter Fourteen

After a busy Saturday night, I decided to sleep in and got up at seven the following day. I put on my chef's whites and went downstairs to help Martin with the breakfast shift. It was busy, we did about forty covers. Then at 10 o'clock Innes turned up for work. As Euan didn't work Sundays, I was going to need to train the two of them up to cover for me when I was away the following weekend.

Martin had told me he had been a head chef in pubs and a sous in various restaurants. He talked the talk and he could certainly cook breakfast to perfection, but I was keen to see how he would cope with a busy lunch.

The hotel did a restricted Sunday lunch menu. Essentially it was a three, three, three menu, those numbers referring to the number of courses for starters, main and dessert. The vegetarian option was spinach and feta börek as a main (layers of filo pastry sandwiched with the filling) and today the option of the aubergine timbales with freekeh, which I'd mentioned before to Lorna. The meat was roast beef with the usual accompaniments; the fish choice: the salmon with a lovage sauce.

This limited menu meant that it was within the ability of two chefs to handle it, provided they knew what they were doing.

I was particularly keen to show Innes how to make the vegetarian options and she was a joy to work with. She learned quickly, had laser concentration and was very deft with her hands. I started looking at her with new eyes. With the right tutelage she could go far. She liked being shown new things, like how to make Yorkshire puddings ('so the oil in the tray has to be very hot when the batter goes in?', 'exactly Innes, practically smoking, that way they rise really well.') and I like teaching the techniques and skills passed to me to those keen to learn. She was confident too, far more so than when I was her age. I began to suspect that there were hidden depths to Innes. Up until now I had just thought of her, slightly dismissively I have to admit, as a naïve young kid. Sweet but lightweight. Now I was beginning to change my mind and treat her with more respect.

The only thing that threw me slightly was the cooking times of the meat. In my restaurant we serve roast beef rosy-pink. Martin shook his head. This is Scotland, he explained, folks will go crazy if you do that, they'll say it's under-cooked. I took his advice. When in Rome…

Well, lunch was a resounding success and Martin proved to be highly competent, so much so that I let the two of them do most of the cooking and plating, restricting myself to the donkey work, veg, desserts, and trotting between the pass and the dumb-waiter to send the food upstairs. I have rarely felt so happy not to be needed. I had no worries now about next week's forthcoming lunch when I was down south.

By half-two we were finished and I sent the two of them home while I dealt with the last few desserts and tidied up the kitchen.

I reflected as I sat having a post-service beer on a crate outside the kitchen door with Ali that the kitchen would be in good hands when I went home the following week.

'She's a good kid, that Innes, Ali,' I said.

He gave me a strange look. 'Aye well… I'm sure she is.'

It wasn't exactly a ringing endorsement, but Ali was old and maybe not a fan of Generation Z/Alpha, Innes' age cohort.

'What's that supposed to mean, Ali?'

'Oh nothing, I was just havering…'

He was lying; there was something but I wasn't going to press him. To be honest, I was disappointed with his attitude. If he had a problem with her that was very much his issue to deal with. She was more than competent in the kitchen and that was the main thing.

I went back to my room, slept for an hour or so, showered and then went down to the bar for a drink. I thought I'd have a couple of glasses of their very good house red and then go and have a curry at an Indian that Ali had recommended, not far from the hotel in Stockbridge, as cheap and cheerful. Well, that suited me just fine.

I chatted a bit to Annie behind the bar. As I watched her cheerfully bustling around, bantering with the customers, expertly and efficiently making the occasional cocktail

(Craig had been right), I reflected on the difference between her and the barista at Number Three. I couldn't imagine Thirties Girl sweet-talking the customers. I wondered what she made of Lorna who was sleeping with her boss. As if by that magical process that when thinking about someone makes them appear, as I finished my wine, Lorna came and sat on the stool next to me.

'Can I get you another?' she asked.

'Please.'

'Let's go somewhere where we can talk.'

She led me to the same corner table that we had sat at before – removing the 'reserved' tag that was on it. It was in a corner of the bar that was partially obscured by a large potted weeping fig. We were hard to see behind the foliage but it gave a great view of the bar and the customers. It was obviously her table where she could keep an eye on things.

'Well, lunch went well,' she said, 'cheers.'

We clinked glasses.

'Innes and Martin did most of the work,' I said, 'I just supervised.'

She nodded. 'Maybe.' I don't think she believed me.

'I was very impressed with the vegetarian dishes,' she said. 'Dave didn't like vegetarians, he was very behind the times in many respects… he…'

She suddenly stopped talking. A man had walked into the bar, that's what had silenced her and I saw the pupils of her eyes dilating with excitement. I peered around the plant to see the guy who had piqued her interest.

I was expecting some hottie, he'd have to be to jolt Lorna's mind off the subject of the Moray Place Hotel.

I was totally wrong.

He was in his fifties I guessed, overweight and balding with a bit of a comb-over going on. He was wearing dark trousers, a sports jacket and a shirt and tie that clashed.

He seemed an unlikely choice of man to ogle. But Lorna wasn't the only one he'd affected. Katriona, the waitress who wouldn't give me the time of day, was kind of all over him, laughing, playing with her hair; it looked very much like she'd undone a strategic button on her blouse. I raised a questioning eyebrow.

'That's him,' Lorna said, her voice quivering with excitement. She was sitting bolt upright, her slender fingers clutching her knees in their expensive dark tights, her knuckles white.

'That's who?' I asked.

'The mystery guest...' she whispered. She turned her head to me, her eyes glowing feverishly, 'That's him!'

Chapter Fifteen

'This is for the mystery guest, Room 23,' Martin said. Just down the corridor from me, I thought.

I looked at the plate on the pass, glowing under the lights. It was faultless, like all of Martin's breakfasts. It was like an illustration from a cookery book, the kind where they are not constrained to use real food.

It was the full Scottish: square sausage (aka Lorne), bacon, fried egg, mushrooms, grilled tomato, black pudding and a portion of baked beans in a ramekin so they wouldn't encroach into the other food on the plate. That would do the mystery guest's waistline a power of good, I thought.

'Better make sure I don't drop it!' I said and carried it over to the lift.

I rejoined him.

'Thank you so much for yesterday,' I said. 'You were fantastic. I don't know why Lorna doesn't just make you head chef and be done with it.'

Lorna had been on my mind for a while. I had reported my discovery that she was in bed (literally and figuratively) with the Cromarty Hotel Chain who owned Number

Three. Strickland had reacted strongly to this. I could feel his excitement through my phone. 'Really! She's trying to get a majority holding, that's why she's raising the money through them. She's a devious bitch. She's obviously the killer, Charlie, you can't let her get away with this, find evidence!'

Then he'd ended the call, I could hear shouting in the background and kitchen noises.

Me, I wasn't so sure.

Martin laughed. 'That'd really be something for Euan to moan about at his men's group.'

I looked at him questioningly. 'Come again?'

'He belongs to a men's group,' he explained. 'They meet in the church hall near the cathedral in the West End.'

'What do they do?' I asked, with interest. I'd once been to a 'Women in Catering' do, tempted by the free wine on offer. I'd gone with this girl I knew called Jo, a shy, mono-syllabic pastry chef.

'I hate things like this,' she told me through gritted teeth. She lasted five minutes then went to the ladies and locked herself in a cubicle with her phone. I was bored stiff.

I couldn't see Euan networking, even with other men, even if they were sci-fi addicts. I couldn't see Euan getting on with anyone.

'Well, it all started a while ago, it's quite a thing in America,' Martin informed me, 'the men's movement. The poet Robert Bly was very influential in their development.'

He went on to explain that some men felt they had been frozen out of life, ridiculed for being a true man, depicted as out of touch Homer Simpson characters, jerked around by a woman/feminist based society whose values were not theirs. Basically, they felt marginalised.

'Really?' I said, disbelievingly. I thought of the men in my life; Cliff Yeats, Graeme Strickland (the reason I was here), the Earl, Francis, my ex – Andrea. None of them seemed remotely the victims of a feminist or societal conspiracy. My sous chef Murdo was intimidated by his girlfriend, mentally and physically; she could have torn him limb from limb, but he kind of liked that. He'd signed up for it after all.

'Do you feel victimised, Martin?' I asked.

He shook with laughter. He adjusted the cap on his bald head. As he did I noted again his tattooed forearm, corded with muscle. He was a strong guy. I couldn't see him being victimised. He was quietly self-confident.

'Do I feel crushed under the heel of Lorna's Manolo Blahniks or your Caterpillar work boots, Charlie?' he asked mockingly. 'No.' Then he frowned. 'But I grew up in Muirhouse, which is nae the most salubrious part of Edinburgh and if you're from somewhere like that, parents who are not exactly what ye might call award-winning – there's a lot of poverty, drugs, alcoholism, crime, violence... those are the issues, not middle-class ones like who wears the trousers, ken? You're lucky tae have breeks in the first place.'

'Yeah, sure...' I'd grown up in a single parent family in a council house. I was lucky, I'd had a supportive and loving father, but I kind of knew what he was talking about. However, I was fascinated by this new aspect of Euan as social warrior in the Gender Wars. I so wanted to hear him talking about how he'd been victimised by women – for the worst of motives I freely admit. I hadn't had a good laugh in ages.

Maybe I was kind of proving his point. Well, you can overthink these things. If there was any benefit of doubt going, I wouldn't be giving it to my sous chef, that was for sure.

'When does he go to these meetings?' I asked.

'Monday nights.' That was tonight.

'I so wish I could go…' I said, wistfully.

He laughed. 'You can if you want.'

I smiled. 'I don't think I would make a convincing man, Martin.'

'You don't need to,' he said, serious now. 'It's a hybrid meeting, they have it in person and on Zoom. You can use my id and log in as me, just don't speak.'

'Really? But they'll see me.'

He shook his head. 'No they won't. Just log in with audio only, keep the camera switched off.'

I mulled this over; what if I got caught? What indeed? Who cares, it was worth a go.

'How come you've got a log-in, Martin? Are you a member?' I was curious to know.

'No, but I am interested in what they have to say. There are some deep thinkers in there, not many I grant you, and unfortunately there's an incel group to watch out for. They're not pro-men, they're just very anti-women. They're the ones to keep an eye out for.'

'I'll be careful not to give myself away,' I promised.

'Enjoy the meeting,' he said. 'I'll send you the meeting code and the password. I hope it proves illuminating.'

'Thanks. I think it will.'

So 8 o'clock that evening found me with my laptop open on the table in my bedroom. Whatever you might or might not say about the men's group they were impeccably techy. The video link was crystal clear and the audio was perfect.

I had no trouble logging into the meeting. I entered the meeting id and the password and, keeping my video camera switched off, logged in as Martin G. There were fifteen other people using Zoom, I noticed.

On my screen, I was looking at about thirty men sitting in rows on folding chairs. In the background was a trestle table with cans and bottles and a small keg of beer. They were all holding a drink of one kind or another. I could also see several banners hanging down. One was Cerne Abbas Man, the chalk figure with a huge phallus. John Wayne was there too and Batman, the Christian Bale Batman, not Adam West (slightly to my disappointment), as was Thor.

None of the attendees would have been mistaken for an all-action hero figure and I somewhat doubted Chris Hemsworth was going to be putting in an appearance.

The guest speaker was a guy called Donovan R. Like many a 12 Step Group whose format they had vaguely adopted, they had decided to lose the surnames. Donovan R told a tale of woe, about how he'd had an affair with a work colleague, his wife had found out and promptly kicked him out of the marital home so now he was living at a mate's house on a blow-up air bed.

'Is it fair?' he asked self-pityingly. 'I paid for most of that house and the children are siding with her and I've still got to pay the mortgage, and then Lisa from HR dumped me. I think she's what they call a home-wrecker... She had her evil way with me and then just threw me aside...' here a tear rolled down his face, perhaps they were pretend sobs, perhaps not, 'like a discarded condom...' he sobbed.

He had one of those red faces and tufty hair that put me in mind of a celeriac. Not that it was grey-brown and slightly misshapen, just the general shape. His eyes were nearly popping out of his face with anger as he spoke. I wondered what Lisa from HR had seen in him in the first place, maybe she looked like a root vegetable too. Like often calls to like.

The secretary gave him a hug and then Donovan sat down, wiping his eyes.

'All of us have been victimised in some way, greater or lesser, by what is laughably referred to as "the gentler sex",' the secretary said sympathetically. 'Now, before we get down to sharing our lives and experiences as men, just a quick housekeeping note.' He looked around. 'Some of us have wanted to burn sage in the meetings; I want to make this very clear, this is church property and we are not allowed...'

'But they do it in sweat lodges in America, I've been...' A tall, bald man with a beard and a Bruce Springsteen T-shirt that emphasised his belly objected, standing up, the better to make his point.

'That may be, but we're not in a sweat lodge in America and this place is owned by the Catholic church not by

Native American shamans.' The secretary had a rather testy tone to his voice now. 'Any other points about sage you can put them in the group chat, okay?' He looked around challengingly; there were a few background grumbles but the sage lobby shut up.

'Good, now, let's carry on' – here he produced a piece of wood about the length of a rolling pin painted with colourful tribal designs; the audience murmured appreciatively, they obviously liked the stick – 'I'm going to pass the talking stick around and those who want to speak please hold the stick aloft and give your name to the audience.'

The stick moved along the row, like Pass the Parcel without the music. A couple of people spoke, one complaining about his ex, another about how hard it was to be a man these days because no one respected you and it was probably because of homosexuality – 'Just look at the Roman Empire,' he shrieked, somewhat camply, and then it was Euan's turn.

I leaned forward to concentrate on the screen.

'Hi, I'm Euan, I'm very much the victim of women.' A murmur of sympathy ran through the audience. 'Wait till you hear this,' he said. He did his usual Euan thing of looking around challengingly. I wondered if he would bring in the Mandalorian.

'I don't just have one woman boss, I have two…' A sharp intake of breath. Horrors! That would be me and Lorna. I was fascinated. 'But it's principally my line manager who's making my life miserable at the moment.' That was me. It's not often that you get the opportunity to find out exactly what people think of you, here was my chance.

'She's absolutely horrible to me.' He looked around aggressively as if someone was going to contradict him. Of course no one did. 'She's a stuck-up bitch who goes out of her way to make my life miserable… I won't say where I work, but I should have been running it long ago, but when my old boss departed, the Queen Bitch,' Lorna I thought, not a bad job title, I rather liked it, 'didn't appoint me to replace him.' He emphasised the *me* heavily. 'Even though I've been there for eleven years and know the job inside out. No, because I'm a man… she brought in this cow… This Charlie woman ridicules,' another pause for effect, 'yeah, that's right, absolutely ridicules, my interests in life…' True, I said to myself, nodding agreement, I did ridicule you, 'and not only that, she physically threatened me in front of witnesses in the workplace! What an absolute bitch!'

Well, it was undeniable, I had threatened to ram a rolling pin up his sorry arse. The whining self-pity was beginning to grate on me though, so I didn't feel any remorse for my actions.

Then he really got my attention. 'I was so fed up with my old boss that when he died, I was actually glad. Women loved him because he was so full of himself. The only good Chad is a dead Chad,' and here he looked challengingly around him, 'it's what he deserved, and when I think how those sluts I work with behave… I'll give you one example. One of my female co-workers, I won't say her name, some Stacey, told me she was going to sleep with one of the guests because she thinks he can advance her career. I know full well she's done it before for money, now she'll do it to get ahead! What chance do you or I stand against women like that, who can buy anything with the offer of their bodies. Hypergaming… it's the 80–20 rule in full action. Well, I think they should get their just desserts too! Thank you for listening to me.'

He passed the stick on and I waited a few minutes then logged out of the meeting. Blimey!

The dislike he had towards me and Lorna I had already factored in. That came as no surprise. What did shake me was his hatred of Dave Holland.

Someone had told me that Euan had resented David for not promoting him. I hadn't understood that this feeling had festered and turned into outright hatred. Nor had I realised how envious he was of Holland's popularity with women. How easy it would have been if he'd come across, or otherwise obtained, a deadly mushroom to have added it to the chef's selection in the fridge. I was also surprised to learn that he had harboured feelings towards Katriona. At least that's who I assume he was talking about when he mentioned the flirting with the guest. I didn't think it was Annie. And there was another revelation.

The guest that he claimed she was going to sleep with had to be the mystery guest. He was the only one I could think of who could advance her career. Of course, that could equally refer to Lorna; she might have suggested to Katriona that if she seduced him to ensure a good write-up of the hotel, a promotion might well be in order.

Either way, I felt I had learned a lot.

I went down to the bar that evening in a thoughtful mood. The mystery guest aka Room 23 was there again. I sat at

Lorna's table where I could get a good look at the bar while being relatively hidden. His face was flushed, his tie slightly askew and when Katriona brought him a drink and bent over to put it on his table, he tried to clumsily kiss her. She said something to him and I noticed him recoil and then reply. The way he moved his hands in a placatory kind of way made me think he was apologising.

She went back to the bar and took her apron off and then I saw her leave. I walked back over the bar and said to Annie, 'Same again please…'

'Of course, Charlie.'

'So how long has Katriona worked here, Annie?' I asked, idly. After Euan's revelation I was curious to learn more.

'About three years. Her sister was here first and then she came along; she kind of got her the job.'

'So she worked here in the bar as well?'

'Oh no, not in the bar, Ellie's a chef.'

'Why did she leave?'

'Dave Holland sacked her a month back, said she was incompetent. Och, you should have heard the row, they were screeching at each other, ye could hear it from up here, terrible noise.'

'Where does she work now?'

'Oh, nae far from here, there's a hotel up the road in St Andrew Square, Number Three it's called, that's where she works… Goodnight Mr Sinclair!' she waved. I turned around to see the mystery guest leave the bar.

Well, yet another connection to Number Three. In some ways it wasn't too surprising that Ellie should have ended up there. She was a hotel chef out of a job and they were a hotel who needed a chef. It's never too hard to get a job in a kitchen, no matter how terrible you are; she must have struck lucky, or pulled her socks up.

Later on when I went up to my room at about half ten I walked around the corner to the corridor that led to my room and suddenly, to my surprise, I saw Katriona from behind.

What was she doing up here? I hung back, and I heard a knock at one of the doors. I peeked around the corner. I saw Katriona walk into a room further down from mine. I knew whose it was, I knew the numbering system.

Room 23.

Chapter Sixteen

The next morning I was working with Euan.

'Did you have a nice weekend?' I asked him.

'No,' he said, shortly, glaring at me as if it were my fault. 'I went to a *Star Wars* special at the Everyman, it was a screening of the first three films,' he paused, 'that's Numbers 4, 5 and 6 chronologically, in terms of production... they are so disappointing after the first three...'

'I'm sure they are,' I murmured. I was batting out veal for Wiener Schnitzel or Cotoletta Milanese as it's called in Italy. It's thinly beaten, then floured, egg-and-breadcrumbed: pannéing as it's known. We would serve it with some chips (matchstick fries or pommes allumettes – posh words for thin cut chips) which was what Euan was doing.

'For example, what is Jar Jar Binks doing addressing the Senate?' he demanded.

'I have no idea,' I said wondering vaguely who Jar Jar Binks was. My mind was still busy processing what I had heard the night before. It looked like Euan's words had been true. I suppose Katriona had slept with Room 23, bald spot, belly and sad sack clothes just for the promise of a leg-up in the industry if she put out.

'And why did Anakin not go back to Tatooine and rescue his mother…' he shook his head sadly.

'I have no idea.'

'Ah well…' He'd obviously forgotten my rolling pin threat or maybe he thought that only applied to the Mandalorian and that with *Star Wars* he would be on a more secure footing.

After seeing him last night moaning about me on Zoom I didn't have the heart to tell him to shut up again. Instead I blanked him out as he started droning on about the size of the Clone Army. Seemingly, four million was nowhere near big enough given the sheer size of the Galactic Empire or something like that.

Anyway, I bravely put up with this until lunch began. Then, mercifully we were too busy to talk.

After service I walked up the narrow stairs to the ground floor and emerged from the door by Lorna's office.

I could hear voices at reception and I didn't want to breeze past guests wearing my stained whites. I peeked round the corner. Katriona was leaning over the front desk, I could just see her back and her tattooed arms. Craig was on duty, he was sitting down staring up at her, ashen faced.

'That's right, you little nonce… cos that's what you are isn't it? A nonce… You make me sick, I know what you're up to…'

'Please leave me alone…' I heard Craig say, pleadingly. He was almost cowering with fear and humiliation. To my horror I saw a tear roll down his cheek.

'That's right, start greetin' batty boy!'

She straightened up and I retreated along the corridor, then I heard her feet on the stairs as she ran up to the restaurant.

I didn't know what to do. I felt disgusted by what I'd seen, and somehow complicit by my non-action. Part of me had wanted to step in and intervene, but this wasn't my workplace and I didn't want to get embroiled in a Moray House Civil War. I already had one battle going on with Euan, I didn't want to add another to the mix. And more than that, I felt it might add to Craig's distress, my knowing how she had humiliated him. I guess Martin might have said that was one of the reasons people went to the men's group you couldn't complain about being bullied by a woman anywhere else, people would think you were weak or pitiful. Poor, gentle Craig.

That evening I was working with Martin. Euan had asked if he could have the evening off to go to a belated fireworks party and I'd said yes. At 6 o'clock Katriona had come down for some staff dinner with another of the waitresses. I noticed she ignored Innes as she fetched her food, a pointed kind of insult. Innes' face was set and resigned. It was obvious that Katriona was the hotel bully. Despite that, I found some kind of sympathy for her. I thought about how depressing it was that she was having to sell herself in a surely misguided attempt to get ahead, and how odd that it was to Room 23 who, balding, overweight and cheery, looked the epitome of a happily married man.

Katriona would turn the heads of most men. She was

coarsely good-looking with a good figure and legs. The tattoos helped. They hinted at, or sign-posted, a wild aggressive femininity. Tonight she was looking quite hot, I thought, wearing a short black skirt and very sheer tights with low heels.

It was the first chance I'd had to talk to Martin since the previous day. Ali was off and we had an agency kp in, a Sri Lankan guy who spoke hardly any English, so we could talk freely.

'I logged in to Euan's meeting last night.'

'Interesting was it?'

'Very. I hadn't realised what a horrible bitch I was.'

He laughed. 'Is that what he said about you?'

'Yes.'

'I wouldnae pay any heed tae what Euan says, he'd be havering as usual…'

'Do you think I'm being a bitch to him, Martin?' I was being quite serious and he paid me the compliment of thinking before he answered.

'No, he's just resentful. I do think you're quite tough though…'

'Really?' I felt a bit disheartened.

'No, that's a good thing.' I felt a bit happier. He continued, 'You're the captain of this ship, someone has to give the orders, or it will sink. And everyone except for Euan is on board with that, so don't worry about it.'

'Thank you.'

'Now, why all the preoccupation with Katriona?'

He must have noticed me appraising her earlier.

I told him what I had heard from Euan last night and

what I had seen with my own eyes, her and the mystery guest. Her spat with Craig I kept quiet about. Martin raised his eyebrows slightly in surprise,

'Well, you cannae be surprised that she didn't go out with Euan when he asked her,' he pointed out mildly, and to my astonishment.

'Euan asked her for a date!'

'Aye, she laughed in his face, at least, that's what I heard and I can well believe it. That lassie is… well, let's just say she has issues.'

'I guess that's true.' Katriona was young, attractive and quite fearsome looking. I was flabbergasted that Euan could have imagined she fancied him, or found his character appealing in any shape or form.

'And would you be shocked if Katriona were augmenting her income with a wee bit of casual sex on the side?'

'No…' Well, I wasn't shocked, more upset.

'What's the problem then?'

I put my other hypothesis to Martin. 'Well, it was more what Euan said about her advancing her career. It sounded like Lorna had put her up to it, maybe bribing her to sleep with the mystery guest to get a good review for her hotel…'

Martin frowned. 'Well, I certainly wouldn't put that past Lorna, she's capable of anything.' He sighed. 'This hotel is her life, Charlie, her passion. She's spent the last fifteen years taking it from a clapped out dump to where it is today, but it's not enough. She can be very ruthless. She'd do anything that she deemed necessary.'

I thought of Strickland's certainty that she had poison-ed Dave Holland. So easy: a visit to the kitchen, a snap inspection of the walk-in for health and safety procedure, a hand travelling from jacket pocket to tub, so easy, so untraceable.

'Even murder?'

He nodded. 'Oh yes,' he said softly, 'even murder.'

Chapter Seventeen

At half past ten the following morning I was making bearnaise sauce (which is a hollandaise sauce with added tarragon) when the phone rang. It was Lorna.

'Charlie, could you please come up to my office, there's something you should know about.'

'Can't it wait?' I said tetchily.

'No. I need you up here right now.'

'I've got to go and have a word with Lorna,' I said to Euan, 'back soon.' He grunted something non-committal at me and went back to making soup. He had huge bags under his eyes and looked terrible, I could smell alcohol on his breath, which, to be fair to him, was unusual. But today he was obviously nursing a humongous hangover. It must have been some night.

I went upstairs to Lorna's office. She was with a woman coming up for retirement age in a uniform who I recognised as the Head of Housekeeping.

'What's the problem?' I said brightly.

'It's Room 23,' said Head of Housekeeping.

'The mystery guest,' said Lorna. They both looked

strangely serious, there was a very strained atmosphere in the office.

'You haven't killed him?' I said with an attempt at humour. Stony faces and a prolonged silence. Sometimes you just know when you've said the wrong thing. Tumble-weeds blew across the small room.

'He's in bed, upstairs.' Lorna's voice was unusually subdued.

'And?' I raised a questioning eyebrow.

'He's dead,' she said.

Chapter Eighteen

'Phyllis found him,' Lorna explained. The Head of Housekeeping nodded.

'Aye,' she said laconically. She seemed totally unmoved by the experience. I guess in a lifetime of cleaning hotel rooms she'd seen pretty much everything.

My next thought was totally selfish: what did he eat? Then I recalled it was the salmon with lovage sauce. There'd been nothing wrong with that.

The three of us sat there in silence. For a weird moment I wondered if Lorna was going to suggest we cover the whole thing up somehow. Maybe try to get me to dismember him and Phyllis could dispose of him in Leith harbour, piece by piece.

'I'll have to call the police,' Lorna sighed. 'Maybe it was accidental death; he was overweight and he did drink too much.'

Hmm, we seemed to be having a lot of accidental deaths; first Dave, now Room 23. Maybe his heart stopped with the excitement of Katriona's body. At least he'd have died happy. He had looked a cheery sort. He most certainly didn't look like the kind of man who filed copy for a prestigious hotel guide. Maybe that was why they employed him; he was the epitome of a mystery guest. And this general unlikeliness carried over into his personal life.

I'd seen copies of the Brook-Schlager Hotel Guide and magazine. Brook-Schlager man, at least the kind who appeared in the adverts, was thin, with cheekbones to die for, expensive haircuts and close-fitting tailored suits. The same went for Brook-Schlager woman, but with expensive designer jewellery. The ads were for fashion house clothes, cars, jewellery and watches that cost more than I earned in a year. Actually, that's not saying a great deal. Sometimes chairs, with an entry level price at around five thousand.

Anyway, Room 23 certainly didn't look anything like that. With his middle-age spread, comb-over, little ginger moustache, glasses and air of general good humour, he looked exactly like the kind of man who lived in a middle-class housing estate with a nice wife and a couple of kids at uni. The kind of man who would be a stalwart of the local golf club and definitely not be having hot sex with a girl young enough to be his daughter. He certainly wouldn't spend five k on a chair or two k on a Ginori tea set.

And now he was dead.

'How did he die?' I asked.

Phyllis shrugged. 'Dinnae ken. He's all tucked up, comfy like… I thought he was just asleep…'

Lorna sighed. 'Well, it'll have to be the police…' She reluctantly picked up her phone and called 999. 'Hello, yes, police and ambulance.'

Chapter Nineteen

'So, you're awa' tomorrow morning?'

'I am indeed Martin,' I said. To show her appreciation of my decision to stay until the end of December, Lorna had decided to give me this weekend off so I would be on the 6 o'clock flight in the morning to London; Jess would pick me up at Heathrow at 8. Tonight at the Moray Place Hotel a busy Saturday night loomed for us. We had forty booked in, which was a lot for the hotel; the dining room was not that big.

'You'll be very relieved to be getting away from Moray Place,' he observed.

'Yeah, you could say that.'

The past few days had been stressful. Room 23's death, that's how we all thought of him, rather than 'Mr Sinclair', which was his actual name, had been ruled suspicious. There had been a lot of drugs in his body seemingly, but cause of death had been asphyxia.

I had this information courtesy not from DS Bain who was leading the investigation at the hotel, but from Lorna who had her own sources that she preferred to keep to herself.

Not only had I been interviewed by DS Bain, in Lorna's office fortunately, not down at the local police station, I'd had the indignity of having my room searched. After what Lorna had told me I guess they had been looking for drugs.

During the course of our interview, Bain had asked me if I had known Mr Sinclair. His manner was quite aggressive; once again I could smell the mouthwash, and his shirt was badly ironed. I began to wonder if he had a drink problem.

'Not really,' I said.

'Not really?' he seemed surprised, almost affronted. 'But he was a very important guest, the most important guest the hotel has had in quite some time I gather.'

'Quite possibly,' I agreed, 'but that doesn't have anything to do with me.' He frowned and looked puzzled so I explained as to how and why I had become the head chef here. 'So, as of the beginning of January, that's it, as far as I'm concerned. I've got no skin in the game as to whether this hotel becomes the number one destination in Edinburgh, or the whole of Scotland – the UK for that matter – or if he'd decided it was a shitty dump to be avoided at all costs.'

'I see.' He looked at me disbelievingly.

Then he said, somewhat slyly, 'Your bedroom is just down the corridor from his?'

'Yes.' I frowned. What was he getting at?

'Did you find Mr Sinclair an attractive man?' Bain asked.

I stared at him in astonishment.

'What!' I remarked, incredulously. I noticed DC Carmichael looking slightly uneasy.

The DS ploughed on in the same vein. 'Well, you have

a lot in common. You're both more or less the same age…
you both work in the hotel and catering business, you're
both strangers in a strange city… what could be more likely
than you would hit it off together?'

What he was suggesting was so outlandish I figured he
had to be kidding. But he seemed to be deadly serious.

'Look, DS Bain, I thought this was a friendly interview…
do I need a lawyer?'

DC Carmichael broke in, almost apologetically. 'You see,
Ms Hunter, the deceased had sexual relations with someone
the night of his death…'

'Well, it most certainly was not me,' I said, crossly.

DS Bain made a placatory gesture with his hands.
'Nobody's accusing you of anything, Ms Hunter,' he said.

'Good,' I said, forcefully.

'But as you may or may not know, there is a CCTV
camera that covers the downstairs hall and lobby, and the
staircase and lifts are clearly visible.' I certainly hadn't
noticed it. He continued. 'Now, nobody who was not a
guest or staff went upstairs from six in the evening on the
night of the murder.'

'So it is a murder,' I said.

'Yes, Ms Hunter, we've had word back from the post
mortem that this was not an accidental death, this is definitely a murder.'

Carmichael joined in. 'So you see, the main suspects
are the hotel staff. There were no single women staying
in the hotel that night, and no strangers came in and went
upstairs.'

I reflected that maybe the police were of a Calvinist turn

of mind, they seemed to imply that such behaviour would be impossible for a married woman.

'Well,' I said, 'you've searched my room – presumably for either a murder weapon or drugs. You found nothing. I was never in his room, so there won't be any evidence linking me to his death. I take it I am free to go?'

'Yes, you are, Ms Hunter, but please do not leave the area.'

'I have to go down south for two days to check on my own business. I'm leaving on the Sunday morning, back on Monday, I take it that's okay?'

The two men looked at each other. I noticed Carmichael nod at his colleague although obviously it wasn't his call to make. 'That's fine,' DS Bain said, reluctantly, 'thank you for your cooperation.'

I stood up. I said my goodbyes. Bain's head was bent over the paperwork. Carmichael stood up too. 'Thank you, Ms Hunter, for your cooperation.'

I guess he wasn't going to be calling me Charlie in front of his colleague.

As I walked back down the stairs to my kitchen all I could think about was Katriona knocking on his bedroom door on the night before his death.

Was I going to tell them? No I wasn't.

I didn't like Katriona but I wasn't going to drop her in it; they could find out themselves, it wasn't coming from me.

Chapter Twenty

I settled back against the passenger seat of the old VW Polo belonging to Jess, my manageress, as we left the torturous exit roads of Heathrow airport and headed towards the motorway.

I filled her in on the situation up in Edinburgh and Jess shook her head as she pulled over into the exit lane of the M4 and headed to the loop of the M25. There was usually a tailback here and even at this relatively early hour of a Sunday morning traffic was still heavy.

She pushed some shaggy dark hair away from her attractive face with her left hand as we joined the motorway that circles London.

'Well, you can't say your life lacks excitement, Charlie...'

'Well, that's undeniably true.' I changed the subject, I'd had enough of speculating who might have killed Room 23. 'What's been happening down here?' I asked. 'How is Francis?'

Francis was Jess's cousin who worked for me as a kitchen porter and occasional chef. He was an exemplary kp and a startlingly inept cook. By way of contrast, Jess was formidably bright, currently doing a PhD at Warwick Uni in some form of IT that I totally did not understand. Maybe it involved Machine Learning and AI, or maybe it was Cyber. I am not exactly computer literate. I can use one, a Windows PC not a Mac, but I have no idea of code or anything beyond using Word. Maybe a vague understanding of Excel for working out my costings.

But I was Tim Berners Lee compared to Francis. It was safe to say that Francis's talents were not cerebral.

It was hard to imagine them as related. Okay, Jess was sturdily built, she had an eye-catching figure but Francis was like a cube of muscle. What he lacked in brains, Nature had compensated for in brawn.

'Francis has read a book,' Jess said wonderingly.

This sounds unremarkable but books and Francis did not belong together. It wasn't impossible, obviously, just extremely unlikely, like Deontay Wilder taking up macramé or quilting.

'A cookery book?' I asked, hopefully.

Last Christmas I had bought him a Delia Smith. St Delia. I had once worked with a chef from a Michelin restaurant who had said, 'A lot of people get very sniffy about Delia, but face it, she owns a football team. Gordon Ramsay doesn't.'

'No,' Jess said, 'it's called *A Snare for Topaz*.'

'What kind of a book is that?' I asked, puzzled.

'It's a bodice ripper.'

'I'm none the wiser.'

'It's like a romantic novel set in Victorian times...' She outlined the plot briefly for me. Topaz was an orphan, she was found outside a jeweller's in Mayfair, in an arcade; the jeweller's shop assistant was childless and brought her up as her own. The only clue as to the baby girl's background was that she was wearing a necklace, with a single stone, a topaz, hence her name…

I marvelled at this. 'And he likes this?'

'Absolutely,' she said. 'He's obsessed with it. There's loads of Topaz books' – she glanced in the mirror, changed lanes – 'Sharon Ransome, the author, very prolific. Other than the book, Francis is Francis.'

'What else?' I wondered, still shell-shocked by my kp's literary achievement. 'How's Murdo doing?'

'Oh, just fine and he gets on really well with Patrick. They make a good team.'

That was the Chef de Partie that Graeme Strickland had sent over. Murdo was doing my job, Patrick doing his.

'So what's Patrick like?' I asked.

Jess turned her head and smiled. 'Insanely good-looking.'

We were in Hampden Green by nine. As I unlocked the door and walked into the kitchen, it struck me that it seemed odd to be in a kitchen at that time and for breakfast not to be cooking. I'd only been away for twelve days, under a fortnight, but it seemed so much longer.

I looked around my own kitchen with proprietorial pride. Murdo had kept the place impeccably. The steel gleamed, the floor was immaculate. On the stove the gigantic stockpot was on the lowest heat, pushed to one side. I went over to it and lifted the lid. About five kilos of browned-off beef bones, plus a mire-poix of onions, celery and carrots ticking away. I felt a surge of affection for Murdo. Jess was watching me with amusement as I checked the fridges, everything covered, labelled and day-dotted.

'Everything to your satisfaction, Charlie?'

I grinned at her. 'It's so nice to be back, Jess.'

'Coffee?'

'Please.'

We went through the swing doors into the dining room. No lifts or dumb-waiters here. While she switched on the old but reliable Gaggia machine I sat at a table admiring the view of the Green through the windows. It was a brilliantly sunny morning, very cold; I could see a heavy frost on the grass. Much as I had grown to love the elegant Georgian architecture of Edinburgh New Town it was so nice to look out at the countryside. It was also nice to see sun. In Scotland I had got up in the dark, run in the dark, finished about three when it was getting dark, started again at six and finished at ten. Rinse and repeat. Today I would see countryside and sun – more to the point I wouldn't see Euan or have to cudgel my brains as to who had killed the former head chef.

Just then I saw a short muffled figure approach the glass door of the restaurant and ring the bell. I walked over and opened it.

'Jesus, brass monkey weather out there,' Graeme Strickland said, striding past me and into the restaurant as if he owned it. I closed the door behind me. He really was an arrogant sod, I thought affectionately.

He turned towards me, pulling off his coat (which looked expensive, Strickland spent a great deal of money on clothes), scarf, gloves and hat. He looked handsome as ever, small as ever too. At five ten I was a few inches taller than he was. Like Napoleon (or Joaquin Phoenix in the movie, I was not a history buff) you didn't tend to notice his lack of height due to his commanding presence.

He looked over at Jess. 'I'll have a double espresso, please, Jess, no sugar.'

She rolled her eyes at me, but, used to Strickland and his brusque manner, acquiesced. He sat down and looked at me. I was still standing.

'Sit down,' he ordered. I exchanged glances with Jess. Whose restaurant was it? He seemed to have forgotten he wasn't in his own place, but that was Strickland all over.

'What's going on up in Scotland?' he demanded.

I filled him in on what had been happening. He listened impatiently, asking lots of questions, not exactly fidgeting but continuously moving in one way or another. The man almost crackled with energy.

'Brook-Schlager, eh?'

'Yeah, I wonder if he'd got round to filing his article,' I speculated. 'He'd been there for three days, he was due to leave when he never did.'

'Just like the Hotel California,' Strickland said. 'You can check in but you can never leave... well, maybe we can find out what he said.'

'How are you going to do that?' I asked.

'Call the features editor.'

He pulled his phone out, searched his contact list, grunted, pushed a button and then, 'Beatrix?' he barked. 'Graeme Strickland, what do you mean it's a bit early? It's gone nine... I don't care if it's Sunday, I've got eighty booked in for lunch.'

'Look, that guy of yours who died in Edinburgh, Mike Sinclair?' he looked at me for confirmation, I nodded.

'He was writing about a hotel up there... Yeah, that's the one, The Moray Place... did he ever send you what he'd written before he died... he did? Could you give me the gist of it?... That would be brilliant, thanks... yeah, come down... I owe you Bea... of course you can stay at my place after service, just like old times... look forward to it... ciao sweetheart.'

He looked at me and grinned then looked back at his phone and handed it to me. I looked at the screen.

Beatrix had emailed him Room 23's review of the hotel.

As I read the pdf of what he had written I had the eerie sensation of a communication from beyond the grave. Sinclair could have had no way of knowing that what he was writing would be one of his last acts on earth, that when he pressed the send icon on his email despatching the attached article it would be literally the final thing he ever wrote.

It was far from ideal reading an article designed for a magazine or a computer on the relatively narrow screen of Strickland's phone but I scanned it feverishly. The first thing I was searching for was what he had to say about the food... skilled hand in the kitchen, classic cuisine with a few modern surprises, a nine out of ten. It couldn't have been more complimentary. I felt a flush of pride.

Phew! Not that it really mattered; it wasn't my restaurant that was on the line, nor would it make a difference to how anyone viewed my restaurant, but I would have known.

I smiled appreciatively at a couple of his comments.

'So he liked your cooking, then.' Strickland had obviously been studying my face.

'Yes.' Then I re-read, this time looking for any clues that might have explained his demise.

I think part of me was speculating, like Strickland, that Lorna might have killed him. It would not surprise me to learn that she had used her body and her good looks to get something she desired in her past and it would not surprise me to discover that she had shared his bed to get a favourable review in the hotel guide. If Bain was to be believed, Room 23 (as I thought of him, it helped to view him dispassionately as an item, a hotel guest rather than a deceased human being) had had sex with a hotel employee. No strangers had been spotted on the CCTV, and it was unlikely he'd picked up a sexual partner from among the other guests. Well, it wasn't me. That would limit the suspects to Lorna, Innes and Katriona, maybe Annie? Or had he somehow managed to smuggle someone else past the all-seeing eye of the camera?

Sinclair had liked the food, the rest of the hotel he had not been so keen on. 'Tired', 'dowdy', 'trading on past glories,' 'clichéd baronial country house'. Just some of the epithets used to describe the place.

'While applauding the friendliness of the staff, we couldn't help but feel that some new blood might give the place some much-needed oomph and a few more millennials/ Gen Z would help to counter the retirement-home-for-wealthy-people vibe that the hotel gives off in stultifying wafts of embalming fluid.'

Ouch.

Well, I figured I could delete Lorna from any suspect list. This review would be meat and drink to her, I would have thought. It more or less underlined and vindicated her opinion that the hotel must change or die. Sinclair was obviously of the opinion that what the place needed were funky youngsters and someone with an iconoclastic designer palette to rip out the wood-panelling, palms and tartan, and drag the place into the twenty-first century.

It was almost as if Lorna had written the review herself.

I also reflected what a dark horse Sinclair himself was. If I hadn't known better, based on his appearance, I would have imagined him to be conservative in his tastes, the kind of man who would like steak and chips, re-runs on *Dave* or the *Yesterday* channel, and an all-inclusive holiday at an upmarket resort somewhere. I had expected him to have the attitudes and outlook of the middle-aged, middle-class, middle-management mediocrity that he resembled. Instead, he was a writer for a taste Bible, with the clout that a TikTok influencer would gnaw their arm off at the elbow for, with a penchant for class A drugs and wild sex.

Also he'd very probably been shagging one of the funky youngsters he'd claimed the place needed so much – although I suppose he couldn't really have added that to the review. Brook-Schlager was not that kind of publication.

I handed Strickland back his phone. 'Thanks.'

'So, any the wiser?' he asked.

I shook my head. 'More confused than ever.'

* * *

An hour or so later, Murdo came down from the flat above accompanied by what looked like a male model in chef's whites. This was Patrick, my good-looking chef on loan from Strickland who had since gone back to his own restaurant across the common.

While they got on with the Sunday lunch preparations, I went upstairs to my bedroom, changed into clean whites, came down and helped repair some of the ravages of Saturday service. I knew my own menu backwards and raced through prepping the starters. Before service I used up a couple of tired looking aubergines and some stale bread and made polpette di melanzane, which were deep-fried aubergine fritters. We'd serve these with a bought in sweet chilli dipping sauce and a rocket salad.

'My days, Charlie,' Patrick had said biting into one with his flawless white teeth, 'they're bloody good…' I noticed Jess staring at him hungrily from the other side of the pass.

'Shall I give Strickland the recipe?' I asked.

He shook his head. 'They're too rustic for us.'

'Aye,' Murdo said, 'they look a wee bit like jobbies.'

What a horrible thought. 'Thank you for your invaluable input, Murdo,' I said, haughtily.

I watched Patrick for a while as he made about forty Yorkshire puddings. Jess was right, he was extremely hot. I guessed I was about twenty years older than he was. Pity, but there it was. Still, I didn't want to be young again. When I was twenty-six I didn't have my current level of poise and confidence, and also I didn't own a restaurant. If memory served me correctly, everything I owned would have fitted into a suitcase. So getting old wasn't all bad.

I wondered if Patrick would find my poise, self-confidence and business skills aphrodisiacal. He had the looks and haircut of a 1960s British film star and by the way he moved it was obvious he knew he was gorgeous. Katie, my head waitress, had now taken Jess's place; she was standing the other side of the pass looking at him over the lights with hopeless longing.

I felt the same way too but stopped short of staring at him the way she was. It wouldn't be dignified. I wonder if he realised that the entire female staff of the Old Forge Café were drooling over him. Probably.

Later, just before service started, I overheard Murdo say, 'So what are you doing this evening Pat?'

'My boyfriend's picking me up about four and we're going to a drinks party in Fulham. Then I'll stay at his place and we'll go to an exhibition at Tate Modern on Monday, a Jeff Koons.'

'Very nice,' Murdo said.

I smiled ruefully to myself. Oh how blind we all had been. Well, Patrick would not be hammering at my bedroom door tonight pleading to be let in, that was for sure.

Chapter Twenty-One

I was back in Edinburgh, revitalised after my trip home. The expensive luxury of the Moray Place Hotel surrounded me again, like being immersed in a strange sea. It was so different from my more homely restaurant. The quality of the tableware, for example. The plates were to die for. The glaze and finish on them compared to my own, perfectly reasonable but bog standard ones, almost made me grind my teeth with envy. The cool linen on my bed, not like my cheap duvet back home.

But the Old Forge Café was a nice place to be. The Moray Place Hotel environment at times felt as dark as the colours of the New Town on a wet November afternoon at dusk, as the rain beat against the bare black branches of the trees in the railed gardens and the shadows lengthened on the slick, black, cobbled streets.

And my staff were friendly and open; here God knows what was going on. I thought of Katriona's persecution of the gentle Craig, like a malevolent cat with a terrified bird. I thought of Euan and his fear and loathing of women. I thought of Lorna and the staff's anxiety that she was going to be handing them their P45s. I thought of the dead David Holland, murdered by someone in the hotel as had, in all likelihood, happened to the mystery guest. A spirit of vindictiveness and dread seemed to spread like a miasma through the hotel; hate, suspicion and tension were as much a part of the environment as the expensive fittings.

So, on the Monday night after I had washed and changed, I sat at the bar, quiet at the beginning of the week, having a glass of very expensive Premier Cru St Émilion Merlot blend, courtesy of Annie who had very generously told me that it was on the house. It was fifty pounds a glass, my budget would normally be to lose a zero from that figure.

'That's very kind of you, Annie.'

'Dinnae tell Lorna,' she whispered mockingly as she slid it to me over the polished surface of the bar.

'I promise not to.'

'Clarty bitch,' Anne said bitterly and went to serve another customer. I savoured my drink while wondering what 'clarty' meant. Nothing complimentary I guessed.

The wine was truly delicious. I hadn't had much very good wine since I'd split up with my ex, Andrea, who, like many Italians didn't drink a great deal, preferring quality over quantity. And he always paid. Not because he was a gentleman (although he was) but because he had a hell of a lot more money than me and when Karl Marx said, 'from each according to his ability to each according to his needs', I was fully behind him. He had the ability to pay, I had the need for fine Italian wine. And expensive restaurants. And I don't mind an exclusive hotel either, preferably one where I didn't have to toil in the kitchen.

Well, those days were gone. Don't get me wrong, I wasn't swigging rotgut reds bought three for a tenner from an all-night garage, but I wouldn't be drinking the likes of this. I didn't even stock it for customers; they would pay fifty pounds for a bottle occasionally, but not for a glass.

Annie rejoined me, having served her customer.

'Aye, well, I have a feeling that my days here are numbered,' she sighed, her normally good-natured expression troubled. 'I dinnae mean on this earth, but here in the hotel.'

'How come, Annie?' I thought of Room 23 or Michael Sinclair's (as he was known to his influential readers) article. Phrases from his review drifted up into my mind as I looked at her pleasant, ageing face, 'some new blood'; 'much-needed oomph'; 'more millennials/Gen Z'.

Reviews could be powerful things and Annie, albeit indirectly, had come off badly.

'I feel like mah neck is being measured fae the chop by Herself...'

I nodded. Herself would be Lorna. Lorna had hired a new barmaid/waitress, a gorgeous Eastern European girl, Angelika, who I'd thought was South American (dark, glossy curly hair, amazing figure, brown skin), but was actually from Bucharest. She was very nice, competent, pleasant, but she had made the rest of the staff nervous; they were (justifiably) fearing a cull.

'It'll be the Clearances all over again...' Annie said, gloomily. 'They're replacing us with younger, sexier workers, we're fae the scrap heap.'

'Now, now, Annie,' I said, 'you don't know that.'

It was more or less exactly what I thought but there was no point telling her that.

The following day we were quiet. Rosa phoned to say one of her kids was ill and could she come in on Wednesday. That was fine by me, we had enough desserts to last. Without her Italian accented chatter, the kitchen had been much quieter than a normal Tuesday. Lunch and dinner were a stroll in the park. Last orders were done and dusted by quarter past nine. I went upstairs, washed and changed and, when I came down I was in time to see the back of Lorna disappearing out of the front door.

I thought of Annie's remark, I wondered if Lorna was off to engage in some clarty business and what that could mean. Maybe Annie had heard she was sleeping with Number Three's F & B Director. Or maybe being clarty meant she had more than one man on the go. I suddenly decided to follow her. Even if nothing came of it, I could reassure Strickland I was keeping tabs on his prime suspect for Dave's death.

She headed in the general direction of the east end of New Town where the St James development and the hotel were located. It looked like there was no new man, that Number Three was her destination. Now I knew where she was going, following her was easy.

It was a cold, blustery, November night and I wondered why she didn't get a taxi or an Uber, but I guess she was getting her steps in for the day. Lorna looked like a gym and exercise fanatic and certainly had the body to go with that. There was no flab there, her fitted blouses betrayed no tell-tale muffin-top bulges.

It wasn't a long walk; in under twenty minutes we had reached the hotel. I watched her go in, gave her a couple of minutes and then trotted in after her.

The Mohican guy was not on the door; tonight there were a couple of saturnine skinheads in crombies, cherry red DMs and bowler hats. They added a kind of *A Clockwork Orange* vibe to the place. Michael Sinclair would have approved. They could hardly have been in greater contrast to the shy, fey Craig and cheery Donald. Inside the lobby the massive disco ball, where a chandelier would normally be, was doing its light refracting thing from a couple of spotlights trained on it. My friend Gav was not behind the reception desk tonight, instead there was a chic, Japanese looking girl, her sleek, glossy hair a waterfall of black. I thought again of the genteel, urbane Donald whom I'd bidden goodnight to as I hot-footed it after Lorna. Obvious whom Room 23 would have preferred.

The soundtrack playing tonight was fifties and sixties style rock and roll. Ironic throwback music from the current generation's grandparents, maybe great-grandparents. I looked around in the semi-darkness of the lobby under the shafts of light from the disco ball for signs of Lorna as Bill Haley rocked around his clock.

I stood there uncertainly as Bill finished his song and Cliff and the Shadows Moved it and a Grooved it. Japanese girl inspected her nails and looked vibey.

'Hi, Charlie.'

I turned round. It was Gav with a girl in tow. Her face

looked strangely familiar, although I couldn't put a name to it. I wondered if it was someone I had worked with at some time. That must be hundreds if not thousands of people over the years, more years than I cared to think about to be honest.

'Charlie, this is Ellie, Ellie Smith.'

More memory bells rang. I knew I should know who she was but I didn't. She was blonde, twenties, slightly dumpy. She was frowning she didn't seem overjoyed to be meeting me.

'Hi, Ellie...'

'How's the Radisson?' he asked.

I shook my head. 'I never said I work for them, I'm the acting Head Chef at the Moray Place Hotel.'

Gav jumped, imperceptible to anyone but me. He was obviously startled by that revelation but managed to suppress it.

'Really, that's a coincidence,' he said. 'Let's go get a drink...'

We went into the bar. There was a lot of noise in it tonight, most of it emanating from a roped off section that I hadn't noticed when I'd last been there.

The three of us sat down in a far corner of the bar next to a large faux bronze statue of a winged woman, Art Deco style. I surreptitiously touched it, it was fibre-glass. I found that surprisingly disappointing, like it was a metaphor for the hotel. Gav waved at the barman and gave a thumbs up. Shortly after, a waiter dressed like a Vegas showgirl, her bust spilling out of her pink corset (just made for Instagram, I thought) brought us a bottle of white wine and three glasses. Gav poured.

'Sláinte,' he toasted us.

We chinked glasses and Gav said, 'Ellie worked at the Moray Place... used to work in the kitchens there.' He was smiling, slightly maliciously, I thought.

'Oh God,' I said, the penny finally dropping, 'you must be Katriona's sister.' The one whom Dave Holland sacked for incompetence.

'Aye.' She kind of scowled at me.

I know your dirty little secret, I thought, you're a shit chef. But I smiled, nicely.

'So,' I said brightly, 'do you prefer working here? The menus look interesting.'

'Aye well, they're twenty-first century, nae nineteenth, ken... but I guess that's what auld folk who go to the Moray Place like to eat.'

There was a contemptuous look in her eye and inflection in her voice lumping me in the 'old' category. Well, I'd tried to be polite and been rebuffed, I wouldn't waste any more time on her. I turned to Gav.

'How about you?' I asked. 'What have you been up to?'

'Work... clubbing, there's a place I go to at the top of Leith Walk; I can be there in five minutes when my shift finishes...Would you like to go?'

'Sure, why not?'

Ellie scowled at me. Don't invite her, the look said.

'It's predominantly a gay bar,' Gav said. 'I see your man from the hotel in there sometimes.'

'Donald?' I couldn't imagine Craig having the nerve to go to a gay bar. He'd be like a terrified shy wild animal, petrified by the noise and commotion, Bambi-eyed with terror.

'Aye, done up to the nines, wee bit tragic really,' Gav sighed. 'He was probably quite the thing when he was younger…'

Poor old Donald, I thought. A sad old has-been in the eyes of Room 23 and now Gav. Save us from pity, I thought, just another word for the judgement of the morally superior. At least I wasn't being pitied by Ellie for being older than her. She just didn't like me.

'Oh' – I remembered Annie's dialect word I didn't know, I thought I'd ask before I forgot – 'what does "clarty" mean?'

'What,' Gav said, 'like clarty besom?'

'I guess.'

'Dirty bitch,' Ellie said disapprovingly. 'Why?'

'Oh, just something someone said at work.'

Just then there was a lot of shouting and laughter from behind the rope, audible over the mixture of house and R&B that was pumping from the hidden speakers. No 1950s rock 'n' roll in here. Thank God for that, I thought.

'That's Pajamaparty,' Gav said, turning his head to look. A couple of young guys staggered out, somewhat the worse for wear, one with those jeans that look like they're falling down around your knees, shirtless with a leather waistcoat, the other with torn skinny black jeans and a Nirvana T-shirt. They headed for the toilets.

'Should I know them?' I asked.

'They've had a couple of big hits, they're all over TikTok as well. They're playing at the O2 the other side of town for three nights, sold out.'

I must make more of an effort, I told myself. Difficult

to do when Murdo had commandeered the kitchen music. Perhaps I should switch the conversation to Death Metal or Black Metal, subjects on which I was better informed than I wanted to be.

'I'm bored, Gav,' Ellie said, looking at him and pointedly ignoring me, she'd been fiddling with her phone. 'Do you want to go to Sugar Town, there's a few of us meeting down there.'

I noticed that I had not been included in the invitation. Gav shook his head. 'Naw, I'll pass.'

Ellie stood up. 'Well, you know where we are if you want to come later... see yez.'

She gave me a sarcastic, tight-lipped smile and left. Thank God for that, I thought, relieved she'd gone.

'I don't think Ellie likes me,' I said.

'She's fine, she's just takes a while to get to know people,' Gav said, apologetically. Yeah right, I thought.

Just then I immediately forgot the Pajamaparty and Ellie. Lorna had walked in.

Chapter Twenty-Two

Lorna was looking unusually tousled and slightly radiant. Doubtless the result of being clarty. Next to her, with a proprietorial air was Ollie, the Food and Beverage Manager. The two of them went and sat down at a table with three men in their forties, well-dressed in a Brookes Brothers casual kind of way. Gav saw me looking at them. Lorna's back was to me so she couldn't see me.

'That's your boss isn't it?' he asked.

'Mm hm, and yours is with her.'

'I bet they're discussing taking over the Moray Place hotel,' he said. I was surprised at him taking me into his confidence like that.

'Really?'

'Yeah, I recognise those guys; two of them are our backers and the other one is from an investment bank.'

I thought, Strickland will be interested in this, God knows why, who cares who owns the hotel.

'Oh yeah,' Gav's tone was conspiratorial, 'it's an open secret round here, we may end up as work colleagues.' He smiled. 'I'd like that. It would be great to see more of you, Charlie.'

I looked at him afresh. I was finding Gav increasingly attractive, his body was slim and appealing and I was quite taken with his slightly sinister shaved head thing. Shame he was gay.

Well, from what he was saying, it certainly looked like a takeover might well be happening. Sinclair's review of the place kind of guaranteed its fate. With Dave Holland, the champion of the old guard, gone, the field was clear for Lorna to lead the way. I thought of the bar here, busy and vibey, the band and their followers, almost certainly running up an enormous tab. Every table was full, mainly on point professionals; youngsters or students were not much in evidence here, priced out by the hefty charges. Then I thought of the bar at the Moray Place, quiet, leather panelled. There was a grandfather clock in the corner and sometimes it was so quiet you could hear it ticking, a requiem for the old times.

And yet, like me, the Moray Place was not yet moribund. It still turned a healthy profit, the restaurant did well, it had even garnered praises from Room 23 before he'd checked out and into the great hotel of the hereafter. Room occupancy was high. There was life in the old girl yet. But that wouldn't satisfy the money-men. Someone would doubtless run the numbers and decide that you could double the restaurant profits by buying cheapo ingredients or using cheaper cuts, hello belly pork, or cheap fish, hi coley. You could maybe partition some of the rooms, vibe them up a bit, and you'd temporarily do well, then sell it off quick before the facelift started to sag and the Botox to wear off.

And above all, it wouldn't satisfy Lorna. Napoleon had ruled France, but he wanted to be an emperor. So did she.

I idly looked at the bar menu again: Mexican sweet potato fries, were they any better than real fries made of the humble potato? I kind of doubted it. Chilli-loaded hot dogs, chilli con quesos (that looked a bit like orange sick), would these have any longevity? Again I had a strong feeling of doubt.

And would the guests at the hotel prefer a kindly, efficient, concierge like Donald or the two skinheads, no matter how decorative they might be?

I wondered if Number Three might be smoke and mirrors, its future as solid as the fibre-glass statues in the bar.

My musings were interrupted by a gentle, but insistent, pressure on my left knee from Gav. I looked at him in surprise.

'You're a very good-looking woman, Charlie…' he said, smiling at me. I raised an eyebrow, not in a coquettish, come on way, but in genuine surprise.

'I didn't think your interests lay that way…' I said. His fingers with their black painted nails intertwined with mine.

He looked into my eyes. 'I identify as someone attracted to beauty.'

'And I make the grade, do I?'

'Oh yes.' He smiled. 'Very definitely.'

I evaluated him as I might a piece of meat. I checked out the quality points. Looks, body, personality. It had been a while since I'd been with anyone. Maybe it was the hedonistic, louche, slightly frenzied atmosphere of Number Three, maybe it was the wine or maybe just good old-fashioned hormones. Maybe I was just a clarty besom as the expression went. I considered what was on offer. On the plus side he was undeniably good-looking and the thought of his young, firm body hard against mine was highly tempting. On the negative side... I really couldn't come up with anything.

'Okay,' I said. I've always prided myself on being decisive.

'Do you want to finish the wine?' he asked.

'No,' I said, 'I want something else.'

'Room Forty-Seven is vacant.' And of course, he had a key.

'What a coincidence,' I said, standing up, 'my favourite number.'

Chapter Twenty-Three

'Late night, Chef?' asked Innes when I walked into the kitchen. I smiled. It certainly had been. Gav and I had been at it until about three in the morning; all that running and yoga had obviously paid off in terms of fitness and stamina. Parts of me were still slightly sore, but in a good way.

'Well, I have slept better, thank you Innes,' I said. 'And how are you Euan?'

My sous was busy making the terrine for the starters, shredding ham haunch with his fingers. It had been simmered for a few hours until it was flaking off the bone; we'd reduce the liquor later so it would set like jelly and bind the terrine together.

'Well, I was watching *Blade 2* last night...' he shook his head grimly. 'I knew it was a waste of time, I should have listened to myself...'

Oh God, it begins. Try and humour him, Charlie, I told myself. 'It wasn't very good?' I asked, cursing myself for doing so. I knew I would be getting far more information than I wanted.

I was squatting, checking my fridges to see that I had sufficient quantities of fish and meat.

'Was it any good?' his voice rose in querulous outrage.

'Bet it wisnae,' was Ali's laconic rejoinder from the other side of the kitchen.

Euan ignored the jeer from the sink. 'Well,' he invested the word with a huge amount of huffy indignation, 'well, let me just say this…You know Blade is half vampire and half human.' I didn't, but so what? 'Well, the filmmakers seem to think that means he can go out in the daylight…'

'Can't he?' I questioned.

'In the daylight? What do you think?' He shook his head pityingly. 'Charlie, vampires do not have enough melanin in their skin to withstand UV rays, that's why they can't go out during the day…' He shook his head in dismay at my ignorance of this biological fact. 'It's a physical impossibility for a vampire to survive in daylight, even a hybrid one. It's a hard fact. It flies in the face of science to say they can.'

Luckily I was saved from any more of Euan's lessons on how these fictitious creatures behave by Rosa wandering into the kitchen and saying, 'Guess what? Katriona's been arrested.'

'Whit fae?' asked Ali.

'Omicidio… murder,' declared Rosa dramatically, giving the r's in the word an extra roll for emphasis, 'she's been arrested for murder.'

After the lunchtime shift, fortunately too busy for us to engage in speculation about Katriona, I left Euan to finish cleaning the kitchen before the evening service began. Euan had been kind of useless during the shift, forgetful, slow; he'd burnt a couple of things.

I bit my tongue and at close I said to him, 'We've only got a few booked in tonight, Euan. If you finish the prep list for tonight you can have the evening off. You should be done by five.'

'Aye, okay then,' he said morosely.

I looked at him in disbelief. I'd given him the evening off, he'd be able to watch sci-fi or go to one of his men's groups (I'd heard from Ali that he belonged to several in the area). I thought, it's probably because you haven't got any friends. I couldn't imagine anyone willingly spending time with the self-obsessed misery guts. Sod you, I thought.

I wanted to train Innes in cooking mains, which is a daunting leap up from doing veg and starters. I'd be her bitch, as the term quaintly used to be, and do her job, while she did mine. If she looked like getting overwhelmed, we'd swap back to our more usual roles. I was looking forward to seeing how Innes would cope. At seventeen, with one year in the kitchen, she was a damn sight better than Euan at his job.

I had been summoned to Lorna's office after lunch and she brought me an espresso from the bar.

'So what's all this about Katriona?' I asked.

'Forensic reports on hairs in Room 23's room were confirmed as belonging to Katriona,' Lorna said. 'There was also signs that he'd had sex with someone; there was lubricant from a condom on his person and said condom was found floating in the toilet.'

I was impressed with Lorna's intelligence-gathering; I wondered where she was getting it from.

'Can they get anything off that?' I asked. I wondered why he hadn't binned it but I suppose he didn't want housekeeping to find it when they emptied it as part of the bathroom clean and know he'd been having sex.

'Seemingly not, the bleach and cleaning stuff in the water would have destroyed the DNA.'

'Oh.' Then I asked, curiosity getting the better of me, 'How come you know so much about it, Lorna?'

'DS Bain is very taken with me,' she said, mock-fanning her face. 'I think he feels that if he shares these bits of info I'll be awestruck by his investigative genius.'

'I hope you're not leading him on,' I said primly, which was a dumb thing to say. She just looked at me. One of those looks. Of course she was, and the policeman hoping to get inside Lorna's pants was putty in her hands. I mentally shivered. Lorna was utterly unscrupulous. When it came to getting what she wanted she would do whatever it took. Sex, or the promise of it, in the case of keeping tabs on the police investigation and maybe that was why she was sleeping with Ollie, oiling the wheels of commerce the easier to raise money for her buyout or partnership.

'What does Katriona say?' I asked. I wondered whether or not I should share my own evidence, her leaving the room, with the police.

Lorna said, pre-empting me, 'She's admitted going to his room, but she says it was to sell him drugs, presumably the drugs found in his system. She never had sex with him and she certainly didn't kill him.'

I breathed a mental sigh of relief. If she'd confessed to being in his room, my confirming it would hardly matter.

'And her hair?'

'Absolutely no idea how it got there, her words.'

I fell silent; things were looking black for Katriona. If anyone looked capable of killing a guest, it was her. She looked aggressive: the tattoos, the slightly intimidating air, the fierceness of her.

'How did she do it?' I asked.

'Well, Sinclair was full of drugs, ketamine and some other opiates yet to be determined, and booze. He was suffocated, seemingly.'

'Poor guy,' I said. 'At least he didn't know it was happening.'

'I think you're right, the DS said there was no sign of a struggle…'

'But why would she want to do that?'

'Who knows?' Lorna said indifferently. 'Who knows?' She gave me a hard look. 'I can't be bothered with the whys and wherefores, Charlie, I have a business to run.'

And that was obviously my cue to leave. As I closed the door I saw her head bow over her laptop. Maybe it was my imagination but I thought, as I closed the door, that I saw a small smile steal across her face.

I was back at work that evening with Innes, who was like a nervous horse, very skittish around the stove. Mains cooking requires a totally different mindset from that of starters and desserts. With those, unless otherwise instructed, you just bang them out as quickly as possible. When you get a bit more experience you start to read the cheques better, more intelligently. For example, you may have ten tickets in the cheque grabber in front of you, the first one has pâté whose accompaniment is a smear of redcurrant reduced coulis, home-pickled seasonal veg, date chutney and sourdough toast. You see this dish occur on cheques three, five and eight. You can plate four portions of this more or less as quickly as one, so that's what you do. You work smart. Otherwise it's straightforward.

Mains are not so simple. They require thought, for one thing. Thought and memory. So much of what we do is highly trained reflexes. But with mains, timing is all. If it's only going to take a few minutes to cook, you have to wait until the starters have been cleared by the waiting staff and the call goes out, 'mains away on table…' If one of the dishes on the ticket is going to take twenty minutes as was the case with the beef Wellington on the Moray Place menu you would do that immediately but not forget the other components of the order.

Things can get really fiendish when you're busy and you end up with twenty-odd meals on the go at the same time. I've known my own mind to crash under the strain like an overloaded computer and you stare at the cheque on the pass wondering what the word 'Hake' means. A horrible sensation. I can recognise the symptoms in other chefs, the blank stare, the lips moving as you try and make sense of it all.

Innes did very well. There was only one major hiccup when she sent out a table of four's orders, two steaks, one duck and a sea bass. I knew what she'd done wrong, I could have intervened but didn't. Sometimes you have to let people make the mistakes that they need to make so that they can grow.

She plated the food on the pass, I'd done her veg and the accompaniments, then she said, checking the ticket, 'Where's the sea bass?'

'Over there,' I said, pointing at a tin tray with the fillets on it, 'right where you left it…'

'Oh Jesus, sorry Chef…what shall I do?'

'I'd cook it if I were you…' I said, 'and quickly.'

Service was over and I was sitting outside with her while she vaped and drank a half-pint of lager that I'd bought her.

She looked ecstatically happy. I smiled kind of maternally at Innes. I could still remember the feeling of my first proper service in charge of a hot section. The serotonin high after the adrenaline rush of the previous two hours, the camaraderie of two people working in total harmony to produce food of amazing quality.

I was having a sip of my white wine when my phone rang with an unknown caller.

'Hello.'

A female voice. 'Hi, I hope you don't mind me calling, it's Ellie. We met the other night…'

'Hello, Ellie,' I said cautiously; I couldn't imagine why she was calling me. She hadn't seemed exactly enamoured of me the last time we had met.

'It's about my sister, Katriona, I know you were a friend of hers… look, could we meet up?'

Friend? That puzzled me, I was no friend of hers, nor she of me, come to that.

'Sure, when?'

'Tonight, at the Campion, it's a bar at the top of Leith Walk, it's open until one...'

I looked at my watch, it was only twenty minutes to ten.

'Sure, I'll meet you at half ten,' I said.

'Thank you, Charlie.'

Innes looked at me interrogatively as I put my phone away.

'That was Ellie, Katriona's sister,' I said.

'Oh, aye.' Her tone was flat, it was very unlike her.

'Did you know her?'

'Aye, we didnae get on.' She said it with the kind of intonation that made it clear she didn't want to discuss it.

I was curious to know why that was but I could see that she didn't want to talk about it, so I let the subject drop. I could sympathise with Innes. I didn't get on with Ellie either.

An hour or so later, showered and changed, I was sitting with Ellie in the bar somewhere at the top of Leith Walk. I gathered from the older guard in the hotel like Annie that Leith Walk, Leith itself, used to be quite scuzzy if not downright off-putting, but had now become quite gentri-fied. Annie was none too happy about this gentrification but I thought it was quite vibey.

Well, whatever the wrongs and rights of the regeneration of this part of Edinburgh, I was drinking a Margarita out of a frosted glass in an upmarket pub while Taylor Swift thundered from the speakers. Courtesy of Jess back home I knew rather more about Ms Swift than I really wanted to.

'So, why did you want to see me?' I asked.

'Cos of Katriona, she said she really liked you.'

'Well, that was kind of her...' Baffling, but kind. We hadn't spoken much, and when we did I had detected no great warmth. But maybe that was just a peculiarity of the Smith sisters. After all, here I was at her invitation and I had been convinced she didn't like me. Maybe they just lacked people skills.

'Aye, well, I just cannae believe that she had sex wi' that guy she's supposed tae have killed.'

I thought of Number 23 with his moustache, his comb-over, his paunchy body. I wouldn't have wanted to go to bed with him and Katriona was half my age. I felt sure that money would have changed hands, must have done, probably quite a lot of it, and Katriona would have self-medicated beforehand. It didn't seem polite to say that I thought her sister might have been on the game, so I kept silent.

'Thing is,' Ellie said, urgently, 'K was badly hurt in a former relationship. She's emotionally bruised, there's no way she would have had sex with that guy, especially given his age' – she shook her head – 'no way at all.'

I considered what she had said. 'But, Ellie, she admits to being in his room.'

'She was selling him drugs,' she said scornfully. 'Lorna almost certainly knew, but turned a blind eye. Most of the big hotels have a dealer, there's a website on the Dark Web you can access for contact names.'

161

Crikey, I thought, using an expression beloved by my kp Francis. I'm so behind the times.

'What about her hairs that they found?'

Ellie waved this aside. 'I think she was framed, Charlie. Please keep your eyes and ears open. If you come across anything, let me know.'

'Okay, Ellie, I'll do that.'

I walked home pensively. Ellie wanted me to clear her sister, Strickland wanted me to prove it was Lorna. They were perfectly reconcilable aims but I was beginning to feel like I had fallen into a briar patch of other people's demands and suspicions.

The rest of the week passed uneventfully. On Friday morning I worked another breakfast shift with Martin. These were killer days for me, working from seven in the morning until half nine at night in the kitchen. I'd done longer days but I'd been younger and more resilient then. What made things easier was that I trusted Martin and I enjoyed his company. He was both charismatic and wise. I've met a few charismatic chefs, Graeme Strickland among them – face it, he was the only reason I was here in the first place – but I don't think I had met many wise chefs. So this was a bit of a first, a welcome novelty. I asked him what he had thought about Katriona.

'Did you think she was a murderer ? Or had the potential?' I added.

'Charlie,' he said gently, 'all of us have the potential to be one. People kill for all sorts of reasons, ideals, honour… a mother to protect her children.'

'I suppose so.'

He broke some eggs into a pan. 'I've known men who would crack your skull open like I just did those eggs, and with as little remorse... but I cannae see Katriona doing that. Maybe a crime passionel, ken, or to protect herself, but no... I don't think she had sex with him and then smothered him with a pillow.'

'Who then?'

'That's for you to find out Charlie, maybe the same person who killed David Holland, which is why you're here after all.'

'But I'd value your input,' I protested.

'That's why I'll haud my wheesht, lassie,' he said as he plated the eggs and I carried them over to the lift for him.

'I'm sorry?' I hadn't really understood that.

'That's why I'm keeping schtum,' he translated for my benefit. 'Woman.'

'I got the "lassie" bit,' I objected.

He smiled. 'If I were to say "X" did it, you'd probably agree and that would be a bad thing.'

'Would it?' I certainly didn't think so. It was what I wanted more than anything.

'Of course. I've been wrong on lots of things in my life, you'll have to find the truth yourself. Something tells me you have a talent for it.'

Just then the ticket machine came into life and viciously spat out four cheques one after another. Martin sighed. 'I wish they wouldnae do that... how many times have I said, no multiple cheques... Would you mind, Charlie...'

'It'd be a pleasure to help, Martin,' I said, and I meant it.

Friday passed, then Saturday, it was hectic but I didn't mind, the end was in sight. I didn't have enough time to ponder Katriona's innocence or guilt. The fact that Martin seemed to think she could be innocent really made me think. I worked, slept with Gav on Friday and Saturday night, crawling home to my own bed about three in the morning.

And on Sunday, like the Almighty, I rested.

Chapter Twenty-Four

On Monday afternoon I went for a walk around the West End of the city. It was only about 3 o'clock but the streets were practically deserted as I walked the short distance from Moray Place up to Charlotte Square, a large square of grass behind the inevitable railings, powerful, light grey, Georgian terraces, and the imposing Bute House, the Scottish equivalent of Number Ten Downing Street.

I crossed Princes Street, the road there an unpleasant tangle of different lanes and traffic lights. Facing this unsightly traffic mess was the Caledonian Hotel. It was a large, ornate, red sandstone building, Victorian gothic, that was now owned by the Waldorf Astoria group. The Moray Place was expensive; I wondered what the Waldorf would cost. Beyond my price range certainly.

I walked along the broad, quiet roads of the West End. There was very little car traffic. Edinburgh seemed to have frozen the car out of the centre, which was a polarising thing to do. I had no views on the matter, it wasn't my fight one way or the other. The area around the Lothian Road was tacky and plebby. I quite liked it, the rarefied air of Moray Place could be stifling after a while. Maybe it was the effect of living in such haughty imposing buildings – it turned you slightly crazy after a while. A New Town version of altitude sickness, attitude sickness. Face it, most of my work colleagues seemed more than a trifle unhinged.

Eventually I turned back, from the grotty but vibrant West End and into the gloomy, dark grey Olympian splendour of the New Town.

And high up above, dominating Edinburgh, was the familiar bulk of the castle, hunched up on its giant rock overseeing the city below.

I walked into the lobby of the hotel and was greeted by Donald. 'Charlie, good to see you.'

Up close I could smell his expensive, sophisticated aftershave. I remembered Gav's slightly dismissive take on Donald, sitting alone on a stool by the bar in the gay club, hoping but ignored by the younger clientele. 'Done up to the nines, wee bit tragic really, he was probably quite the thing when he was younger…'

A cruel thing to say. Donald was still a very attractive man, much better looking than average and with quite a lean body. He was still a catch. More to the point, professionally as well as personally he had great people skills. He might not be cutting-edge but he was still a hell of an asset and, I had seen with my own eyes, greatly loved by the repeat customers. Not like the haughty cow the other day at Number Three.

I wondered what he would do if it came to pass that the Moray Hotel did become a trend destination for the Instagram/TikTok generation. Unlike the enormous

Mohican-haired doorman or the matching skins with crombies and bowlers, Donald, attractive as he was, was not imageworthy. He was just nice and reliable and helpful – qualities no longer appreciated, it would seem.

'I'm not working tonight,' he said. 'Join me for a drink at ten?'

'Aye,' I said. God, what was happening? 'I mean yes, I'd love to. See you later.'

I walked up to my now familiar room, conscious of the camera that monitored the base of the stairs with its unblinking eye. It's amazing how your behaviour changes when you know you're being watched. My back straightened, I held my head higher, and when I was round the corner I slouched again. Weird.

I slept for a bit then showered and did some yoga to unwind. As I did so, looking around it struck me that this was how a bigamist might feel. I was leading two lives. I was running two separate kitchens, in two separate establishments, with two sets of work colleagues. I even had a lover stashed away up here; I hadn't told Jess about him. Like many Gen Z she was a bit prudish. Or maybe it was because I was, in her eyes, too old to be behaving like that. It was like a secret other life. And, equally, nobody up here knew anything about my life down south. It was all quite strange. I liked it. I was feeling an odd sense of freedom despite the burdens being placed on me by Strickland, and now Ellie.

I changed into clean clothes and went down into the lounge.

It was only half nine but the bar was surprisingly busy.

167

Another surprising thing was seeing Innes there. I had never seen her in the bar before, surely she was too young to be allowed in. I guess Annie was turning a blind eye, and there was no sign of Lorna. Innes was talking to a middle-aged couple and a youth that I guessed was their son. The two men, senior and junior, were enormous, maybe six-six, or nearly two metres, for a more modern girl like Innes.

I sat at the bar. Annie gave me an enormous smile and brought me a glass of my favourite red wine. I reached for my bag and she shook her head. 'On the hoose.'

She served another couple of people; waitress service was courtesy of Katriona's Eastern European replacement. Then she came over to talk to me.

'Who's Innes with?' I asked.

'They're Americans,' Annie said. 'Texans seemingly, doing the heritage trail.'

'What's Innes doing with them? They seem to be getting on very well.'

They were. Innes looked remarkably attractive. She was wearing a black metallic tank top that was see-through to a black bra, and a light grey denim maxi skirt. No guessing where Innes' slender paycheque went. The boy was craggily good-looking, the father roaring with laughter at something Innes had just said. The mother looked serenely on, probably happy that everyone was getting on so well, not always the case on a holiday.

Annie shrugged. 'She met the boy in town, by chance, and got talking. He invited her to have a drink with him and his parents... I don't think they've actually spoken to a Scot before, you know how it is in a foreign country, you never meet the locals unless they're serving you wherever.'

I nodded; it was true. Whenever I'd been to Europe I just spoke to hotel staff, taxi drivers, waiters. I'd never had a chance to use my schoolgirl French, which was just as well maybe. The French would never know how close they had come to hearing their lovely language mangled by me. I am, quite frankly, shit at languages.

Innes was looking very animated, her face was slightly flushed. I realised I had never really seen her look so happy. I felt a twinge of despondency. Surely working with me in the kitchen was an unalloyed joy. Maybe I was deluding myself.

'Hi Charlie.' It was Donald, now at my shoulder, also looking oddly happy. What was it with everyone tonight?

'Annie, get her another drink please…'

She gave him an oddly complicit look and he led me over to a table in the corner. Oh God, I thought suddenly, this is going to be serious.

He sat down beside me. His eyes measured me in an evaluating way, 'So, Charlie…glad to be home?'

I looked at him slightly suspiciously. 'Er, yes…'

'I think you've settled down brilliantly here,' he said, saluting my achievement with his glass.

'Thank you.' I wondered where this might be leading.

'Everyone agrees that your cooking has been a triumph. I hear the comments from the guests, even Lorna sings your praises and she's notoriously hard to please.'

'Well, that's very nice,' I said. I drank some wine.

'You know Lorna has plans for this place don't you? She

wants to turn it into either the Soho House of the north or alternatively the NoMad or the Battersea Power Art Hotel.'

'Kind of, she is very ambitious,' I said. I had no skin in the game, all I wanted to do was find out who killed a chef and a mystery guest, not get involved in the war for the future of the Moray Place Hotel.

'Well,' Donald said, grimly. His face was serious for a change. 'Two can play at that game. I know more than a few of the stakeholders in the hotel. Her plans would involve raising a lot of money for a risky refurb. Quirky is fine, but it comes at a big cost, and Edinburgh is not a party city, it's not trendy like Berlin or Barcelona, or even London. We don't have a great nightlife scene… we're heritage, more than anything.'

'I guess,' I said neutrally.

His voice swelled with enthusiasm now he was talking about the Moray Place Hotel. It suddenly occurred to me that the building seemed to cast quite a spell on those who worked here. They all seemed more than slightly obsessed with the place. He continued, 'It's like the architecture of the New Town, it's classic… Dave Holland understood that. Look at his menu – that could have come from any classy restaurant in the last fifty years. Things endure if they're good, fads come and go.'

'Uh, hunh.'

'What I'm saying Charlie is,' his eyes were feverish with excitement, 'let's capitalise on what we've got, go for the heritage market…'

I wanted to clarify the situation. 'So you want Lorna out and for you to run the place?'

'Exactly, Charlie.' He had the bit between his teeth now, he continued elaborating his theme. He wanted to make it a kind of highly polished old-fashioned hotel, the equivalent of Savile Row tailoring. I guessed it could well succeed, what he had said about chasing short-lived fads was very true. I'd worked a few years ago in a couple of, at the time, talked about night clubs, the kind of place Royalty were papped in, eye-wateringly expensive, now defunct. Face it, the Savoy and the Ritz were not hip, not vibey with the young, but still very much going concerns.

'And you could run the kitchen,' he said, 'we'd pay very well…'

Oh, Donald, I thought. Et tu Brute. Another person wanting me to bend to their wishes. You've forgotten I have my own business. It would be like leaving a reliable and loving spouse for the toy boy you were having a meaningless fling with. With eerie timing my phone vibrated, it was Gav wondering when we could meet up.

'Sorry, Donald, I've got to take this,' I smiled. 'Tomorrow?' I texted. He sent me a thumbs up.

I looked at Donald. 'I can see it working,' I said, cautiously.

'Then you're in?' He suddenly looked very excited.

'You misunderstand me, Donald,' I said. His face fell.

'I'm already taken. Sorry.'

I left him sitting alone at the table looking desolate. Not, if Gav were to be believed, for the first time.

Chapter Twenty-Five

The following day things got off to a bad start. I turned my ankle when I was out running at about seven in the morning. The cobbles were slippery and wet, and stupidly I hadn't been paying attention. I stood up and a flash of agony ran up my leg. I sat down on the pavement for a couple of minutes, my backside getting cold and wet, the drizzle running off my fluorescent waterproof jacket, my hair soaking under the sodden wool of my beanie hat. The cold Edinburgh wind froze it painfully on my wet forehead. It was like an iron band tightening. I stood up slowly, wincing. I could just about walk. I limped back to the hotel. Luckily I hadn't gone too far, I was at the end of an adjoining square that connected to some main road or other in the West End of the city.

Craig was on duty as I hobbled up the steps; he hurried out from behind his desk to see if I was okay. I assured him I was and took the lift the two floors up to my room.

There I pulled my shoes and socks off and examined the damage. The flesh was puffy and red, sore to the touch. I swallowed a couple of painkillers and kind of hopped to the bathroom where I showered. I dressed for work, the high sides of my steel-toed work boots gave some support and the tablets were kicking in. It would have to do.

Time down in the kitchen went slowly and painfully. I was back in the full swing of things. Euan was being even more infuriating than usual, huffy, sulky and hostile. Ordinarily I could have coped with this but today I was very much not in the mood. I was tired and in extreme pain, but I couldn't leave the kitchen. Food trumps pain.

Then Euan nearly cremated a piece of duck. If I hadn't noticed and intervened it would have been ruined. That in itself would have been liveable with, but it was one of four mains on a table for four. Either three people would have had to start while duck guy waited for his lunch, or the other three dishes would have been hanging around far too long. They'd have had to be redone.

Halfway through service I had enough of him. I had a pain in my ankle and a pain in my arse which, although metaphorical, was causing me more grief. I suddenly came to the end of my tether with him. I snapped, 'Get outside, now, Euan please.'

He looked shocked, suddenly frozen to the spot, his mouth open, his fair, almost white hair sticking up and his eyes round with amazement.

'Innes… take over from me,' I ordered, advancing pain-fully, limping towards the useless sous.

'Er, yes, Chef,' she said and hurried over to the stove.

'What's going on!' Euan protested.

I grabbed him by the sleeve of his jacket and shoved him, hard.

'Get outside now!'

I was incandescent with rage. I think there is a term in psychiatry called 'affect' when your response is wildly out of proportion to the stimulus. My leg was in agony, I was tired, I was trying without much luck to solve two crimes but most of all I was fed up with Euan and his constant whining.

We stood outside, glaring at each other in hatred. I was taller than he was so had the satisfaction of looking down on him.

'What's the matter with you?' he said, angrily. Well, since you ask, I thought...

'You're shit at the best of times, Euan,' I barked. 'Today you've surpassed yourself, you're shittier than shit...'

'You can't say that to me!' he protested, his face turning red.

'I just have, Euan,' I said, ominously.

'Who the hell do you think you are?' he blustered. I knew exactly who I was, the Head Chef.

'Euan, shut it,' I said. 'You're no use in there' – I pointed at the kitchen – 'go and get changed, go home and I'll see you tomorrow.'

'You can't do that...' then desperately, 'I've got rights.'

'Don't we all, Euan,' I said, acidly. 'Now I suggest you do us all a favour, exercise your right to silence and fuck off.'

'Okay then.' He turned and walked off to the changing room, then stopped and turned back, pointing a warning finger at me.

'You'll regret this, Charlie Hunter,' he said angrily, 'you'll rue the day... I've got friends...'

ALEX COOMBS

'I doubt that very much.' Boy, was that ever true. 'Goodbye Euan, you can come back to work when you've had an attitude review.'

He didn't bother to answer that, just slammed the door behind him by way of a response.

I walked back into the kitchen. Innes looked at me with awe.

'Well said, Chef,' Ali said, smiling at me from his sink. 'Someone should hae done that years ago...'

'I wasn't too harsh do you think?' I was beginning to regret my actions. Had I been a tad hasty?

Ali's tough old face crinkled as his smile broadened. 'Naw, that wisnae harsh, that was braw.'

Chapter Twenty-Six

Euan didn't turn up for the evening shift; Innes and I handled it between us. My foot was killing me by the time we'd finished. I took a couple of painkillers and went to bed. What a day, I sighed to myself, pulling the duvet over me.

My ankle woke me up at three in the morning. I lay in the darkness listening to the wind howling around Moray Place. I stared at the ceiling willing sleep to come, but it didn't. A car drove slowly by, rattling across the cobbled surface of the road. This was no good, I decided.

I reached a hand out for my handbag, picked it up then dropped it back on the floor. There were no painkillers in my bag, I suddenly remembered. It was a horrible realisation. I needed them badly. Reception had a supply, but I didn't want to wake Donald up to find me some. Then I recalled there were some in the medical cabinet in the kitchen.

I pulled the logoed hotel dressing gown on over my pjs, put my room key card in the pocket and made my way downstairs. Padding silently along the richly carpeted corridors and then the stairs at this time of the morning made me think of Katriona and Room 23.

I'd had a couple of furtive hotel experiences, was actually having one now with Gav up the road at Number Three. They are weirdly exciting. It's not like popping round to someone's flat. It's the slightly sleazy, secretive nature of the assignation that makes it such fun. The discreet click of the bedroom door as it locks behind you, whispered endearments, the strange bed... This wasn't fun though. I was having to lean my weight on the banisters to help me hop down the stairs. I could have taken the lift but it would have roused Donald.

I looked up at the security camera at the bottom of the staircase. I waved briefly to the stag's head, Hi Staggie. Then I headed down to the kitchen. The internal door at the foot of the stairs was locked, but I had the code to the keypad.

I made my way over to the work area in the darkness and I switched on the lights to the pass. The rest of the kitchen was a black void and I could feel the hairs on the back of my neck prickle. An empty, silent kitchen is a weird place at the best of times. At three in the morning, in three-quarter blackness with odd-looking slightly fright- ening shadows cast by the central low strip of lighting, it was strangely scary.

I located the pills I wanted in the first-aid cabinet, slipped them in my pocket and switched off the pass lights. Now it was totally dark apart from some external light filtering through the window and the glass in the kitchen door to the yard. There was a glimmer of blue from the gas on the stove underneath the stockpot. As I turned to go, a green light on the far wall came on. I nearly jumped out of my skin, stared at it wondering what was happening, then I realised that it was the light for the dumb-waiter.

I crossed over to the wall; sure enough I could hear the motor as the lift moved downwards.

What was happening? Was it malfunctioning? Surely this didn't happen of its own accord?

I suddenly had a flash of inspiration; maybe someone was inside and was lowering themselves into the kitchen.

Thoughts raced through my mind. Who could it be? My first thought, primitively and stupidly, was that it was some horrible entity out to get me. Then reason took over; whoever it was, it would be human. And at this hour it had to be someone up to no good, and it had to be someone who knew the hotel and how it worked.

Euan, I thought, it has to be you. Out for revenge. I glanced over at the huge stockpot ticking over on the range; he'd do something like tip a couple of hundred grams of salt in there to ruin it, or worse, he might have some old chicken at home that had gone off, that he'd brought it in to rub on ours, trying to cause an outbreak of food poisoning, or maybe slip a used condom into the poached plum compote.

Well, we'll see about that. I went over to the pastry section and picked up a hefty rolling pin (often a weapon of choice) then I crouched, invisible in the darkness, near the hatch to the dumb-waiter.

Come and get it Euan, I thought, tapping the long, round, plastic cylinder in my hand. I'm Anakin Skywalker to your Darth Vader. Din Djarin to your Moff Gideon. Dr Who to your Davros.

It was the only language he would understand.

Chapter Twenty-Seven

I could hear the noise of the motor change as it slowed and then the final bump as it settled. I kicked off my slippers. I would crack the pin hard into the backs of his legs, flooring him. If I hit him over the head with it I was liable to fracture his skull.

The doors rattled slightly. Then I heard the sound of them opening. My grip on the heavy, plastic shaft tightened. My heart was pounding and I could hardly breathe, my chest felt so tight. I swallowed nervously. Suddenly I saw a foot appear, and a leg, then a complete figure emerged in the darkness. I crept forward silently in my bare feet, the lino of the kitchen floor cool underneath.

They had their back to me. I smelled perfume and sweat; I paused, confused. That wasn't an Euan smell surely. My hand felt for the wall switch and I pressed down on three of them simultaneously, flooding the kitchen with bright, white light, raising my rolling pin aloft like a sword.

The figure jumped out of its skin and turned. I was looking into the terrified features of my apprentice.

'Innes!' I couldn't believe it.

'Chef!'

She looked very frightened indeed. Her hair was a tangled mess, her eyes wide. I dropped my hand holding the rolling pin down by my side.

'You, young lady,' I said severely, 'have got some explaining to do...'

By the bright light of the pass, my arms folded, Innes staring at the floor like a Victorian painting, The Chastened Child, the story came tumbling out. She'd fallen for Chet, the Texan boy, he was on the fourth floor. She didn't want to be seen going up there, not by Donald, who would still be up until one or two, and not by the CCTV camera.

'So I thought about the food lift. I left the hotel, came round the back, let myself in the kitchen. I know the back door code, and used the lift to go up to the dining room. From there I took the stairs... Please don't tell Lorna, she'll fire me... it's not allowed to have contact with guests...'

I marvelled at her ingenuity and the depth of her desire. I looked at her, so sweet and innocent looking, so young. Hard to believe that underneath lurked a passionate woman.

'No, I won't say anything, Innes... just don't be late tomorrow morning, I mean this morning,' I corrected myself. 'I'm already a chef down.'

'I won't, promise.' She smiled at me. 'Thank you, Charlie, for being so understanding...'

I let her out of the back door and limped back upstairs to bed feeling the comforting shape of my box of painkillers in my pocket.

* * *

The ibuprofen kicked in and I fell asleep. Two hours later I was awake at my usual time. I experimentally flexed my ankle, it was still painful and the tissue surrounding it was swollen slightly and sore to the touch.

I toyed with the idea of getting up and running on it, 'run through the pain', as we runners like to (stupidly) say and then hobble off to a physio once we've damaged it some more.

I sensibly decided not to, but by now I was wide awake and had no desire to lie in bed, staring at the ceiling. I got up, put my work clothes on and went down to help Martin in the kitchen.

It was 7 o'clock and he was bustling around, cooking off some sausages and bacon; they would keep warm under the lights.

There was a dish of precooked mushrooms on the pass as well and I said, 'Mind if I have some of those?'

'Be my guest.'

I cut myself some bread and had mushrooms on toast with three rashers of Ayrshire bacon; it was of a superb quality.

We did a few breakfasts, well, he cooked them and I carried them over to the dumb-waiter that Innes had used for her midnight tryst. I smiled at the memory. I looked at the space critically as I put the plates in. I'm pretty flexible but I think I would be too tall to fit.

'So, Charlie, what's been happening?' Martin asked.

I looked at his wise old face. I say 'old': he was about sixty I guess, that was only fifteen years more than me. I had a horrible, lurching feeling of mortality. What would

183

I look like when I was his age, a mad old hag? Then I thought of Anna Bruce; no, I would be like her, wise and old and beautiful. I felt comforted.

'How old are you, Martin?' I asked.

'Sixty-five.'

'And still working!' I marvelled.

He shrugged. 'It's my own fault. When I was younger, I didnae plan for the future… However, I'll show you something.'

He dropped down to the floor in one graceful movement so he was in plank position, and then lowered himself to the floor, did a couple of one-armed press-ups before standing up again.

'I figure, Charlie, if I can do that and run a sub-thirty minute five k, I can probably cook the odd breakfast without worrying unduly about my unfortunate life choices…'

I grinned at him. I felt hugely cheered by Martin's take on ageing.

'Fancy some overtime?' I asked.

'Maybe, why?'

I told him of my run-in with Euan. He rolled his eyes.

'So you want me to cover lunch as well?'

'Time and a half, Martin,' I dangled the financial carrot over him, 'plus the excitement of working with moi…'

'Well, that's set my pulse racing… make it double time and it's a yes.'

'Done,' I said, denting the profits of the Moray Place kitchen significantly. 'Thank you, Martin. I'm sure Euan will be back soon.'

He frowned. 'I'm no' so sure.'

'Don't be ridiculous, Martin,' I snorted. 'Of course he'll be back, nobody else would have him, would they?'

He laughed. 'That wasn't exactly what I meant... no, he is a deeply disturbed man, there's no telling what he might do.'

'Kill himself?' He was too egomaniacal.

'No, Euan's not suicidal. But he could get violent.'

'Him!' I said incredulously. If Francis was here he would have said, 'he couldn't knock the skin off a rice pudding'.

'You misunderstand me; he does hang around with some psychos.'

'Who?' I said scornfully. 'People from Star Wars conventions?'

He shook his head. 'I'm no' worried that you'll be attacked by a guy in a Chewbacca costume, no, it's his men's group friends.'

I thought of the people I had seen on the Zoom link. 'Those losers!' I called to mind Mr Celeriac Head, fatso in the Springsteen T-shirt and a couple of others. 'What are they going to do? Waft sage at me?'

'You're being unfair on the men's group concept, Charlie,' he said, shaking his head. 'They do have some valid points... but, like any group they attract undesirables. I have no doubt that Euan is there because they're one of the few places that could stand him, but as I mind I told you before, there is a sub-set of men who actively hate women' – he looked at me meaningfully – 'particularly females who are successful, and even worse, successful in a profession with very few women. There are some hard-core incels in there among the normal; I'd be wary if I were you.'

'Like in catering?' I had come across some real arsehole chefs in my time.

'Exactly, like catering. So, Charlie,' he warned, no hint of levity now, 'watch your back, just in case. It's not Euan, but his friends.'

Martin's dour words didn't worry me. I was either in the kitchen, in my bed, occasionally in Gav's bed, or running the streets of Edinburgh. It didn't leave many opportunities for a hate crazed, anti-woman nutjob.

I was interested, nevertheless, in what Euan was up to. Martin had said there was another meeting on Wednesdays at five in the evening. Euan would not normally be able to make that, he would be on his way to work, but as he wasn't coming in, early that evening I joined his men's group meeting using Martin's log in and password again.

This time, the chair gave a talk on how his wife had left him for another woman. A frisson of pantomime-like horror ran over the men at the very thought. Lesbians. Furtive looks were exchanged; where would the madness end? Could they trust their own wives not to run off with another lady? Face it, women were everywhere, some were even running things, and who knows what they might be thinking. No one was safe. The barbarians were at the gates.

The talking stick went round. One man, once he had the stick, said it was like ancient Rome; Scotland would be hollowed out by sexual deviants who were everywhere, particularly on the BBC, and then we'd be overrun by barbarian hordes. Almost certainly non-white Lesbians. Or homosexuals.

'Have you been to London recently!' he thundered. 'Sodom and Gomorrah!'

Someone else blamed the internet for putting ideas in women's heads. 'Women are easily swayed. I read a scientific paper from a university on Facebook and they are sixty per cent more likely to believe in unscientific falsehoods than men, and seventy-five per cent more likely to believe in made-up statistics. It's a fact.'

'TikTok,' said another man. 'It's the Chinese... and they're listening in via Alexa.'

'Aye, and they all have women's voices. Alexa, Google... and they say there's nothing going on... well, look around you, drink the coffee, not the Kool Aid.'

'Too true, take the Black Pill, sheeples!' said another. 'Whores...'

'Now that there's sat navs in cars these days, women know where they're going, they know how to get there. Before they were limited by their inability to read maps properly.'

The stick had reached Euan. I was fascinated to see if he would join in the Lesbian witch hunt: had they taken over *Star Wars*? What was the Sith's position on this?

Euan was of course, Euan. He hadn't been paying any attention whatsoever to the heated Sapphic discussion.

'I've been suspended by my bitch boss from Hell,' he announced dramatically, waving the stick for emphasis. I raised my eyebrows. I kind of liked that description of me, maybe I should have it printed on business cards. (I still used them, it was convenient if a customer asked if I did catering, quicker than getting phones out.)

187

Charlie Hunter
Bitch Boss from Hell
For all your catering needs

I think that had quite a ring to it.

'Do you know why?' he said in an aggrieved way. Polite disinterest was the best word to describe the group's reaction. Euan was obviously known to all of them and even here he was not popular. Also, his work problems were dull. This wasn't a patch on Conspiracy Lesbians. It was obvious no one really cared. Euan's problem in a nutshell.

Gross incompetence, that's why, tell them about the duck, Euan, I mentally urged.

'Because I showed her up, because she couldn't take being put in the shade by a man.'

This elicited a round of nods. He passed the stick to another man and I left the meeting.

Well, I thought as I walked down the stairs to join Innes at the stove, Euan was as big a prick as ever, but he sure didn't look dangerous to me.

'Everything okay for this evening, Chef?'

'Yep, full send Innes, just the two of us tonight. Euan's still nursing his pride.'

The evening went just fine.

The following morning I was working the breakfast shift with Martin. My ankle was still not a hundred per cent and I was doing the sensible thing and resting it. I made some remark about Innes and the American boyfriend, about how surprised I was, given Innes' rather demure, choirgirl appearance.

Martin sighed. 'Yon Innes is not the wee innocent that you seem to think she is, Charlie.'

'She isn't?' I was surprised. Okay, there was Chet, but what girl isn't occasionally swept off their feet? She was only a teenager still.

He shook his head. 'No. For one thing, she was having an affair with Dave Holland.'

My jaw must have dropped. 'What! But...'

'But he was twice her age? Get real, Charlie... this is a kitchen, you don't need me to tell you how things are in a kitchen.'

No, he didn't. Working cheek by jowl, in hot, sweaty proximity, quite literally, bathed in sweat from the heat and the stress, the adrenaline surging through you as you struggled to cope with the remorseless flow of orders, sexual feelings were heightened. Then there is the hero-worship element that you feel for a head chef at the top of his or her game, the fact that they are so much better than you are when you're a lowly apprentice.

Dave Holland at fifty should have shown more moral fibre in my view than shagging a girl young enough to be his daughter, grand-daughter even. My view of him plummeted. It must have shown in my face because Martin said, 'Don't be too hard on Dave. Innes made all the running. That girl's got a fantastic body as well as a pretty face...' he shrugged. 'I'd say he was helpless in the eye of the storm.'

Well, I wasn't so sure about that, but I let it pass.

Innes was working twelve until finish that day so I had plenty of time to evaluate the new side of her that I hadn't even suspected existed. As she worked beside me on the mains section – Martin effortlessly filling in on the starters and desserts – her face devoid of makeup and her goddess figure concealed under her chef's whites (I could still remember her see-through tank top), it was hard to imagine her as some kind of juvenile femme fatale.

But it had led to nagging suspicions in my mind. Someone had put poisonous mushrooms in Dave Holland's personal supply, that was a hard fact. Innes had been involved with him. She was also capable of seducing (this was a guess on my part, maybe it had been the other way round) a young, male guest and sneaking up to his room using the dumb-waiter. The Dave Holland thing had me wondering as to whether or not Innes harboured feelings towards older, successful men. In other words, men like Room 23. If you can hero-worship a successful chef, you can do the same with a successful restaurant and hotel critic.

We sent the last cheque out about half past two and gave the kitchen a clean-down. I went through the afternoon prep list with her and said, 'Okay, Innes, I'll be back at six… have a good afternoon.'

'See you then Chef.' She hesitated. 'Thank you so much.'

'What for, Innes?'

'For having faith in me.'

I smiled, hoping it didn't look as guilty as I was feeling, and left the kitchen. I felt a terrible hypocrite.

Upstairs in my room, I drew up a revised suspect list for Dave Holland's death.

Innes – motive: love gone wrong, jealousy.

Euan – resentment and rancour for not being appreciated. Maybe envy for Holland vis à vis Innes.

Not to mention Rosa. Maybe others? Lorna?

Lorna – with Dave Holland gone her plans to revamp the hotel could go through largely unopposed. If she had had a relationship with the head chef, maybe she was seeking revenge?

Rosa – the Italian lady chef who made the desserts, and reputedly Dave Holland's former side-piece. If she had found out about Dave and Innes, who knows what might have happened?

Katriona – the police thought she had killed Mike Sinclair. If she had killed him, maybe she had killed Dave Holland too. Maybe she had been sleeping with him, everybody else seemed to be.

Then I turned my attention to the other death, Room 23 aka Mike Sinclair.

Katriona – again. Currently on remand somewhere. Her DNA in the form of hair had been found in the room, she had admitted selling him drugs. Had she been selling sex too and something had gone wrong?

Lorna – she still seemed the most likely person temperamentally to have slept with Room 23. Katriona was money hungry, drug dealers are. But Lorna had an even more pressing motive: her career, which I suspect meant everything to her, it defined her. Someone had sex with the man in Room 23 and that person had then suffocated them. Lorna would do that if she deemed it necessary (I was sure of that), and a glowing review from Brook-Schlager would be incentive enough.

Innes – did she have a taste for powerful, older men or was Dave Holland a one-off? That was something to find

191

out. Then I recalled her dislike of Ellie, maybe it was over the Dave Holland issue. Well, I could find out.

I texted Ellie to see if she would like to meet for a drink on Saturday. She replied almost immediately. I watched the little dots dancing around on my screen then, yes, she said but late. Sounds good, I replied. She texted me with an address, a bar in Rose Street and a time, half past ten.

See you then.

I looked again at the list I had made. One name appeared twice: Lorna. Strickland's favourite. He'd gone crazy on the phone when I'd told him about Lorna and the bankers. See, he kept saying, she's killed one person, now she stands to make a killing. Get some bloody evidence Charlie!

So I felt I had to concentrate on her more than anything else. What would that mean in practice? Following her, I guess. It had worked once, maybe it would again. Most nights she finished round about the same time as me. She didn't have a car in Edinburgh and like me she seemed to prefer walking to cabs. The problem was knowing when she left the building.

If only I had a camera alert every time she left the hotel.

Then I remembered I kind of did.

Chapter Twenty-Eight

'Donald, I was thinking about what you were saying the other night...' It was Thursday night and I had just finished my shift. I had decided to enlist his help on my way to my room.

'I knew you'd come round, Charlie...' he looked hugely relieved. But it wasn't his plans for the future of the hotel I wanted to discuss.

Following Lorna before had paid handsome dividends, I was going to try it again.

'Umm, I wouldn't say I'd gone that far...' I said cautiously, 'but I do think that Lorna is up to something...'

'Absolutely,' he nodded passionately, 'she is up to no good... I'm sure it was her who did for Dave. And Number 23. She tramples anyone who gets in her way.'

'Possibly, Donald,' I said, levelly, 'but if you could let me know when she finishes for the evening and leaves the hotel, or, better still, is about to leave, I'd appreciate the heads up, just text me, okay?'

'Okay, Charlie, I will do... and Charlie...' his gentle face looked so excited, 'thank you so much.'

Poor Donald, I thought, like Strickland, he so much wants Lorna to be guilty.

The following night, Friday night, I struck gold. We sent the last orders out at half past nine, it was a dessert cheque, which Innes did. She had also volunteered to do the ordering for the following day. That meant checking the amounts of fish, meat and veg we had in stock; I'd done the bakery order earlier in the day. There was a checklist I had made so all she had to do was measure the quantities that were left against the various items, and then once that was done, email the order to the various suppliers for next morning delivery. It was a big responsibility for her and she was nervous and excited.

I went upstairs to my room, showered, changed and, while I was drying my hair, my phone pinged. It was Donald to say that Lorna was making arrangements to leave.

'Stall her for five minutes.' I texted.

I pulled on some shoes and a jacket and ran lightly downstairs, my ankle was definitely on the mend, and out through the kitchen door, down the alley at the back and arrived on the corner of Moray Place as Lorna left the hotel. I followed, at a distance.

I like following people, it's the thrill a hunter gets when the prey is in the cross-hairs of his sight. And like a good hunter, I appear to have a knack for it. Tonight the animal I was stalking, to carry on the hunting metaphor, was still wearing heels, she strode forward on them, a movement I admired. I could never have moved so well in shoes like that. Her sleek dark hair gleamed whenever she walked directly under a streetlamp. I hung well back, keeping to the shadows, but there was no need, she didn't look round once.

She was walking uphill and in towards the West End of Edinburgh, the opposite direction from St Andrew Square and Number Three. We walked into Charlotte Square, on the far side stood the illuminated bulk of Bute House. Next to it the green dome and golden cross of some church or other; I have never been anywhere so full of churches as Edinburgh, other than Italy. Then down towards Princes Street. I glanced up at the castle. The clouds were low and lights reflected off them, so tonight the black battlements silhouetted against the night sky looked to be surrounded by swirling pink and purple mists, like something from a fairy story.

I watched as she crossed over at the lights and went into the large, Gothic, red-brick bulk of the Waldorf or the Caley, as people called it still. It had been the Caledonian for about a century before being bought by the chain.

I followed her, under the awning and, nodding a good evening to the liveried doorman, I went inside. I was in time to see her back disappear into the bar.

The lobby area was very congested. Congested, jostling and shouty. There was a big sign, 'Edinburgh Welcomes Invest in Scotland Initiative'. There were trestle tables with brochures and an information point. There was a whisky bar with a banner, 'Caledonian Distillers Association, proud sponsors of the I.S.I'. Businessmen and a sprinkling of businesswomen were milling around it excitedly, like expensively dressed ants around a sugar bowl.

I slipped through the corporate crowd, loud and fuelled with free whisky, and into the bar. Lorna was sitting at a table with DS Bain. His tie was loosened and his collar buttons undone, his hair slightly rumpled. I thought to myself, he's drunk. He sprawled in his chair rag-doll style. Maybe he too had been sampling the Distillers' free bar. I saw him lean forward and kiss Lorna clumsily. I was fascinated. I stared at them wondering what she would do. You're playing with fire, DS Bain, I thought. I expected her to slap him. To my surprise she returned the kiss, not passionately but with a deft and economic display of sensuality.

Bain, encouraged, put his hand on her knee. He was obviously quite pissed, in a drunken world of his own where nobody would notice, or maybe Police Scotland conducted their investigations in a more people-centric way than in England.

Nobody did seem to notice. I guess they were both wearing suits and this blended them seamlessly into the background. I wasn't wearing a suit. I was wearing a short, bright red tailored puffa jacket, ripped black jeans and red Doc Martens. I was hardly camouflaged. I stood out from the crowd. I realised this because when Lorna removed DS Bain's hand from her knee and her tongue from his mouth and turned her head slightly, she saw me.

Lorna was not best pleased. A look of violent fury crossed her face and she jumped to her feet and headed straight towards me. A woman spoiling for a fight.

'Hello, Lorna,' I said brightly. 'What a surprise meeting you here…'

She drew herself up to her full height, even with the heels she was shorter than me.

'Have you been following me?' she demanded, angrily.

'No,' I said. Even to my ears it sounded like a blatant lie.

'Well, what are you doing here then, hey! Or is this a coincidence?' She had beautiful eyes, I thought as they burned into me, dark brown.

My mind raced. I could have said, 'I've always wanted to invest in Scotland, ever since I was a teenager it's been my dream…'

I could have said, 'I'm checking out the Waldorf hotel menu, in person, rather than online.'

I could have said, 'I was just passing and really fancied one of their cocktails.'

'I'm waiting…' Lorna said, through clenched teeth.

'I'm meeting my ex,' I said, with a calm I wasn't really feeling, 'to see if we can patch things up.'

'Oh really,' sneered Lorna, not taken in by this obvious lie. 'Investment banker, is he?'

'Yes,' I said. 'I'll introduce you.'

I walked over to a man standing with his back to me. He had black hair, the kind you get in Mediterranean countries. It was streaked here and there with silver. He was wearing a beautifully cut dark blue suit and expensive looking brown shoes.

I tapped him on the shoulder and he turned around. I saw his eyes widen in surprise and before he had a chance to speak I put my arms around him, and kissed him on the lips.

'Hello, darling,' I said.

Chapter Twenty-Nine

'Charlie,' he muttered, 'che cazzo…!'

I could feel the muscles on the back of my ex under my palms tense and harden. I smiled at him, my grey-green eyes gazing into his brown ones with an unspoken plea, just go along with this please!

I squeezed his back firmly, willing him to cooperate with me. The fabric of his suit felt really good, maybe a cotton/silk mix. Strange, the things you notice when you're hyped up.

To say I was chancing my arm was putting it somewhat mildly. The last time our eyes had met was at a distance of about five metres, the distance between the bedroom door, where he had been standing, and my bed, which contained me, which was fine, and another man, not so great. We hadn't seen each other since. If the roles had been reversed right now in the Caley bar, I might well have just slapped his face.

Fortunately for me, Andrea didn't. It was one of the things I had loved about him, his calm gentleness, his unflappability. Very un-Italian.

'I'll see you at the bar in ten minutes,' he murmured to me, 'you can explain then,' and turned back to his companions who were looking at him with a mixture of bemusement and envy. These Italians… you could imagine them thinking – a woman in every city.

I rejoined Lorna, feeling somewhat triumphant. That had gone far better than I had any right to expect.

'He's busy right now,' I told her. 'To be honest, I'm not sure how things are between us…' Well, that was certainly true, the understatement of the year.

DS Bain had disappeared. That was Lorna's doing, I was sure. She looked suspiciously at Andrea. Then at me, then at him again. Like someone watching tennis.

'So he's your ex?' She finally said, accepting the situation begrudgingly.

'Yeah,' I confirmed. 'I heard he was going to be here in Edinburgh so I thought I'd surprise him.'

I'd certainly succeeded there.

'Hmmh.' She frowned, still reluctant to believe me. 'Well, let's talk about this tomorrow, nine o'clock in my office.'

'Okay,' I said brightly, 'see you then.'

She marched out of the bar. More than a few heads turned to watch her go. It wasn't simply that she was an attractive woman, she generated a kind of magnetic forcefield of power round her that compelled attention.

I bought myself a drink, a Diet Coke, and stood near the bar for a few minutes looking down at my phone, avoiding eye contact with anyone until there was a touch on my shoulder and I turned round to face Andrea.

It had been a few months since I'd last seen him and he

looked much the same as ever. Good-looking in that North Italian way, a commanding presence in his dark suit (with its nice fabric as I had ascertained). His eyes regarded me in an unfathomable way. I was happy with that, at least it wasn't naked hostility.

'So, Charlie… what's going on?' If anyone was entitled to ask it was him.

It was now quarter to eleven and the place was thinning out. I guess the free bar outside the door had shut down.

'Let's talk over there…' I said, pointing to an unoccupied table.

We sat down and I told him what had brought me to Edinburgh. He nodded as I explained, asking one or two sensible questions. I finished and looked at him questioningly. 'And you?'

'Well, I'm currently a freelance,' he explained. 'I was hired by a Milanese bank to look at the possibilities of investing in a couple of online gaming companies based here in Edinburgh, and also a Torinese hotel group interested in investing in a property here, so I added the conference on at the end. They were happy to pay… I'm not sure anything will come of it, but that's not my concern.'

'And are you dating?' I asked, casually.

'There was someone,' he said, 'but she wanted commitments I was not willing to make, so, not like you, Charlie then.' He smiled thinly at me. It was a telling shot.

We had split up, partly because of my flagrant infidelity but mainly due to Andrea wanting to, as I saw it, control my life. The M word, I suspected. I'm not Mrs anybody. I suppose he was used to running things and had wanted me to go along with his plans. But I was used to running things too, therein lay the problem. You can't have one ship with two captains or one kitchen with two chefs.

'No,' I said, 'not like me at all. I'm the Bitch Boss from Hell!'

'What?' he was perplexed.

I told him about Euan and he laughed.

'Well…' That kind of broke the ice. Up until then there had been a kind of formal, awkward tension between the two of us, uncertain of our positions with each other, of where we stood. This just dissipated that tense atmosphere, like clouds being blown away by the wind.

For a while it was like old times. He wanted to know all about my business, life in the village, my financial situation, my employees.

'And how about Jess and Francis?'

I filled him in on what they had been up to. (Jess was a huge Andrea fan, she had been furious with me when we had split up.)

'Well, Charlie…' he looked at the clock on the wall, it was half eleven and we were the only people left in the bar. The staff were discreetly cleaning around us, almost certainly willing us to be gone. 'I'm tired. Can I see you again?'

'I don't see why not,' I said. Our surprise meeting had gone well. I hadn't expected it. After the split-up, I thought I might see him again, but only in the context of perhaps being invited to his wedding (do you invite exes to such things? We had spent quite some time together after all, most of it happy). I examined my feelings towards him, I didn't quite know what to think or feel. I knew that inside me emotions were churning like clothes in a washing machine; later I'd open the door and sort them out, but not just yet. I wasn't in the mood for introspection.

'Dinner?'

I shook my head. 'I'm working.'

'Tomorrow?'

That was Saturday. I thought of Ellie. I had the feeling that if I cancelled her she'd be furious.

'Are you still here on Sunday?'

'I can be.'

'I'll meet you at the Moray Place Hotel at three then. The lunch shift will be over and the others can clean down.'

'Thank you, Charlie…' he leaned over and squeezed my hand, 'I'm glad we can still be friends.'

I stood up. 'Ciao then, Andrea…'

'Alla prossima, Charlie.'

I walked out of the Waldorf. My phone rang, it was Gav. 'Hi!'

'What have you been up to, Charlie, I've been messaging you for the last hour? Don't you ever look at your phone?'

'Sorry, I was busy.'

'Can I see you tonight?' I thought of St Augustine's prayer: 'Lord, give me chastity and continence, but not yet!'

'On my way.'

I dropped the phone back in my pocket.

I looked up at the castle and the night sky; a tram hissed by on its way out to the airport. I saw a cab with its light on driving down the almost empty Princes Street and flagged it down.

'Top of Leith Walk,' I said to the driver and settled back in the upholstery.

Right now, I didn't want friendship, I wanted action.

Chapter Thirty

On Saturday morning I woke up early. My ankle was still sore so I didn't want to risk a run. Besides, I was tired; I'd crawled into my bed at half past three in the morning. There had been no sign of Donald; I guessed he was sleeping on his inflatable mattress in his office.

I went down to start prep and chat to Martin. He greeted me cheerfully and made me a bacon sandwich while I told him of my encounter with Andrea.

'What are the chances!' I marvelled.

'Synchronicity,' he said, shrugging, 'if you know the expression.'

I nodded; I did. It was one of Anna Bruce's favourites. A meaningful coincidence, often with spiritual consequences. I told him about Anna. He nodded approvingly. 'She sounds like my kind of person,' he said.

'You'd get on with each other.' It was true, they were both wise.

The talk turned to Euan, whether or not he was a danger to me as he had stated.

'Maybe I should get Uncle Cliff to mind me,' I said.

'Who's Uncle Cliff?' he asked, bemused.

I showed him a photo of Cliff Yeats on my phone from the summer. It was taken in the beer garden of the Three Bells. In the photo you couldn't see the rickety wooden furniture, the bald spots in the grass (mostly weeds and moss) and the dandruff and scurf, the detritus of umpteen cigarette butts.

Cliff had been wearing one of his horrible crimplene work shirts, white, with short sleeves showing his massive tattooed biceps, the fabric straining at his gut, the sunlight playing on his bald head with his few strands of gingery hair lovingly combed over the gleaming scalp and glued down with Brylcreem. Sovereign and onyx signet rings on his fingers. He was 130 kilos (20 stones to Cliff) of muscle overlaid with fat. And I adored him.

He was holding a pint of lager in one hand, the glass looking dainty in his massive grasp, the tattoos on his knuckles spelling out his name, his eyes sparkling behind his heavy glasses.

Martin's eyes widened slightly.

'He's your uncle?' he said wonderingly.

'Well, kind of; he was my dad's best friend and so he's that kind of uncle,' I explained. 'He's been there all my life, he's very protective.'

Cliff was chivalrous, my very own Parfit Knight, but not so Gentil.

'And what does he do for a living?' Martin asked.

A slightly odd question, I thought.

'Security. Cliff Yeats Security Solutions... basically, he's a bouncer, and much in demand.'

That was true. Cliff Yeats had quite a reputation. He may have been a bare knuckle boxer, but he wasn't stupidly violent. He did know how to defuse situations. His times spent in prison had never been the result of excessive force in a professional situation – they'd been GBH and armed robbery for purely commercial, albeit criminal, reasons.

'Och well.' He changed the subject back to the more prosaic matter of lunch and the prep list.

At nine I presented myself outside Lorna's office. It reminded me uncomfortably of being back at school and having to see a teacher, and not for a good reason. I knocked and went in.

'Hello, Charlie, have a seat.'

I did so. Lorna looked at me aggressively. 'So you're probably wondering about last night. Me and Ryan.'

Who? I frowned.

'DS Bain.' She had read my puzzled look correctly.

'I guess.' It was another confirmatory sign in the case against her. Attempting to pervert the course of justice. An innocent person would not have set out to seduce the investigating officer. She had.

'Look, Charlie, this hotel is my life more or less,' she said. 'Dave Holland and I took it over about fifteen years ago when it was on its last legs and we built it into a successful establishment; we won awards… Lately of course we had our differences as you know and then this… his death and then the murder… I don't mind telling you, it has shaken me.'

She didn't look very shaken. With her flawless makeup,

her immaculate clothes, her hair tied back in a tight ponytail from which no strand had escaped and her habitual steely air, she looked totally formidable.

'I'm... I'm sure it has...' I concurred.

'DS Bain may or may not be a very good policeman,' she said firmly, 'but he is a tragic wreck of a man. His wife's kicked him out, he's living in a Travelodge on the outskirts of Edinburgh, he's evidently got a drink problem...'

Then why are you seeing him, I wondered.

'I'm leading him on, Charlie,' she said, with brutal candour. 'I want to know what his investigation is unearthing and where it's headed.'

'What have you found out?' I was interested despite myself. Maybe I was as bad as she was.

'Nothing that we didn't know before.' She looked a bit cross at that. 'Katriona Smith is still the main suspect. There is the evidence of her hair in his bed, her prints in the room, her confession that she was indeed there to sell him drugs. She has previous convictions as a juvenile for violence and a search of her flat revealed drug paraphernalia, not to mention five thousand pounds worth of ketamine. And three thousand in cash.'

'And the motive?'

Lorna shrugged. 'They don't really know. They're guessing maybe a row over money, but they, that is the Procurator Fiscal's office, are confident enough to go ahead with a trial.'

'And how about Dave Holland?'

'Misadventure,' she said, decisively and approvingly. 'Case closed.'

So there we left it and I went back to the kitchen and the prep.

Later that night I walked the cold, wet empty streets of Edinburgh New Town to the bar in Leith Walk to meet Ellie, hoping to find out more about her relationship with Innes and the late Head Chef. I kept off the two main roads that ran west to east and wound my way through the residential Georgian cobbled streets. Although it was Saturday night I met hardly any pedestrians. Either the young folk were staying at home or they were all using Uber on this rainy, windy and dreich night.

The bar was heaving. I saw Ellie over in a corner. She stood up and waved at me. She was wearing tight black leather trousers (God knows how she got them on over those thighs, I thought uncharitably), a black sweatshirt that said 'Moschino', and a sour expression. There was something about the designer shirt that didn't look quite real, something made me think 'knock off.' It was kind of sad, I thought, wearing a copy of an expensive logo, pretending to be something you're not. It didn't make her look wealthy and sophisticated, it made her look like she'd been shopping down the market.

I squeezed through the scrum around the bar, bought myself a gin and tonic and sat down opposite her.

'Hi, Ellie, how are you?' I asked.

'I'm just fine,' she said in a way that made it clear that she wasn't. 'And you?'

'Good thanks.'

'What did you want to see me about?' Ellie asked.

I replied, 'I just wanted to touch base, really.' It was kind of meaningless but Ellie didn't seem to notice, she had an agenda of her own.

'You're in that hotel, you know more about what's going on than me, tell me, is my sister is still a suspect.'

'She is in prison, Ellie,' I pointed out.

'Aye but often it takes time for people to realise they've made a mistake. Naebody likes to admit they got it wrong, ken… especially the polis.'

'Well, that's very true, Ellie, but who do you think might have killed him then, if not Katriona?'

'Innes.' It was said definitively.

'Innes!' I exclaimed incredulously. 'Why on earth do you think she would have done it?' Innocent little Innes, impossible to believe.

'Because she's a crazy bitch…' she said, with sneering certainty. 'She looks like butter wouldnae melt in her mouth, but she's sex crazed, she's mad for it. She was knocking off Dave Holland, and he's older than her dad, he was certainly older than the guy who was kilt in the hotel.'

'Okay…' I stretched the word to indicate my misgivings, 'but, Ellie, sex is one thing, murder quite another… So you think she killed two people. Why would she?' I recalled that Ellie was no friend of Innes, but it was certainly true about the Dave Holland relationship. Then there was Chet…

'Because her mum is crazy,' Ellie stated with more than some satisfaction. 'She's a paranoid schizophrenic… she was locked up somewhere in East Lothian, Haddington I think it was, in a loony bin in the early noughties; she'd have been about Innes' age now... she went raj at a bus stop wi' a knife.'

She looked at me with an air of triumph as if this were a trump card that would get her sister out of prison.

'Sorry for sounding stupid, Ellie, what does raj mean?'

She gave me a scornful look. 'Raj means crazy, what else did you think it meant?'

Good point. I thought about this. It was undoubtedly interesting (if it were true) but did it have a bearing on the case? What I did know was that Innes was capable of accessing the upper floors of the hotel without anyone knowing; it was true that she could have gone to Room 23, had sex and killed him without anyone knowing.

Ellie shook her head. 'That girl is seriously bad news, Charlie. I'm very glad I don't work in that kitchen any more... all they knives, like mother, like daughter...' She lifted her glass. 'Here's tae Crazy Lorraine McDuff, sláinte,' she said, witheringly.

I got back home before midnight and, in my room, immediately booted up my laptop and looked up the local newspaper for Haddington, which I found easily enough. It was called the *East Lothian Courier*. I registered as a user and logged onto their archives which seemingly went all the way back to 1700. I didn't need to go back that far, just a few years.

The search was time consuming; it took me about an hour. 'Lorraine McDuff' had thrown up an awful lot of matches, none of which was the Lorraine I was looking for. But eventually I found what I wanted.

'Knife wielding woman terrifies High Street.'

The article described how a 'visibly distressed' woman identified as a Lorraine McDuff of Alder Road, Haddington had suddenly produced a kitchen knife from her bag and threatened passengers queuing for a bus on the High Street. After a stand-off with police, which closed the High Street for an hour she was arrested and taken into police detention. A spokeswoman for Police Scotland later confirmed that a young woman, Lorraine McDuff, a barmaid at the Campbell Arms, had been arrested and was now undergoing psychiatric evaluation.

And that was it.

I searched for the Campbell Arms, found it on the internet and logged onto its website. It boasted that it was family owned and run, and had been awarded a Bib Gourmand for five consecutive years and that the head chef, Baxter McIlchere had been there for over twenty-five years.

So he would have certainly known Innes' mum. They'd worked together. Maybe slept together, like mother like daughter. I filed that information away in my head for use later. I was too tired to think now.

I rubbed my eyes, it was 1 o'clock. Time for bed.

Chapter Thirty-One

I walked up the stairs to reception. Donald was working.

'Hi Charlie, good to see you. I heard from Lorna that the kitchen was on fire today.' He smiled warmly, it was a nice smile, sincere and good-humoured. 'So many compliments about the food.'

'I'm pleased to hear that.' I looked at the clock on the wall, next to the stag's head.

The stag seemed pleased to see me this afternoon, I thought. I blew him a kiss.

'Donald.' I leaned over the reception desk. I could smell his cologne. His hands were resting on the desk surface and I noticed how well kept his nails were. 'A friend of mine is coming here soon, a guy called Andrea di Stefano. Could you send him up to my room when he does, I don't want to keep him waiting.'

He raised his eyebrows, his eyes widened, and I realised how that must have sounded.

'Perish the thought! I'll send him straight up, I promise.'

'I mean…' I suddenly thought, like I care what Donald thinks.

ALEX COOMBS

'It shall be done, Charlie.'

'Thanks… Oh, and could you ask Annie to send a bottle of champagne and two glasses up to my room, I owe him that at least.'

He nodded. 'I'll do it myself, right now.'

'Thanks, Donald, I'll be in the shower; just leave it on the table.'

'I'll do that.'

'Thanks.'

In my bathroom I stripped off and kicked my clothes into a corner and washed the kitchen off my body and out of my hair. I thought of Innes. I couldn't wash away the feelings of guilt I had for suspecting her, nor the feeling that maybe I was right to do so. I dried myself, pulled on a big, white fluffy bathrobe and went back into my room.

'Hello, Charlie.'

Andrea was sitting in the chair by the table. No suit today. He was wearing black jeans, a grey cashmere sweater and black shoes. A classic tan Burberry trench coat was hanging on a peg on the wall. Andrea was, as always, dressed appropriately for the occasion.

Andrea's demeanour, however, was far from relaxed. He was perched tensely on the edge of the chair. His voice was edgy too, brittle with suppressed emotion.

'Shall I open the champagne?'

'Please do, it's for us.' I sat down on the bed as he opened the bottle and poured us both a glass. He looked around. 'Nice room.'

'Nicer than the Waldorf?'

He shrugged. 'I've got a suite.'

214

I laughed. 'Of course you have.'

He laughed too. 'One of the things I really like about you, Charlie... you're not impressed by money are you?'

'I don't know...' I guess it was true. I don't really have time to spend it.

'I do,' he said. 'I've been dating... it's quite dispiriting...' he pulled a face, 'people just seem interested in your salary or status.'

He looked at me levelly. 'And you've never done that, Charlie.'

'Done what?'

'Used me for money.'

'You did buy me a bed,' I pointed out.

'I was being selfish.'

Silence fell. We looked at each other for a while, wondering what to say and do, trying to make some sense out of the maelstrom of memories, shared experiences and emotions that had arisen in both of our breasts.

'Charlie...' his tone was exasperated, 'you and me...it's just, we complement each other so well... it's a perfect fit.' He sighed. 'Why isn't it working?'

'Because I don't want to be Mrs di Stefano,' I said, brutally honest, 'which is what you seem to want.'

He nodded and drank some champagne. 'Only because I want to be with you.'

I looked at him over my glass. I suddenly felt very strange, slightly faint. I never had unloaded the washing machine of feelings. Well, now its door was open and everything was over the floor tiles in clean sight. I realised what I had known for some time, that I had missed him. I don't think

I had realised how much until I'd held him against me in the Waldorf two nights ago. Now I suddenly knew that I wanted to be with him again.

'Can't we try again?' he asked, looking at me anxiously. 'I promise I won't propose or ask you to move in.'

I thought this over. 'Promise? No pressure?'

He smiled. 'No, just the pleasure of your company, when I can get it... besides, I've missed your Bavarois.'

'So,' I said, primly, 'you want cake with privileges?'

'I guess so.' He nodded his head.

'You're asking a lot, Andrea. I don't bake just for any old man, you know.'

'I know.'

I put my glass down and stood up. I tugged the sash at my waist so the bathrobe opened. I shrugged my shoulders and let it fall to the floor.

'Suits me,' I said.

Thank God I had remembered to close the shutters for once.

Chapter Thirty-Two

'Martin,' I said at breakfast, 'do you mind if I took the lunchtime shift off?'

I had decided to go to Haddington and see if I could discover any more about Innes and her background. It was Tuesday and it was a reasonable bet that the Campbell Arms would be open and the head chef working. I was hoping he could shed some light on things.

Martin looked at me calmly, nothing seemed to surprise him, and said, 'Not at all, lassie. So, what are you doing this lunch time that's so important?'

'I'll tell you when I next see you, Martin.'

'I guess that'll be Wednesday morning then.'

I nodded. 'Then that's when it will be.'

'Well, whatever you're doing today, I wish you every success. You'll be in for the evening shift?'

'I will indeed. Tell Innes I'll see her around six. Thanks again, Martin, you're a sweetheart.'

I kissed him on the cheek.

About half nine I walked up to St Andrew Square where the lone statue stands forever high on his enormously tall plinth, like a secular St Simon of Stylites or a proto David Blaine. Who is he? No one knows, well, I guess there's a plaque, but a poll of my co-workers indicated one hundred per cent ignorance.

I found a bus going to Haddington easily enough. I stared mindlessly out of the window watching the scenery go by, grotty dormitory towns outside Edinburgh, Musselburgh and Tranent, then eventually Haddington.

I got off in the town centre. It seemed an attractive, old-fashioned market town, prosperous, with wide streets and Victorian, or Victorian-style, ironwork in the forms of streetlights.

The Campbell Arms was easy to find. It was more or less bang in the middle of town, a sizeable building painted white, with grey woodwork around the windows. I looked at my watch, it was half past eleven.

I walked up to the front door; the bar opened at twelve, but the door was unlocked and I walked inside.

I stood in the carpeted vestibule for a moment or two. There was a flight of carpeted stairs, a tartan pattern, running upwards. There was a map of East Lothian on the wall. The door to the lounge bar was open and I could smell stale beer and floor polish, the smell of a pub. I closed my eyes and savoured it, the way you might bury your head in a loved one's sweater or scarf, inhaling the scent of their body, their perfume, their essence. I love the aroma of pub.

At the end of the corridor was a sign saying, 'Restaurant.' I could hear the sound of hoovering from down there so I walked up to the glass door and went in.

218

A young girl was vacuuming the carpet. She looked up. She was slim and pretty with dark, bird's nest hair scrunched up into a ragged bun.

'Oh, I'm afraid we're not open yet,' she said.

'That's okay, I just wondered if I might have a quick word with Baxter if he's in.' I smiled a winning smile.

'Aye, he is, he's in the kitchen, I'll go and get him for you... is he expecting you?' she enquired.

'No,' I said, I reached into my bag and brought out a business card, the one saying, 'Charlie Hunter, Head Chef/Proprietor The Old Forge Café.'

'Could you give him this and ask him if he's got five minutes.'

'Surely, may I ask what it's about?'

'Yeah, Lorraine McDuff and her daughter Innes.'

'Okay, I'll just be a minute.'

She disappeared through the swing door to the kitchen. I could hear the brief sound of a morning kitchen prepping as the door swung open and closed. Male voices, a radio playing, the clang of a pan being banged down on the stove, the rat-a-tat sound of chopping.

I waited a moment. I was fairly confident he would speak to me, we were both chefs after all, brothers under the skin. He'd wonder what this was about, simple curiosity would do the rest.

The girl returned.

'I'm sorry,' she said apologetically, 'he said that he's busy and doesn't want to see you.'

My face fell; I had not been expecting this.

'Oh, maybe later, after service?' That was an unexpected

setback. I wondered what I would do in Haddington until 3 o'clock.

She shook her head. 'I'm afraid he won't see you, period.' She raised her eyebrows and shrugged, embarrassed by the turn of events. 'Sorry about that.'

'That's okay…' I said, defeated. Well, there was nothing more to be done, nothing I could do. 'Thanks for your help.'

I left the pub. I was mystified and in truth, slightly hurt. Why didn't he want to see me? Maybe it was my business card. If it had said,

Charlie Hunter
Bitch Boss from Hell
For all your catering needs

we might have got somewhere.

I walked back towards the bus-stop. It was about an hour's wait for the next one back to Edinburgh. What a complete and utter waste of time that had been.

Chapter Thirty-Three

I'd only gone about fifty metres down the road, when I heard a voice from behind me.

'Hi, excuse me…'

I turned around, it was the girl from the pub. She was slightly breathless, she'd obviously run to catch up with me.

'Hi, can I speak to you a moment…'

'Sure,' I said.

'May I ask why you're interested in Lorraine McDuff?' She was scrutinising my face carefully, to make sure I gave a satisfactory answer.

'It's not her specifically, it's her daughter.' I couldn't very well say that I was wondering how likely it was that Innes was a murderer, so I said, 'I'm a chef and I'm considering her for a job, and I'm doing due diligence on her background, and that includes her family.' That sounded faintly plausible, although in truth nobody really cares much about you in a kitchen apart from your ability to cook.

The girl nodded. 'I was at school with Innes, the Knox Academy, just up the road. I'd be happy to answer your questions.'

'Have you got the time?' I wondered if she had to be back at work soon.

'Aye, I'm no' waitressing today, just doing a spot of cleaning there.'

And so we had lunch at a small, cheap Italian owned café with formica tables and perfectly reasonable food in the centre of Haddington.

Lizzie McEnery opposite me, was eighteen and had just started a psychology degree at Edinburgh Uni.

'It was because of Innes that I first became interested in the mind,' she said. 'In her case it was of course Lorraine's mental illness.'

'What's wrong with Innes' mum?' I asked.

'Paranoid schizophrenia,' Lizzie said. 'Very serious indeed.'

'Was there some incident here?'

'Aye,' she nodded. 'It was before either of us were born. Her mum had to go into a secure unit, but she was released after a year or so; with medication and therapy she'd quietened down.' She pulled a face. 'But sadly she took her life four years ago. Poor Innes had to go into foster care. I kind of lost touch with her after that.'

'So you'd have been both, what, fourteen?'

'Aye.'

'What was Innes like?'

Lizzie frowned. 'Complicated...' She hesitated as if wondering whether or not to trust me. She drew some symbol delicately on the formica surface where she had spilled some Coke. She looked up from the pattern that she had traced. 'The thing is, Charlie, she was man-mad, and not in a guid way. I know that she was sexually active from the age of thirteen. She'd get made up – she had developed early – and she hung around with these older guys who'd been at school and then kind of dropped out... I suppose, the local bad lads... What I'm saying is that she would fling herself at men, sometimes much older.'

'I see.' This sounded terrible. I felt both very sorry for Innes and increasingly concerned by what she might have been up to in the hotel.

'In a very needy kind of way. It was sad, and a wee bit scary too. I mean, her mum was obviously unbalanced, you kind of wondered about Innes sometimes.'

'I see.'

'Well, Charlie, the reason I'm telling you this is because Innes definitely needs help in some form. Personally I think it's because she was always looking for a father figure, and that's why she would go for older men, and when they didn't live up to that, to the fantasy she had created, there would be trouble.'

'How do you mean?'

'I know that just before she left Haddington she'd been' – her fingers sketched quotation marks in the air – '"seeing" a guy called Dougie Grant. She smashed up his car with a hammer when he left her and then had a go at him with it. Dougie was terrified. He thought he might go to prison for having sex with a minor – that was from the legal side, or have his head battered by Innes on the other.'

She sighed. 'I know Dougie, ken, it wasn't his fault. He wasn't much older than us, a couple of years... he thought she was sixteen for the month they went out, because she'd told him she was doing highers at Knox Academy... When he found out she was under-age, that's when he dumped her. After she got over it she took up with a traveller from Fife who knew her age but didnae care, or was maybe excited by it.'

A waitress took our plates and I thanked her. Lizzie continued, 'So that's what she's like. She was a lovely girl except where men are concerned. There's something gone askew there, and as her employer you should be aware of that.'

She looked at the clock on the wall. 'Right, Charlie, I have to go. I've got your number on your card, I'll call you later so you have mine; I'd like to get back in touch with Innes. Now I'm at the Uni and know people who work in therapy, and know ones I can trust who are good, I could do something to help her. Christ knows what we'd do about funding but we can worry about that later, I'm just worried she might do something stupid.'

I nodded. 'Okay.'

She squeezed my hand as she stood up. 'You seem like a nice person, Charlie Hunter, I'm glad she's working for someone like you. You seem to care. So few people do. I hope we meet again.'

I watched her as she left the restaurant. The staff behind the counter called out to her as she left, she seemed very popular here. Deservedly so, from what little I had seen of her.

I paid the bill and walked to the bus-stop. On the way back to Edinburgh I thought of Innes' open, pretty face. I also thought of the not very long ago incident where the young child had trashed a boyfriend's car with a hammer and then had a go at him with it.

I thought of what Lizzy had said about her, how she would go for older men. Dave Holland, for sure. Maybe it was not so far-fetched to imagine she might have been in Number 23's room too.

I thought she may well have had something to do with their deaths, and the fact I did made me feel despicable.

Chapter Thirty-Four

'So, did you have a nice day, Chef?' Innes asked me brightly. 'What did you get up to?'

I had bounded into the kitchen at six in the evening, looking alert and energetic and raring to go, to mask my real feelings which were guilt, despondency, suspicion and gloom. It was hard to believe that this pretty, fairly quiet girl was capable of going berserk with a hammer, but she had. Equally, it was hard to believe she would sneak into the hotel, squeeze into the dumb-waiter and go up to the American boy's bedroom for wild sex, but she had.

'Oh, not bad. I had an unexpected chance to see a bit of Scotland that doesn't come along too often...' That was certainly true. 'I thought I'd better take it.'

'Where did you go?' Innes asked, curious.

'Errrm...' I was saved from having to answer by the arrival of the first cheque.

We were crazily busy that night, and I was profoundly glad. There was hardly time to draw breath, let alone waste it on conversation.

Both Innes and I were dripping with sweat from the heat

of the stoves, the exertion and the effort and the sheer mental strain of trying to keep up with the flood of orders. Ali too got roped into the general carnage of the service, having to juggle the washing up with running dishes over to the dumb-waiter, emptying it and doing the desserts as well.

In the odd moment when I wasn't cooking, plating up or getting things ready I would steal evaluative glances at my junior chef.

Innes' concentration was faultless, she didn't put a foot wrong, which was a hell of an achievement. There are so many things going on simultaneously in a kitchen it's easy to break down or start making mistakes. Her plating of the starters was impressive, they didn't deviate from the photos in the spec file that the late David Holland, her ex of course, had created. There were not only no mistakes, there was no hint of sloppiness about them.

Her features were immobile. Before, I had noticed how well she could concentrate, but now it seemed to me that she had withdrawn into a world of her own; it was as if an impenetrable, invisible bubble surrounded her.

Was this what she had been like when she had smashed that guy's car up before threatening to turn the hammer on him? Was this what she was like when she was making love, a mask-like, inscrutable face?

Had this been her face when she had gone up to Number 23, had sex with him and then, with serene detachment, pushed the pillow down over his face while he lay semi-conscious in a drink and drug fuddled state? Then calmly made her way downstairs to the dining room, climbed into the dumb-waiter and exited unseen via the kitchen back door.

I couldn't even begin to fathom what reason she might have had for killing him but it seemed horribly possible.

We sent the last mains at 9.20 and the three of us went out into the yard with huge grins on our faces. Innes' detachment had vanished to be replaced by that incredible adrenaline of a chef's high when the terrible strain of a hard service is over.

I had phoned the bar earlier and now Angelika the foreign waitress brought us six bottles of lager.

We sat on the plastic beer crates outside. It was cold so we'd put our coats on against the winter chill. Ali lit a cigarette and Innes and I clinked bottles. She took her cap off and ran a finger through her dark hair that was plastered to her skull like she'd been swimming.

'Euuch, my hair's minging.'

I smiled, so was mine. Utterly sweat drenched.

I stood up. 'I'd better go and change.' I was finding the strain of carrying all this new knowledge around with me seriously hard. 'Thanks, Innes, you were great tonight, I really mean that.'

'Thank you, Chef.'

'Charlie,' I said, I pointed, 'you can call me Chef in there.'

'Thank you, Charlie.'

'See you tomorrow.'

Chapter Thirty-Five

The next morning I was down early with Martin for the breakfast shift. I started my mise-en place for the day; I knew it was going to be fairly busy. Thank God for Rosa, I thought as I checked the section in the freezer for desserts; we were okay for sorbets and parfaits. You can't knock out a parfait in a hurry, or a sorbet come to that. I grimaced. I can remember once having to send out a sorbet I'd made well before it was properly frozen; it looked like one of those slush puppy things children drink at swimming pools. The waitress had looked at it dubiously.

'Tell them it's supposed to be like that,' I'd ordered her, desperation in my voice, 'tell them it's demi-gelé.'

'Okay…'

I'd made up that word from my schoolgirl French, hoping it meant 'half-frozen', which was indeed an accurate description. There were no complaints, but I sometimes still wake up sweating at the memory.

I closed the freezer door and brought my mind back to the present.

'Martin, did you know about Innes' background?' I asked.

He looked at me thoughtfully as he finished sending out another couple of breakfasts.

'You mean, her mum and her mental health?'

'Er, yes.'

He nodded. 'What of it?'

'You didn't think it worth mentioning?' I asked, somewhat incredulously.

He turned to me. 'Charlie, we all have a right to a private life. There are things about me I never told you.'

'Really, like what?'

'Okay then.' There was a charming grin on his face. 'I was a career criminal for about twenty years, a wee hard man frae a shite council scheme. I learnt to cook in the slammer during my last five years in there.'

'Oh,' I said faintly. Well, I had asked. 'What were you…'

He laughed. 'What was I in for? Grievous Bodily Harm. My lawyer argued it down from attempted murder, but it was actually attempted murder indeed. I'd tried to kill him but luckily for both of us, I failed. That's what I used to do.' He shrugged. 'Gangland enforcer and occasional hitman.'

'I had no idea…'

'Obviously not. Does it change anything between us?'

I looked at him. I still liked and trusted him, all the more so now. 'Absolutely not, no.' And I meant it.

'I'm delighted to hear that… Behind the persona, the face we put on to meet the world, we all have secrets Charlie, from the mundane, to those deep, dark secrets we don't like to tell ourselves exist. The ones that surface in your dreams or in your projections, to just practical ones, like lying on your CV, or cheating on your partner…'

'Mm, hm,' I said. This was all drifting a bit close to home. I thought of last night with Andrea. I certainly hadn't told him I was seeing someone in Edinburgh. Not that it was important but the fact that he was only a mile or so away geographically seemed to make matters slightly worse.

'So,' he concluded briskly, 'let's not worry too much about Innes' past and concentrate on the present, shall we?'

'Okay, Martin,' I said equally briskly. 'You're right.'

But I did worry.

The day wore on. I'd told Martin that his criminal past made no difference, but that was a lie too. If I hadn't been invested in discovering who had killed Dave Holland then maybe it wouldn't have mattered. But I was looking for a killer and now I had two people in the kitchen with a history of violence.

During my break from three to six, I searched online for Martin Ridell, GBH. After a lot of faffing around I found an article from the *Daily Record*, a Scottish newspaper. 'Greenock Man Sentenced to Ten Years.'

Basically Martin Ridell was found guilty of having beaten a guy called Tom McConnachie to within an inch of his life before dumping his body on a football pitch in Motherwell. Luckily for McConnachie, he was found by a dentist walking his dog, who was able to keep him alive until an ambulance arrived.

Ridell's lawyer had argued that McConnachie had started the fight by bragging in a bar about his part in a brawl in a Parkhead shopping centre in which a friend of Ridell's had been severely injured. This had provoked Ridell into retaliation.

I closed the tab and stared into space. Poisoning someone with mushrooms was different from the usual modus operandi of a hit man, but killing someone is killing someone. Who knows if Lorna had maybe decided to ask her breakfast chef if he wouldn't mind removing Dave Holland who was blocking her path from the scene. But why would he want to kill Number 23? That made no sense whatsoever.

Then my phone signalled a message. It was Gav. I sighed. I guess I would have to end it.

That night was busy, but I relished the work. Innes had grown into her role as sous chef. She was immeasurably better than Euan and the two of us dealt with the forty-five covers with almost casual ease.

Another couple of messages from Gav. I frowned. I wasn't looking forward to finishing with him but it had to be done. I toyed with the idea of just texting him, but I thought that seemed a bit cowardly.

I told him we'd meet at the bar at the top of Leith Walk about eleven, and he agreed to that.

I got there about ten past the hour. He was sitting at a table with Ellie who looked somewhat the worse for wear. Gav brightened when he saw me. He stood up and went to put his arms around me. I forestalled him by putting my hands on his shoulders and sliding them down, effectively pinning his arms to his side.

'Can I get you a drink?' he asked, looking slightly hurt.

'I'll have a red wine,' I said. I really wanted a Pils but I needed a drink I could neck quickly once I'd said my piece.

I couldn't break up with a man, down a bottle of Pils in one and leave without burping loudly, which would kind of ruin the desired effect of quiet, adult dignity.

He went to the bar and I sat down opposite Ellie. Tonight she was wearing a shocking pink and black shirt that said Prada on the breast. It clashed badly with her pinkish face and fair hair. She gave me a sharp look.

'Something up, Charlie?'

'In a manner of speaking. Look, Ellie, when Gav comes back could you give us a moment please...'

She stiffened; she immediately knew what I was going to do.

'You're breaking up with him?' She was certainly shrewd. She also looked very angry; I didn't see what it had to do with her.

'Yes.'

'Sure? It'll really hurt him, Charlie.' Her voice made it sound like a veiled threat.

'He'll get over it.'

'You really are a callous bitch,' she said. She stood up. I noticed she was unsteady on her feet and was slurring her words slightly. She was quite drunk, combative.

She leaned over the table. 'Euan was right about you.' She spat out the words venomously. 'I'm going to the ladies, you'd better be gone by the time I get back.'

I watched her back disappearing through the crowded bar. She'd been talking to Euan! Why? This was weird. What could those two have in common? I guess they had both been work colleagues, but why keep in touch?

Gav came back with my drink. I thanked him.

'Where's Ellie?'

'Gone to the loo.'

'Oh.' He suddenly frowned. 'Look, Charlie is something the matter?'

'In a way, Gav.' I took a deep breath. 'There's no easy way to say this.' Actually there was, I thought. I could just shout, 'Bye Gav, I'm off, nice knowing you,' and leg it out of the bar. That would be easier.

'I'm getting back together with my ex...' I spread my hands wide apologetically, 'I'm sure you understand.'

'What!' he looked thunderstruck.

'I'm afraid we're through, Gav.'

'No...' he looked really shocked. 'No, Charlie...'

I was beginning to get a bit tired of this. What bit of 'I'm afraid we're through' didn't he understand? Man up. I stood up, drained my wine and put the glass down on the table.

'It's been nice, but ciao, Gav.' I walked out of the pub into the cold rain of a November Edinburgh night.

I was unsure of how to get home via the back streets in this part of Edinburgh, not through any safety concerns but because I didn't know them well enough to take short-cuts. I don't like walking late at night with a phone in my hand staring at the screen following a suggested route. So I went to the top of Leith Walk and at the busy junction with Waterloo Place took a side alley by the Guildford Arms and cut across to St Andrew Square. Nodding hello to the guy nobody had ever heard of on top of his stupidly tall column.

I walked down a narrow road called Thistle Street. It's

one way, a pretty lane with some interesting little shops in it. It's very restricted, room for a car and two narrow pavements. The buildings crowd in on it from either side. It's arrow straight and you can see it stretching away in the distance for about, I guess, a quarter of a mile. It was there that I realised I was being followed.

There was nobody else in the street, and it was about 11.40 on this cold, wet November night. I could hear footsteps behind me. I walked faster, the footsteps sped up. I looked round over my shoulder.

Two guys, youngish, one with long hair, wearing the kind of grey, crappy tracksuit that is known in Scotland as a jobby catcher, presumably because it's gathered at the ankles. The other was wearing a kilt. Not a common sight except in the Royal Mile and other visitor hotspots. Something in his demeanour told me he didn't work in the tourist trade. I could see a sudden glow as one of them drew on a cigarette. Then I smelt it, it wasn't a cigarette, it was weed.

I broke into a jog, they followed suit. Now I knew they meant business. I was wearing trainers, not my running shoes, very nice new Nike Air Jordans, high sided. They were certainly good enough for running short distances. My ankle initially protested but the adrenaline surging through my body now, brushed any objections aside.

I ran faster, lengthening my stride, trying to be careful not to stumble on the irregular and slippery cobbles. I could hear their feet thudding behind me. I was praying that the weed would slow them down. The sound of footsteps grew louder. I lengthened my stride, upped my cadence. I was flying now.

237

Thistle Street runs parallel to Princes Street, the capital's main thoroughfare that runs below the castle. At the end of the narrow street I turned left into Hanover Street and headed towards it. I thought there would be plenty of people around, they wouldn't dare attack me in such a public place.

The castle on its gigantic rock dominated the city, lit up like something from a fairytale. I was in no mood to appreciate its beauty. I still had my pursuers uncomfortably close, I could hear their laboured breathing. Then I saw what I needed. There's a road that curves up from Princes Street to the castle and the top of the Royal Mile. The Mound. It's steep and floodlit. I thought, I can run up hills fast, I doubt they can.

I hurtled across Princes Street, devoid of traffic apart from a tram in the distance, the National Gallery and the Royal Scottish Academy with their pillars and porticoes lit up on my left. Now was my chance. I increased my pace, gritting my teeth as I pounded uphill, fire in my lungs, fire in my thighs and calves but most importantly fire in my belly.

Halfway up I was aware that they were no longer behind me. I glanced over my shoulder. No one there. I slowed and stopped and looked back.

I could see them in the distance. They'd given up. One was doubled over and I saw him throw up. I felt a huge triumphal surge run through my body.

I remembered something Jess had taught me, one of her unusual words. Semiotics, the science of the language and philosophy of science, invented by some bloke called Saussure.

'Bitch!' The shouted insult floated up to me, borne on the breeze.

Time for a display of semiotics.

I bent the four fingers of my right hand together, placed my thumb on my index finger and raised my hand aloft, vigorously working it up and down.

Saussure would maybe have approved.

I jogged on up to the Lawnmarket to get a taxi home.

Chapter Thirty-Six

On Thursday morning I was telling Martin about the events of the previous night. His face full of concern, he suggested I call the police. I shook my head.

'What are they going to do about it, Martin? Nothing, we both know that.'

'But you could have been...'

I stopped him there. 'A lot of things could have happened, but they didn't. What did happen, Martin, was that I got away, and quite frankly, humiliated those two arseholes.'

He saw that my mind was made up.

'Okay, so what are you going to do?'

I laughed. 'Avoid Ellie Smith and Gav. I reckon it was Ellie who set them on me for hurting Gav, or whatever mad reason she might have. So, I shan't be meeting her again in a hurry I can tell you.'

'Well, all I can say is, you'd better take care. They might be back for a second bite of the cherry.'

'Martin, I'm only here for another month and most of

that time I'm safe in the hotel. I don't think I'll be seeing any more of those two thugs, or Ellie for that matter.'

And there we left it.

The next few days passed in a work blur and on Sunday morning I flew down to check on my own restaurant and relax for a couple of days, leaving my troubles, at least the physical ones, far behind, to the tune of 400 miles.

To my surprise Anna Bruce, not Jess, met me at the airport. I rounded the curved corner at Arrivals and noticed her immediately: short, white hair, blue denim jacket, radiating a charisma so powerful it turned heads.

'Where's Jess?' I asked as we embraced. She smelled of expensive perfume and self-confidence.

'She had to go back to uni for a conference. I volunteered to pick you up.'

'Thank you.'

'It's always a pleasure to see you, Charlie.'

We had a coffee before we went to the car. I was craving espresso, and I told her what had been happening up in Edinburgh, well, the edited highlights.

We got out of the lift and walked across the crowded floor of the car park to her car. It was one I hadn't seen before, a Porsche, one of those classic sports cars, I think they're a 911. Like the emergency telephone number in the USA familiar to me from TV.

We got in. She started the powerful engine and we listened to it throb.

'You look tired, Charlie,' Anna Bruce noted.

'I'm getting very fed up of all of this,' I sighed. 'It

wasn't my idea to go up to Scotland and now I'm trying to work out how the chef died, running someone else's kitchen and then the guy in Room 23 getting murdered and now there's all this emotional wear and tear with everyone's problems, and then someone tries to attack me… I'm tired of all this shit.'

Anna Bruce regarded me sceptically. I could tell she was sceptical because her expression, if you were being charitable, was one of doubt, or more plausibly, borderline contempt.

It wasn't the reaction I had expected. I'd wanted overwhelming sympathy, not an expression as soft and forgiving as the concrete framework of the car park.

She drove us with easy competence out of the Heathrow multi-storey and through the complex road system that I find horribly intimidating, with almost nonchalant skill. She was silent until we reached the motorway.

'Okay,' she said, 'I've heard you out…' She overtook some cars with brisk efficiency. 'I'm sorry, I don't buy this "St Charlie" schtick… I just don't.'

I stared at her blankly. Not only was it not what I was expecting, I didn't really know what she meant.

'You're not a victim, Charlie, in fact you're a very selfish woman, in many ways.'

'What!' I was astounded. I very much begged to differ. 'I'm up to my ears not in my shit, but in trying to sort out other people's. How is that selfish?'

'Because you want to do it,' she said, exasperated. 'You're not doing it for them, not out of the innate goodness of your heart.' She continued, 'You like solving other people's problems, don't you, Charlie, because it suits you, you like interfering. I think you even enjoy the violence you seem to attract, like a magnet. Above all, because it means you don't need to think about your own difficulties… and you're good at it, I'll give you that. Shall I go on?'

We drove up the elevated section to drop down onto the M25 London orbital, for once relatively traffic free.

'By all means,' I said indifferently, and shrugged to really prove I didn't care what she thought. But I did. I respected her, and her opinions, too much not to.

'Okay, I will…' Damn, me and my big mouth. 'Let's take your restaurant, Charlie. You're forever banging on about how hard you work, how many hours et cetera, but face it, you love being your own boss, you can do what you want. Work when you want, and when you don't want…'

'It's almost as if you're calling what I'm doing in Scotland a holiday…' I protested.

'For any sane person, no,' she laughed, 'for you, yes… You love investigating people and you love cooking. You use food as a double-edged tool, Charlie, you attract people with it – and you distance people with it.'

We were turning onto the M40 now. I could feel the car vibrate as Anna put her foot down to speed up, no cameras on this bit of road.

'And doubtless there's some man stashed out there up in Edinburgh?' she added. 'For your entertainment?'

'Yes,' I muttered, thinking of Gav. 'Kind of.'

We were driving past Beaconsfield now. Soon we would be on the backroads leading to the village of Hampden Green.

244

'What was it you said about men, Charlie?' she said innocently. 'Ah yes, I remember. "Men are like ovens, you should always have two of them on the go, in case one malfunctions." It was supposed to be a joke, but y'know… grains of truth, eh Charlie?'

Well, it was true. But I felt I didn't want to admit it. I sat silently, sulking.

We finally pulled up outside my restaurant. I felt horribly deflated. Maybe it was what I needed to hear, but it wasn't what I wanted to hear.

'So, Charlie,' she said, 'less of the self-pity. You seem to have been put on this earth to do two things: cook like an angel and track down criminals like a blood-hound. I suggest you fulfil your destiny and stop moaning about it.'

Positive advice at last. I got out of the car. Weirdly, I felt better in some strange respect. Shriven, was that the word?

'Thank you for the lift, Anna and thanks for the character insight.'

'That's okay. Give my love to Andrea when you see him.'

I nodded silently, closed the door and watched her drive off.

How could she know these things?

Chapter Thirty-Seven

I walked into my kitchen yard, everything looked orderly. I patted a wheelie bin appreciatively. I noticed the rosemary in the tub was looking good and I pulled off the tip of one of the small branches and crushed the needle-like leaves in my fingers and inhaled deeply. It smelled so good.

I looked at my watch. It was only just gone nine in the morning. The kitchen door was locked. I unlocked it and went inside. I looked around. Once again, neat and tidy. There was a stockpot on the stove ticking over, and I peered inside, it was simmering perfectly.

I felt an overwhelming sense of gratitude sweep over me. This was my kitchen and my restaurant. Above was my flat, where Murdo was sleeping in his room and Patrick was on the air mattress in the living room. It was mine. It wasn't a swanky establishment like Number Three and it wasn't a beautiful Georgian terraced house in the centre of Edinburgh worth millions and it wasn't the Waldorf Astoria – but it was mine and I loved it fiercely.

I then felt a weird stab of empathy for Lorna. If my restaurant were threatened, would I kill to protect it? Yes

I would, in a heartbeat. With very little remorse. Maybe it's because I didn't have children, I'd become maternal over the Old Forge Café. But then I thought, no. I doubted Lorna had any affection for the building and its history; for her it was simply a step on the way to making money.

I thought of the looming, gloomy grandeur of the Moray Place Hotel with its Doric pillars and its huge sash windows and porticoes. It had a brooding presence which my place didn't have.

I checked the walk-in and the locker fridges. Everything perfectly labelled and day-dotted. I peered into a couple of unfamiliar tubs: 'Marinated Pork Steaks 01/Dec'. So, from Friday. It wasn't on the menu, must be a Murdo special. I sniffed: soy, honey and star anise if I wasn't mistaken. It smelled good. I replaced the lid and put it back.

I went into the cubbyhole where my office was. There was one of my jackets hanging on a hook, the one I change into if I have to leave the kitchen and go into the restaurant. You don't want to see the head chef emerge splattered with bits of sauce, jus, blood, whatever they've been cooking. Some things should remain behind closed doors.

I put this on now. It had my name embroidered on the white cotton fabric: 'Charlie Hunter, Chef/Proprietor'. I felt a surge of pride, tinged with arrogance. Why not? I can cook like an angel, Anna Bruce had just said so. Okay, so I'd cherry-picked that from the less flattering things, but I'll take what I can. I stood for a moment, breathing deeply, marinading in the glow of my achievements like the pork steaks in their soy and honey I'd seen just now in the walk-in.

I kicked off my Cuban-heeled suede boots, pulled on my

spare pair of Caterpillar work boots and went back into the functional part of the kitchen on the other side of the pass. There was an MEP list taped to its metal. It was a long list in Murdo's laborious handwriting. Like many chefs, spelling was not his strong point, he was so much better with a knife than a pen. As indeed was I.

I walked over to the huge stockpot and turned the gas off. I thought I'd strain it and then start reducing it; I'd begin work on his list until he appeared at ten. He'd appreciate it.

I wrapped an oven cloth around my hands to protect them from the hot metal of the handles and slid the pan forward from the back of the stove. It weighed a ton. I frowned. I'd have to fish out all the heavy bits in situ so only liquid was left, to lighten the load before I could even think of moving it. Then a voice behind me said, ''Ere, Chef, you wanna hand with that?'

I turned around. To my delight it was Lucy, Murdo's girlfriend.

It had been a while since I'd last seen her. She had a pretty face with shoulder length blonde hair held in a net with a cap jammed on top, cornflower blue eyes and a determined chin. You could immediately see that fools would not be suffered gladly or any shit taken. She was shorter than me – for a start she didn't have much of a neck; her head looked as if it had been just placed on her body, which was much heavier than mine, like a female shot-putter or hammer thrower. She was wearing chef's whites and a butcher's striped apron, her sleeves rolled up to reveal her powerful forearms.

'Lucy!' My voice full of pleasure.

We hugged each other, those strong arms crushing me against her massive chest.

She let go of me and walked over to the stockpot, lifted it effortlessly and walked it over to the workbench near the sink.

'That better?'

'Perfect, Lucy,' I said, and began ladling out the bones while she looked at the list. 'So how is everything these days?'

'Yeah, all right… I thought I'd give Murdo a bit of a hand before he comes down with Patrick.'

She switched the fans on and lit the oven. It gave a kind of welcoming whoompf as the gas ignited.

'How is Murdo?'

She laughed, her huge bosom wobbling as she did so. 'Prince Charming's still sound asleep up there, boys of today, got no stamina…'

As she checked the MEP list I reflected that she was all of two years his senior.

It was nice being back in my own kitchen and although it had only been a fortnight I felt almost a stranger in it.

Murdo and Patrick came down together at ten, and both greeted me enthusiastically.

'How's my home town treating you?' Murdo asked.

'Oh, fine,' I said.

'Have you seen the town spread out at night from the top of the Mound?' Murdo asked. 'It's magical.'

'Yeah, I have actually,' I said. I thought of the other night and shuddered. 'It's truly memorable.'

'I'm glad about that,' he said smiling. 'I love Edinburgh, but I'm no' sure I could live there any more, too many memories ken from when I was younger.'

At eleven I left them to it. We had fifty booked in for lunch and then in the evening he and I would prep for Tuesday's start of the Christmas Menu. We had no party bookings for the first week but I was replacing one of the meat dishes on the main menu with turkey and trimmings; the fennel and chickpea tagine with saffron rice would be the vegetarian option. It would save prep time, we'd get economies of scale, and hopefully it would cut any waste to virtually nil.

I went upstairs to my room in the flat above the restaurant. I checked the living room, it was untidy but relatively clean, liveable. I unlocked my bedroom door and threw myself down on my bed. Tiredness washed over me.

I pulled my boots off and napped for half an hour. When I woke up, I lay in bed, warm and safe, listening to the noises from the kitchen, filtering up through the floorboards. I stared at the ceiling that felt like just a few centimetres above my head after the grandiose height of my bedroom in the hotel.

It was fantastic to be home.

Chapter Thirty-Eight

The Moray Place Hotel had put up its Christmas decorations while I was away. It seemed a little late in the day but I guess all the drama had impacted on the festive planning, or possibly it had been Katriona's job. There was a tall tree in the bar, rather nicely decorated with white lights and gold balls, surprisingly minimalist. That was the only concession to the festive season, if you discounted the Michael Bublé Christmas album drifting from the speakers. Well, it was better than Slade or Mariah Carey, which was all I had been hearing blaring out of shop doorways.

I sat in the bar of the hotel, closed my eyes and recalled the conversation with Strickland that had taken place on my return to Hampden Green. When I'd debriefed him, he'd been gratifyingly concerned about my welfare.

'Are you sure you want to carry on, Charlie? This sounds like it might be getting dangerous.'

'Yeah, of course, those two meatheads…' I snorted contemptuously, 'probably just a one-off.'

'I'm not so sure,' Strickland had said. 'The Moray Place is worth money, people kill for less.'

'What have I got to do with that?' I asked. 'I'm only a temporary chef, the future of the hotel hardly lies in my hands?'

'It does if you find a murderer,' Strickland pointed out. It was clear to me that by 'murderer' he meant Lorna.

'I'll take my chances,' I said.

'Hello, Charlie.' I looked up from my phone, surprised to see Lorna. Speak of the devil. She had interrupted my reminiscences.

'A quick word?'

'Hello, Lorna.' I was sipping a glass of the exceptional house Cabernet Sauvignon that Annie had generously provided on the house. I was allowing myself just the one drink before bed.

'Sure.'

I put my phone down. Lorna was not wearing her usual black skirt, jacket and white blouse combo tonight. She was casual in pale blue designer jeans and a cream cashmere sweater that looked expensive even for cashmere. She was wearing white training shoes and looked very petite. Without her heels and the business clothes, which she kind of strapped on like armour I guess, she seemed softer and more vulnerable, maybe even nice. I wasn't fooled.

'I just want to check that you are definitely not taking up my earlier offer from a while ago of a permanent job here?'

I shuddered at the thought.

'That's right.'

'Well, on Friday and Saturday as well as next Tuesday, I've got a new head chef and sous to trial. Sorry about springing this on you at such late notice.'

I shrugged; good luck to them, I thought. 'I don't mind. So do you want me to guide them through the menu?' I asked.

She shook her head. 'I'm sure they'll cope.'

I blinked in surprise. No matter how good they were, I thought she would have wanted to show them the way things were plated and cooked for continuity purposes.

'Tomorrow of course we start the Christmas menu,' she said, 'so that's simplicity itself... they'll work round the other dishes okay.'

I shrugged again; well, it wasn't my problem. It was her hotel. 'Who is he? The new head chef?'

'He's a guy called Paul MacPherson, comes from a place called Villiers Terrace in Glasgow, they're rosetted. He's sous there, and he's bringing some junior with him, so they're used to working as a team.'

'Well, that's great news, Lorna.' I meant it. I was pleased that the kitchen would be in what looked like good hands.

'So, Charlie – you've got Friday and Saturday off as well as Tuesday. You needn't come into the kitchen.' She smiled. 'In fact, that's an order, don't come into the kitchen on those days.'

'Can I go back down south then? Since you won't need me for five days?'

She shook her head. 'No, I'd rather you didn't. Just in

case… I know they'll be fine but, well, as we all know, shit happens.'

'Okay by me, Lorna,' I said, I toasted her with my glass. 'Here's to my replacements.'

Chapter Thirty-Nine

Although I had been given the time off, the habit of a lifetime of getting up early was not easily shaken. I was up at 6.30 on Friday, the day of the new chefs' trial. I pulled my running clothes on, my ankle seemed to be healed now, and, holding my running shoes in one hand, since they were dirty and I didn't want to track mud over the hotel's carpets and make more work for the hard-pressed cleaning staff, walked down to the front lobby.

Craig was at the front desk, now decorated with some tinsel and a mini Christmas tree. Someone, I suspected Annie, had wrapped coloured fairy lights around Staggie's head and antlers. He didn't look happy about it. I knew the feeling, I don't like Christmas much either. Craig smiled shyly at me as I greeted him. 'Have a lovely run, Charlie.'

I ran out of the hotel into the street-lit circle of Moray Place. The enormous Georgian terrace with its grandiose pillars and porticoes was dark and forbidding, despite the lighting, and slick with rain. Quite a few of the ground-floor flats had Christmas lights and wreaths up. The occasional car drove past on the cobbled streets.

I headed down the terrace towards Stockbridge and then descended a steep lane that I guessed had once been a mews for carriages and then passed a couple of cafés and the cheese shop, which we used as suppliers. I reached the small river they call the Water of Leith. I stared for a moment at the Antony Gormley bronze statue of the man in stream, the water of the shallow river flowing around it. Here I ran upstream along the footpath by the side of the swollen waters.

I was thinking as I ran about last Wednesday's attack on me by the two young thugs. 'You'll rue the day… I've got friends…' Euan had threatened me, and Martin had been at pains to point out he did have violent acquaintances.

I didn't know how they had known I would be there. Maybe Euan had followed me from the hotel? That Braveheart could be a friend of Euan's, or at least an acquaintance, someone in the lunatic fringe of the men's group, would come as no surprise.

Of course, another possibility existed. It was Ellie who had set Braveheart and his mate on me as revenge for upsetting Gav. Calling him from the toilets to come and get me. But if Braveheart was Euan's friend from a men's group, how could she know him?

I resigned myself to being in the dark for the time being, hoping enlightenment would come eventually. But even if she hadn't been behind the attack, I reflected as I ran along the river path, I was no friend of Ellie's. I got back to the hotel, showered, changed and went down to the dining room for breakfast. It was the first time I had eaten in the place. I had cooked enough meals and sent them here so it was a peculiar sensation to watch the system in action.

Angelika and another waitress whom I didn't recognise were working the room. There were about ten other people in so they weren't busy. The dumb-waiter procedure worked well enough; when my Full Scottish arrived it was still acceptably hot. I suppose it only took under a minute for the plates lift to travel the relatively short distance from the kitchen straight up to the dining room, and as soon as it arrived they were taken immediately to the table. Toast was made by the waitresses in advance of the breakfast's arrival, and there was a table laid out with croissants and pastries, together with a fruit bowl and yoghurts. The restaurant manager was in charge of this. That had been Katriona but was currently being handled by Annie who was training up Angelika.

While I was in the restaurant I used the time to catch up on my correspondence on my phone and then idly I searched for Villiers Terrace in Glasgow where the new guy had come from.

'17 Villiers Terrace,' I read, 'is an award-winning 3-rosette restaurant attached to the hotel which is simply known as #17. #17 is part of the Cromarty chain of hotels owned by Michael Dundas and Ollie McDougall which includes Number Three in Edinburgh's St Andrew Square and a yet to be announced third hotel, currently under acquisition, also based in Edinburgh.'

So, I thought, you and Ollie are moving in downstairs then. I put my phone down. Another thought struck me.

Angelika came up to me to take away my plate.

'Was everything okay, Charlie?'

I smiled. 'It was great. Compliments to Martin, first class as always, and beautifully served, Angelika.'

'Thank you, Charlie.'

'Angelika,' I asked, 'did you work in the industry in Scotland before you came here?'

'Oh yeah, I was in Glasgow for two years in a restaurant in the West End, called Villiers Terrace. Why do you ask?'

'Oh, no reason, just curiosity I suppose.'

I watched her as she carried my plate back to the lift. It looked like Lorna was gradually filling the hotel up with her boyfriend's employees so that the takeover would be effortless. The key players would be in place. Manager, restaurant manager, kitchen team. Maybe they would bring in Gav to supplant Donald. I felt a twinge of sadness for him. I finished my coffee and went back to my room. I stood by the window and looked out at Moray Place, the pale stone almost a pearly grey and austerely beautiful in the watery morning sunshine of an Edinburgh winter's day.

I called Andrea; he answered immediately.

'Ciao, Charlie…'

'Hi Andrea, do you happen to know anyone in Edinburgh who can tell me about the hotel industry in Edinburgh?'

'Yes, I do.' I thought he would; Andrea was a tireless networker, he knew people in every corner of the business world. 'He's a financial journalist whose speciality is the hospitality industry. You'll have to buy him an expensive lunch though, if you want any information from him.'

'That's okay,' I said. 'I'll do that.'

'I'll send you his number and I'll call him, let him know who you are.'

'Thank you, Andrea. I'll buy you lunch too.'

'Where?'

'At my place, very soon.'

'And can I stay over?'

'You bet your sweet ass you can,' I said. I ended the conversation and stared some more out of the window. Nothing had changed down below in the circle of Moray Place. I opened my laptop and attended to some business matters relating to my own restaurant and then at 9.30 I went downstairs.

Craig was still sitting at the desk, looking fresh-faced and innocent. Would he survive the takeover? I had a feeling Gav would take an instant dislike to him. I thought he would find Craig a wimp, and make his life hell. There was a certain cruel streak in Gav, I'd noticed.

'Hello, Charlie!' Craig whispered as I walked past, then blushed.

'Hi, Craig.' I didn't stop to talk. I walked past Lorna's office and then down the stairs to the kitchen where I let myself in on the keypad.

Martin was cleaning down and mopping the floor ready for the arrival of the new head and sous chef.

'Hiya, Charlie, come tae see your replacement?' he grinned.

'Yeah,' I admitted, 'I'm kind of curious.'

I walked over to the glassed in cube of the chef's office and fiddled with the pc, basically pretending to look busy.

A few minutes later I heard the kitchen door open, the

sound of Martin greeting someone and the rattle of the fly chains as they passed through.

I stood up and left the office cubicle, a welcoming smile on my face for the new arrivals. I saw my breakfast chef, and looming over him a tall, thin guy in his thirties, with receding dark hair and a close-cropped black beard. He looked almost priestly.

Then the smile on my face disappeared. Not because of him. The new sous chef had stepped into the kitchen and was looking around proprietorially.

She noticed me and swaggered over, smiling sarcastically. 'Hello, Charlie,' Ellie said, 'this is our kitchen now.'

She pointed at where I had come in. 'There's the door. I suggest you use it.'

Chapter Forty

John Anderson, the financial journalist, was a nice guy. He was in his sixties, overweight, avuncular in a rumpled suit and rumpled grey hair to match. We were at the Stane Bothy, the restaurant where Murdo, my sous chef had trained. They were fully booked but when I had told them that Murdo was working for me, they immediately became more affable and found me a table. Murdo was one of those kids who could be bloody annoying, but he was essentially so sweet-natured that he tended to be forgiven his transgressions. They obviously remembered him with fondness.

The girl on the phone had asked after him with genuine affection and when I arrived I was given a complimentary glass of champagne, as was Anderson. He glanced at the wine list and ordered a Malbec. The Stane Bothy had made only a few concessions to the coming festival with the odd hint of tinsel. But I had spoken too soon, Frank Sinatra started singing *White Christmas*. My spirits dipped.

Anderson looked around him with approval. 'It's three months' waiting list to get a table here,' he marvelled. 'When did you book?'

'Half ten this morning,' I said, smiling.

'You,' he wagged a finger and chuckled, 'are an amazing woman, Charlie Hunter.'

A dark-haired waitress came over to our table. 'Compliments of the chef,' she said. 'Some canapés: these are confit duck vol-au-vents and this is a potato and leek velouté with a chive oil garnish.' The soup came in a tiny, black glazed bowl that looked Japanese in its styling and glaze, the chive oil a brilliant green emphatic line on the thick pale soup which, like its name, was a velvety texture.

'Wow,' Anderson said, his eyes glistening, 'I must come here more often with you.'

Over our starters, a haggis bon bon with a whisky sauce for me and a fishcake with cucumber and chilli coulis for him, he asked me how I knew Andrea.

'We're sort of an item,' I said.

'Lucky you, he's a wonderful man.'

'Tell me more,' I said. I was curious to see how Anderson viewed him. 'How did you meet him?'

'Oh God, it must have been about ten years ago. We were introduced at some corporate do in London and I needed some information on Nastro Azzurro who were then owned by SABMiller and then bought by Asahi.'

'Asahi own Nastro Azzurro?' It seemed strange that something so Italian should be owned by something so Japanese.

'Yes.' He looked at me wide-eyed at my financial naivety. 'Anyway, we kind of hit it off and he is so knowledgeable about the markets. Also, if he doesn't know, he'll find someone who does.' He refilled his glass. Anderson could pack it away, I reflected. He continued. 'The main reason I like him though is he's genuinely modest, I get to meet so many assholes who are convinced they're masters of the universe because they get a percentage for playing with someone else's money...' he rolled his eyes, 'and for God's sake don't let anyone tell you that the markets are a good indicator of anything, Charlie, they're driven by greed and fear.'

Over mains, confit duck for him, a hake dish for me, he asked what I wanted to know.

'The Moray Place Hotel,' I said.

He nodded. 'Andrea said you'd probably want to know about it. Well, currently it's owned by a consortium – Cobalt Investment who have forty-five per cent, and two individuals, Lorna Hobson, twenty per cent and the deceased David Holland, thirty-five per cent.'

'So if Lorna buys Dave's stake, she'll be the chief shareholder?'

He nodded. 'Yes, and she'll be fully in charge. Cobalt's stake is purely financial, they'll go along with whatever she says. An offer has been made by a company called Cromarty Hotels, it's on the low side but spearheading it is their finance director, who's well respected and its current manager, Lorna Hobson. They might get it at the price they want, there's been a bit of unease in the sector with the adverse publicity surrounding the hotel. Things like that spook investors.'

'I see.' So, Lorna was trying to buy it at a knockdown price in cahoots with her boyfriend. Nice to have that confirmed. Once she and Cromarty, the owners of Number

Three, bought it, she would then have carte blanche to do whatever she wanted.

They cleared our mains.

'And how was everything?' asked the waitress.

'Great,' I said.

'Exquisite,' murmured Anderson.

'Desserts?'

'I'll have everything on the menu!' he said. For a moment I think we both thought he was serious, but then he laughed and said, 'The Îles Flottantes, please.'

'I'm fine,' I said.

She walked away and he carried on. 'When I was looking into it, sniffing around, I discovered someone else is interested.'

'Who's that?' I asked.

'It's a company called Naphill Holdings. I heard that they were approaching Cobalt to buy their share... they're... oh, hang on.'

His dessert had arrived, followed shortly by the head chef, a guy called Jason Monckton, at least that's what he had written on his jacket in scarlet piping.

'And how is my young protégé behaving?' he asked me, apropos Murdo. Jason sat down next to me on the banquette. 'Don't mind me,' Anderson said. I got out my phone and showed him pictures of Murdo in my kitchen and some of the food he had made, and filled him in on what he'd been up to (omitting the drug abuse and the overdose that had nearly killed him).

'Does he still listen to that godawful music?' Jason asked.

Frank was now on 'Adeste Fideles'. I'd have preferred

Murdo's latest discovery, Darkest Hour to this, even if 'Perpetual Terminal' wasn't very seasonal. It was refreshingly free of the 'ho ho ho' factor.

'Oh yes.' I smiled, recognising a fellow sufferer. 'But I've grown quite fond of Cannibal Corpse, you should give "Chaos Horrific", that's their last album, a listen… I'll get Murdo to send you a copy.'

He laughed. 'I'll pass, thank you… good that the wee guy is doing so well.'

He stood up. 'Nice to have met you, Charlie.'

'And you.'

We shook hands and he went back to the kitchen. Our waitress returned with petits fours and two glasses of whisky.

'Compliments of the chef,' she said.

'My God, this is good,' Anderson said, inhaling the whisky with the same greedy air that Murdo used to stuff coke up his nose before he got clean.

'It's a twenty-year-old Macallan,' the waitress said. 'I'll tell Chef you appreciated it.'

'Appreciate it,' Anderson said. 'Put it in a skirt and I'd marry it, with no pre-nup…'

She left and I slid my glass over to him. 'You can have mine.'

'Are you sure?'

'Definitely.' Too early in the day for me.

'You're a wonderful woman, Charlie Hunter…' Anderson said, lifting my glass, 'Sláinte.'

'You were saying?'

'Ah yes, Naphill. They're a small company, just own one property, a pub called The Kings Head, weirdly profitable…

maybe it's a restaurant... are you okay Charlie? You seem a bit agitated.'

'Who owns it?' I took my glass of whisky back from him and took a sip. The burning liquid tasted good.

'Some guy called Graeme Strickland... Are you sure you're okay?'

Chapter Forty-One

I got back to my room about three in the afternoon. All I could think about was that treacherous snake in the grass, Strickland. Best mate my arse. He had wanted me as his eyes and ears in a property he'd been interested in. I knew kitchens and he trusted my judgement. He was using me to evaluate the state of the hotel and kitchen and staff. A financial report can only tell you so much, and any claims by Holland could be verified by me. If he was satisfied, then Strickland, with his name in the industry, would be able to raise the money needed. Then he and Dave Holland would own eighty-five percent. No wonder he wanted Lorna found guilty of murder. I was furious with his deceit.

I did some yoga breathing exercises to calm my raging heart and thought of other things. I wondered how lunch had gone, not that that was anything to do with me.

I was disturbed from my reveries by a hesitant knock on my door. I got up and opened it. Innes stood there, still in her chef's whites clutching a large sports bag in one hand and her knife box in the other. Her eyes were puffy and swollen, it was obvious that she'd been crying.

'Innes,' I said, 'come in...'

She did so.

'What's the matter?'

'I've just had the most horrible day of my life, Charlie, and on the whole my life has been fairly full of shit but this has been the shittiest of all those shitty days... by far...'

She sat down on my bed and I sat beside her with my arm around her as she poured out her tale of woe.

Arriving at work to find Ellie there had been horrible, and as the day went on, Ellie had got nastier and nastier to her. Basically criticising everything that she did, telling her that she was rubbish and, when the chef's back was turned, saying sotto voce not only was she a useless chef but she was crazy too, like her pathetic, insane mother.

'What did the head chef do or say about this?' I asked.

'He didnae ken the extent of what she was saying,' she said, 'and near the end of shift she told me that this was only the start of things and that it would get a lot, lot worse so I'd better leave now.' She gestured at her bags. 'So I did. I walked out, went into the changing room, grabbed my stuff, shoved it in there and went out the back gate, came round the front and up to your room.'

'Well,' I said, 'let's not be too hasty, Innes...'

'I'm no' working for that bitch, end of!' she said, forcefully.

'I don't blame you, but Ellie is not yet employed here. Not officially. Take tomorrow off, call in sick and then come back to work on Sunday – Ellie's not working then, take Tuesday off and come back to work on Wednesday when they're gone and I'm back. You never know what the future will bring.'

DEATH OF A MYSTERY GUEST

'Okay,' she said doubtfully.

'There are some really nice people in this hotel,' I continued, 'it's not a hostile environment. In the kitchen there's Martin and Rosa, you like them…'

'Aye.'

'Ali of course.' I decided to leave out Euan (who had been off since I bollocked him citing 'stress'). 'And out of the kitchen, there's Donald, Annie…' she nodded and, encouraged, I went on, 'Craig… he seems okay.'

'He'll no' be pleased to see Ellie back,' Innes said. 'She and Katriona had really got it in for him, poor wee soul. They hate gays, but they don't pick on Donald because he'll give as good as he gets, it's poor Craig who gets it in the neck.'

'Look, Innes,' I said, 'you're a good chef and you've got the potential to become very good. Let me see if anything can be done about the Ellie situation, okay? Meanwhile, leave your knife box in my wardrobe and I'll bring it down to you on Sunday morning so you can get changed for lunch.'

I could see her eyes moistening, 'Charlie, you're so kind…'

I thought she was going to cry again. I gently shooed her out of my room.

Later that afternoon, my phone went. I looked at the screen, it was an unknown number.

'Hello, who's calling?'

'It's Euan.' His voice sounded sulky. I wondered if he had recovered from his 'stress' and was going to apologise

271

and ask to come back. I suddenly thought, he'd have to work under Ellie, how much would he hate that.

'What do you want?' I said. I wondered if he had heard about her and that's why he was calling.

'I thought I'd call you.' His voice had that familiar, slightly truculent, edgy tone to it that I was used to in the kitchen.

'Have you heard the news?' I asked him.

'No.' Just a flat 'no'. That was so typical of Euan, I thought. Zero curiosity in what was going on around him. Why was he calling then?

'I've got some information you'll be interested in.'

I very much doubted that.

'Really?'

'If you want to know who killed David Holland meet me at the Spoons near Waverley at half past ten on Sunday night.'

He ended the call.

Chapter Forty-Two

The bar that Euan had selected as our meeting place was on a road by the taxi entrance to Waverley, the central station for Edinburgh. I walked down Princes Street, empty at this time of night on a Sunday. The centre of Edinburgh was looking very festive, the Christmas lights stretched across the broad road and the Christmas Market, empty and shuttered now, in Princes Street Gardens. Above me, the Mound reared up, the same Mound that had saved me when I had outrun my pursuers nearly a fortnight ago. On top of the Mound was the bulk of the castle, everything a castle should be, crenellated and majestic, dominating the skyline and the city. To its left the former Bank of Scotland, a fantastic temple to Mammon, with a green dome and a golden statue on top. Floodlit at night, it looked gorgeous. No wonder people fell in love with Edinburgh.

Waverley, the station, was a kind of rabbit warren of a place, smelling of old soot, full of stairs and gantries and confusing signage. Running down to it was a kind of tarmacked maw, currently blocked to traffic, whether permanently or temporarily who knows, and at the top of that was the pub in a converted ticket office. It was okay, nothing special, and there I found Euan nursing a pint of lager.

I had pretty much discarded Euan as the instigator of my previous assault. I was absolutely sure Ellie lay behind it. Strickland's theory, or so I guessed from the other day with his remarks about money, that Lorna was behind it, was absurd. If she wanted me gone she could just tell me, and I would.

The pub was half empty. A selection of Christmas songs were playing over the speakers, the jaunty, up-beat happy music at odds with the depressed looking customers and staff. End of the night on a Sunday in a bar by a station is a pretty depressing experience.

Euan was sitting on a tall stool at one of those small high circular pub tables, wearing a dark blue anorak and crappy jeans with matching crappy trainers. He looked pallid and unhealthy in the bright light of the pub and somewhat furtive. I bought a Diet Coke and slid onto the stool opposite him.

'So, Euan, how are you?' I said to get the conversation started.

He considered the question carefully. 'Well, I've got bleeding gums,' he said after a while. 'Maybe it's gum disease, maybe I was just brushing too vigorously... I suppose I should go and see a dentist. I'm also going to see *Dune* again at the cinema but I wasn't that struck with it the first time I saw it to be honest.' He suddenly looked animated. 'There is so much unsaid in that film... I mean what is the science involved to get the spaceships across the galaxy? Where is it? Proper sci-fi deals with these issues, but not...' he shook his head sadly, '*Dune*.'

'Oh dear.' I tried to move him on to the real world and the 'important information' he had for me. 'Now...'

He held a hand up to silence me. 'I know what you were going to say. David Lynch touched on that with *Dune*, but Villeneuve dodges the issue.'

I reflected that's not what I was going to say at all, I hadn't got a clue what he was on about.

'And it's all very well riding the worms and using grappling hooks, but, Charlie...' he looked earnestly into my eyes. I realised with a guilty start that Euan was truly passionate about sci-fi. No wonder he'd got so cross with me trampling over his dreams. It was almost touching the way he cared so much. I almost found him likeable. A child who had never grown up, in a world he couldn't understand, taking refuge in fairy stories, which is what I think sci-fi is.

He carried on. 'A sandworm is (a),' he raised a finger to emphasise the point, 'enormously powerful and (b),' his second finger, 'enormously heavy. You wouldn't be able to control it with a grappling hook and a rope any more than you could use a piece of cotton to steer a horse...'

I sighed mentally. Enough was enough. 'Euan,' I said, 'who poisoned Chef?'

'Lorna.' He turned back to more important matters '... And worms live underground, their instincts are to dive down... they wouldn't obligingly plough along the top of the surface for hundreds of miles, would they?'

'Euan, I've had a long day... can you please tell me what happened?'

275

'In the kitchen, or on Arrakis?'

I looked at him in amazement, but for Euan this seemed a perfectly sensible question.

'In the kitchen?'

'Yes.'

'Okay.' He looked faintly surprised that I should prefer to hear about this rather than the imaginary planet.

'Lorna put those poisonous mushrooms in his tub in the walk-in.'

'When?'

'On the day before you arrived, the Saturday. He ate them for breakfast on the Sunday. Innes cooked them for him, I'm sure Innes didn't know they were poisonous...'

'Why?'

'It's obvious isn't it?' he looked surprised at the question. 'She wanted him out of the way so she could turn the hotel upmarket, we all know that, Charlie.'

I remembered what he'd said ages ago when we had discovered David Holland was dead: 'I wonder when the police will get around to finding Chef's real murderer, we all know it's a woman.'

'Okay, Euan...' I was not shocked or surprised by what he'd said, it all made perfect sense. But was it true? I'd certainly need very convincing proof.

'Do you know anything about the other death, the mystery guest?'

He shook his head. 'Absolutely nothing.'

'Have you got any proof, Euan?' The vital question. 'Proof of Lorna's guilt.' I added just in case there was any confusion.

'Yes.'

Thank God. 'What kind of proof?' I asked.

He nodded. 'I've started writing a book, well, to be accurate, it's a five volume space series...' Oh God, here we go... 'the Bachiotes, they're the aliens, they look like ropes, you know, the kind you get in a gym, thick ropes... You see, the problem with most aliens...'

'The proof?' I jogged his memory. Typical Euan to be side-tracked by sci-fi.

'Oh.' He looked hurt. 'When I get an idea, I use the audio record function on my phone. I'm a slow writer and you can't just start writing in the middle of service anyway. So, there's a sub-species of Bachiotes, the Jallaad, who look like leathery tea towels...' I mentally rolled my eyes, where was this going? 'I was going in the walk-in to photograph the big piece of pork belly on the meat shelf; it was on a tray, we hadn't cut it up yet. Cos it was about the right size and shape for an average Jallaad, I wanted to get some ideas...'

'So you followed her in?'

'I'm getting to that... don't you want to hear more about the Jallaad?' He sounded disappointed.

'In a minute.' I reassured him.

'So my phone was on camera mode, on video. I was going to record the meat; it was the audio function I was concerned about, and any descriptions that came to mind, like how it felt, how it smelled... You may not know this, Charlie,' he said sternly, filling me in on the mysteries of writing, as if I cared, 'but these things are important in books, it's the little details that people notice. Like how a Jallaad smells.'

Like pork belly, presumably.

'Go on…' I encouraged him.

'So I've actually got Lorna on film doing it, mushroom in hand.'

My eyes widened with excitement and interest. 'And she doesn't know you were doing this?'

'Why should she?' He looked cross. 'I didn't tell her I'd filmed her. To be honest I'd forgotten myself until later that evening when I made some Jallaad notes and looked at my phone and realised I'd actually filmed her doing it.'

I could picture it now in my mind. Lorna wandering into the kitchen, 'just checking the fridge, weekly review…' Maybe she wouldn't need to provide a reason, who would dare challenge her? Besides, Euan was always so wrapped up in himself it probably hadn't registered.

Then Euan wandering in, phone in hand, not an unusual sight. Lorna turning, hand in tub; he didn't realise he was filming her, his mind locked on his fictitious aliens looking like sentient leathery tea towels (did they even have hands?). She would have laughed it off if challenged, but she probably assumed he hadn't noticed, which indeed had been the case.

'Can I see?' I asked eagerly.

He shook his head. 'I haven't got my phone with me.'

'What?' I felt terribly cheated. And yet, what an Euan thing to do.

'I left it at home,' he clarified. 'I had a lot on my mind. Deciding to tell you was a big decision. I could get into a lot of trouble for this, maybe lose my job – but I guess I'm going to lose that anyway…'

Probably, I thought.

'But I'll come round to the hotel tomorrow and bring it with me, promise.'

'Good, and you'll be prepared to go to the police with this?' Not DS Bain, I thought, remembering him with his tongue in Lorna's mouth. Hardly blindfold justice.

He looked uncomfortable. 'Do I have to?'

'Yes, Euan,' I said firmly, 'it's your duty… One last thing, Euan. Why have you decided to tell me this?… And why now?'

He gave me his Euan look, the aggressive tilt of the chin, like steeling himself for the rejection or contempt from others that usually came when he opened his mouth.

'Because I'm sick of women getting away with things because they can. It's always the man's fault isn't it. Lorna thinks that just because she looks pretty nobody will ever suspect her. I told you once a woman had done it, no one believed me… well, now they'll have to, won't they!'

'I guess you're right,' I said. What a weird world he lived in.

He sighed. 'This is the Way.'

'I guess it is.' I now recognised this as a quotation from the Mandalorian, I slid off my stool. 'Okay, then Euan, thanks.' I held out my hand and he shook it, rather limply in my opinion, but you can't have everything.

'I'll see you tomorrow.'

'See ya,' he replied; he looked totally miserable. Maybe understandably so, it must have been a difficult decision to reach.

* * *

I walked out of the pub. The National Gallery and the Royal Academy at the base of the Mound were floodlit. Christmas music was coming from some party or other, drifting down from the Gothic skyline. It was incongruous. 'Last Christmas I gave you my heart...' coming from the high, dark gloomy buildings above.

Rather than walk along Princes Street, I thought I would walk along the road that led from Waverley Station to the top of the Mound and enjoy the panorama over Edinburgh while I savoured my victory.

I strolled down the broad, taxi-only, thoroughfare towards Market Street. It was quarter to eleven and the streets were totally empty. The music grew louder as I drew closer to the heights above. It was too loud for a pub, I thought, it must be students. I felt a tremendous sense of accomplishment. I had finally done what I had been sent here by Strickland to do, I had discovered who had killed Dave Holland.

Strickland had been right all along. Of course it was obviously Lorna and that was why she had been having that affair with DS Bain, leading him on to discover how his investigation was going. I'd make sure Euan took the phone and himself to another police station, far away from DS Bain. He was not going to be a happy bunny. If word ever got out he had been sleeping with the murderer in the case he had declared closed, trouble would be a mild word for what would engulf him.

That led me to wonder what had Lorna's role been in the death of Room 23. Had it been her, not Katriona, that Sinclair had been having sex with? Had she bribed him with her body to write that review, which basically played into her hands, saying that the hotel needed to modernise or die? It could almost have been dictated by her.

That thought led my mind into all sorts of odd, laby-rinthine possibilities. Sinclair dead while she, stark naked, held his laptop up to his unseeing, glassy eyes to open it with facial recognition, her fingertips with their brilliant red nail-varnish, nimbly racing over the keys while she wrote the review for him and pressed SAVE.

The smell of cannabis. I stopped dead in my tracks. I had just turned onto Market Street. I looked back. Sure enough there was Jobby Catcher guy walking towards me, no sign of Braveheart. He stopped and looked at me. Then he was joined by a man I'd never seen before from round the corner of Cockburn Street. Jobby Catcher pointed at me and they started walking towards me. No mistaking the menace there.

'Are you hanging up your stocking on the wall…' The song floated down from above.

Euan, you bastard!

Followed by, Charlie, you moron.

'So here it is merry Christmas, everybody's having fun….'

I turned and ran. I saw on my left a broad flight of steps that led straight up in the direction of the illuminated former bank building at the top of the Mound just down from the castle. There was a sign, 'The News Steps'.

I sprinted up the steps towards the top, on my left some sort of budget hotel. Immediately in front of me was one of Edinburgh's enormously tall Gothic tenements, this one with faux circular castle turrets at roof height. On the first

281

level of the stairs, like a landing, I paused and looked back. They were following, walking up the steps towards me, in no hurry. I frowned and then shrugged. Well, by the time they got to the top I would be gone.

How did they know that I would be there? It had to be Euan; the Lorna story was a lie, a lure to get me to the pub. The stairs, broad, shallow and smooth, albeit steep, veered right. I sprinted up them. I was nearly at the top of the News Steps now. Far below me, through the railings I could see Jobby Catcher and his mate still plodding up after me. In a moment I would be on the Lawnmarket below the castle then I'd run towards the university and hang a right and cut over to the unlovely Lothian Road and then back to my hotel via the Caledonian Hotel and the West End.

Just a few steps to go, then I halted and my confidence turned to frightened despair. The song continued, 'Will you land upon your head when you've been slayed...'

Stepping out of the shadows at the top of the granite steps, was Braveheart. He stood for a moment, framed against the skyline, then stepped down towards me. I was trapped between him and my pursuers below.

Chapter Forty-Three

I was rooted to the spot with terror. I suddenly, desperately, needed the toilet. Light from the illuminated splendour of the old bank building gleamed on the wicked-looking blade. They're called zombie knives I think. I shrank back against the wall. Braveheart took a step towards me, savouring my fear like a connoisseur the smell of a fine wine.

'Not so cocky now are we, hen?'

He grinned; he had a gold incisor that shone in the light. Then he paused and glanced round. I stared over his shoulder. I could smell smoke now, not weed but cigarettes. The bulky form of a man in a black raincoat had materialised behind Braveheart.

'Evening...' he said to the thug, conversationally. 'Out for a stroll are we?'

He was elderly, big and overweight, the buttons of the raincoat tight against his belly. He wasn't local; he had a London accent, a bald head glistening with moisture, with a few strands of hair combed over it, held in place by the fine rain that was beginning to fall. One large hand held a cigarette, the other was behind his back as if he were scratching an itch.

'On your way, fatso...' Braveheart said, gesturing with his knife.

The old guy didn't seem fazed by this. He cocked his head to one side.

'Oh, like that, is it...?' His voice expressing nothing more than mild interest.

I was aware of a blur of movement, and the next moment Braveheart was sprawled on the ground, his head making a loud thunking noise as his skull hit the granite step. The zombie knife had fallen from his unconscious hand onto the step by my feet. The old guy picked it up and examined it.

'Nasty,' he said, almost approvingly in his rasping cockney accent. In his right hand was the baseball bat that had knocked Braveheart out. Then, 'You okay, Charlie?'

'Cliff...' I nearly burst into tears I was so pleased to see him, 'but how—?'

'Just a minute Charlie.' He was looking over my shoulder, 'They with him?'

I nodded.

Jobby Catcher and his friend were coming up the steps. They halted, staring in astonishment at Cliff Yeats, cigarette in mouth, knife in left hand, baseball bat in right, dressed in black like a bald, overweight Angel of Death, their ring-leader lying vanquished at his feet.

Cliff Yeats pointed the baseball bat at them.

'Fuck off Bonnie Prince Charlie' he said to Jobby Catcher, 'and take Flora MacDonald there with you...'

They hesitated and Cliff shrugged and took a step towards them.

Jobby Catcher raised his hands, palms outstretched in a gesture of surrender and the two of them retreated down the steps.

'What the hell are you doing here, Cliff?' I stared at him in disbelief. It was like a miracle. I put my arms around him, felt his comforting bulk, smelt his familiar smell of Old Spice, cigarettes and lager overlaid with the damp smell of the wet fabric of his raincoat. I wanted to make sure that he was real as much as anything, and not some dying fantasy as I lay bleeding to death with thirty centimetres of metal inside me from the zombie knife. My arms just about encircled him, he was real enough.

Then a familiar voice from above us.

'I called him up here a couple of days ago.' It was Martin. Answering my question. 'I'll explain everything later, now's no' the time.'

Chapter Forty-Four

In the back of the black cab, Martin said, 'I was concerned about you after the attack. I had done time with Cliff. Before we reformed, we said we'd meet up, keep in touch, like you do, but, of course, we never did... so when you showed me that photo...'

Cliff chipped in. 'Yeah, Marty contacted me straight away, got my details off the internet. Told me you was in trouble. I came up.'

'He's been staying on my sofa,' Martin said simply and the two men grinned at each other like delighted schoolboys.

'We're here,' the driver said.

Granton, or at least the part where Euan lived, was not the nicest of neighbourhoods. The taxi had dropped us off on the corner of a small housing estate, the buildings low-rise, brown pebble-dashed. There was a communal grass area with three swings, two of them broken, and opposite a high metal fence, originally painted white but now rusty and peeling and heavily graffitied.

'It was his mum's flat where he lives now, but she died,' Martin explained.

Cliff and I followed him to a ground floor flat in a small, low-rise development with a low wall and a scrubby hedge. The front garden was a small, weed-grown plot. Martin unlatched the gate and we walked up the cracked concrete path to the front door.

The curtains were drawn but there was the flickering of lights behind the fabric. Someone was obviously at home.

I rang the bell. You could hear it but there was no answer. Martin sighed and rapped on the window.

'Let us in Euan,' he said wearily, 'or we'll break the door down.'

Then we heard footsteps and the sound of a chain being drawn. The door opened and Euan's pallid, worried face peered around the corner.

'What? What do you want?' his tone was one of aggrieved innocence.

'Your friends sent us,' Martin said. 'They told me you would explain why you wanted Charlie taught a lesson.'

'That's simply not true,' Euan looked outraged. I believed him then, it was the same look as when he had asked me how it was possible that in *Star Wars*, Padme didn't know Jar Jar Binks was a Gungan when they came from the same planet.

'Well,' I said, 'let us in and you can tell me exactly what did happen, Euan.'

'Okay then.' His voice was sullen as he opened the door. 'You can come in, but I'm not making you tea or coffee,' he added in a tone of defiance.

Led by Euan, the three of us trooped into his living room. It was every bit as depressing as one might have imagined.

288

There was a shabby, worn grey three-piece suite, a coffee table with magazines and fanzines heaped high, all sci-fi as far as I could see, *SFX*, *Doctor Who Magazine*, *2000AD*, Marvel comics. They were carefully grouped by title. He obviously hadn't done much with the place since his mother had died; there was still a calendar on the wall from 2018, Scenes of Scotland. I guess that she had died in May – that featured Glamis Castle. Either that, or he liked the picture.

There was an old sideboard with some artificial flowers in a vase and a framed photo of Euan in school uniform. Next to that was a stack of takeaway pizza boxes, flyers and free local newspapers. He had arranged them in order of height and size. A large flatscreen TV hung against the wall, a cable connecting it to a DVD player, and a bookcase full of sci-fi films. I knew they would be alphabetically arranged. I wandered over; they were.

'So what do you want?' he said truculently.

I figured that I'd be better off talking to him alone.

'Could you wait in the kitchen,' I said to Cliff and Martin. The latter nodded and the two of them vacated the living room, leaving me with Euan.

I sat down. 'Take a seat,' I said. No harm in establishing the parameters as to who was in charge here.

'Your mate from the men's group threatened me with a knife half an hour ago; he was backed up by another couple of guys.'

Euan shrugged, he made no attempt to deny it. 'And?'

I breathed deeply, I could feel my temper rising. 'It wasn't a prank, Euan. Now, you said it wasn't you, who was it then?'

He was silent for a moment then he said, 'It's all right for you, you're a Stacey.'

'I'm sorry?' What was he on about now?

'You're a Stacey… you're gorgeous… you've never had to struggle, not like me…' he said bitterly, 'people like me never get anywhere with girls, we are blackpilled…'

And gradually and then more and more quickly it all came out. How he'd never had a girlfriend, how he'd been bullied at school, how he'd resented Dave ('he was a Chad… all the women fancied him… Rosa, Innes, he could have his pick'). Ali had been right; he had been envious of Dave's success with women and then Ellie had come along.

'She wasn't a Stacey. Katriona was the one the men fancied, her not so much.' Then he told me how Dave Holland had fired Ellie for her attitude. He'd noticed how she was bullying Innes. 'I think Ellie was jealous of Innes, she was a Stacey, one hundred per cent and she was the one who had the power…' Then, in a rare moment of reality he mentioned that Innes was a lot better than Ellie as a chef. 'Ellie had even tried it on with Dave; she got nowhere. He didn't fancy her.' So another reason to hate Innes. Humiliated, then fired, Ellie had turned to Euan for revenge.

'She gave me the mushrooms. She said they'd make him sick, it was supposed to be just that… and if I did, she'd sleep with me. She even showed me her boobies…' His eyes widened. 'I'd seen boobs often enough' – he waved a hand at his TV – 'on pornos… but never real ones… my God…'

He'd done as she asked, then Dave had died as a result.

'That wasn't in the script. That was hardly my fault, was it?' Back to being a victim again. 'And meanwhile I'd introduced Michael Robertson to Ellie, he was my friend from one of the men's group I belong to, the guy in the kilt. Then she backed out of our deal. She started going out with him. She could control him, you see.'

'And why me? What has she got against me?' I asked.

'For a start, cos you're a Stacey and she's not,' he said. 'She's had the hots for Gav since she saw him. She got nowhere, then you come along and bang, you're in his bed. Lorna thinks you're God's Gift, that would piss her off. Katriona must have told her.' He looked around in his familiar way, slightly aggressive as if someone was going to challenge him. 'Ellie's envious of you. You're successful in the kitchen, you've got your pick of the men, things she doesn't have. That's why she hates you. She told Michael to cut you, bring you down a peg or two.'

So now I knew. Euan obviously felt no guilt. None of this involved him, in his view.

'And why did you call me to meet you at the pub tonight? If you'd fallen out with her after she started dating your mate?'

He took his phone out. 'Cos of this.'

He went to his photos and showed me the screen. A fully naked Ellie this time.

'I'll give you this,' the accompanying text read. Fingers helpfully pointing. 'Just get her there...'

'So you did?'

He nodded. 'Then I called her after you left, told her I'd done what she said, I wanted to claim my reward.' He frowned angrily. 'You know what she said? She said she never wanted to see me again, that I was pathetic, that I wasn't a real man… and she wouldn't do it with me if I were the last man on earth…Well' – huffy look – 'I thought, typical woman. Then I had another thought: I'm not taking this. That's why I'm telling you.'

I felt a surge of excitement 'Will you go to the police?'

He nodded. 'Yeah. I'll tell that DS Bain how I did what I did and who made me.'

'Let's maybe not go to DS Bain,' I said, 'let's go to a different police station.'

'Ok, there's one just round the corner.'

'That'll do,' I said.

'Ok. Fine.'

Good, I thought, then, no one will believe him. Ellie would just say he's lying. There's no proof that she made him do it. I guessed a good defence lawyer could come up with an innocent explanation for the naked text. And there was no doubt in my mind that Euan had been acting under duress. Thirty-odd years of sexual frustration and he was one step away from entering the Kingdom of Heaven and Ellie controlled that gate. How could he do otherwise? I still didn't like Euan but I didn't want him carrying the can for Ellie. I thought to myself, I'd better get in touch with DC Carmichael, just to be on the safe side.

Then Euan spoke. 'You remember when I lied to you about Lorna and how I'd recorded her putting those poisoned mushrooms in Chef's special tub?'

'Vividly.'

He smiled, picked up his phone. 'Listen to this.' He pressed a button and I heard Euan's voice, with that slightly hollow, tinny quality that you get on a dictation, or voice memo, app played through the loudspeaker on the phone.

'Izor 3 sprinted across fine sand of Skerrandarra towards the open, dented door of the shuttle.'

I looked at Euan. 'What?'

'This is what I was dictating at the time, just be patient.'

'He could hear the laboured sound of his own breathing from the partial ALF…'

Euan paused the recording. 'That's Augmented Lung Function… the atmosphere of Skerrandarra is not that of Earth, this is a detail that so many sci-fi films get completely wrong…' His voice was cross now, 'how many films have we seen where they land on an alien planet and they can breathe the atmosphere?' Truculent look again. 'Well, I ask you, is that credible? No…'

'I guess so…'

'Izor 3 could hear—'

'Hello, Euan… I've brought the special mushrooms for you…' A woman's voice.

'Are those really poisonous, Ellie?' Euan's voice, sounding both petulant and doubtful.

'Yeah, they'll give that arsehole the shits really badly, he'll be boking his guts up too… here, take them.'

'Won't Dave know?'

'He won't know… Little Miss Big Tits will cook them for him, and he'll get what's coming to him.'

'They won't kill him, Ellie, will they?' Euan sounded anxious.

'Who cares if they do? It's what the big arsehole deserves the way he's treated me. I hope they do!'

'Och, I don't know, Ellie...'

There was a pause; Ellie's voice dropped to a husky kind of whisper. 'Speaking of tits... do you want to see mine... oh, I see you do... here, you can do the buttons...'

'That's me, taking her jacket off,' Euan said proudly. I really didn't need that detail. He pushed the phone with a finger; Ellie again.

'So when are you going to do it?'

'Tomorrow...' Euan's voice, 'sure they won't kill him?' Nervous laugh.

'Of course not, they'll just make him sick... now don't let me down and you'll get a whole lot more... I'll show you the rest... and then some.'

Euan stopped the phone. 'That's recording one. I have two more, I think the police will be interested in that, don't you?'

I nodded. 'I do indeed.'

'Tomorrow I'm going to Drylaw Police Station...' he hesitated, 'will you come with me?'

'Yes,' I said, 'I'll come with you, Euan.'

Chapter Forty-Five

At 9 o'clock on Tuesday I was knocking on the door of Lorna's office.

'Come.' Imperious as ever. I walked in. She looked me up and down in frank astonishment. I was wearing my chef's whites.

'What is this, Charlie?' she asked, the expression on her face would best be described as irritated. I knew she'd be cross when she saw me; she'd told me not to come in and here I was. She was not used to being disobeyed. 'Didn't I make myself clear the other day? What do you think you're doing?'

'Digging you out of the shit, Lorna,' I said.

She frowned. 'What do you mean?'

The TV monitor on her wall now flicked from the bar area where Annie was crouched by the glass fridges on the rear wall, bottling up, to the reception area. Four police officers were walking in, two of them I recognised, DS Bain and DC Carmichael. Two uniforms brought up the rear.

DC Carmichael had tipped me off. After Euan had disappeared into the clutches of the police, I had called him on the number he'd given me when we first met. I didn't entirely trust Bain; I wanted to alert Carmichael whom I trusted, just in case Bain tried to hamper things.

I pointed at the screen of the monitor. 'That's what I mean.'

I saw Donald leaning over the desk talking to them and then he nodded and picked up the phone.

'Lorna, could you come to the front desk please, the police are here.'

'What's all this about?' Lorna turned to me. For once her composure was shaken and she looked worried.

'They're here to arrest Ellie and take her in for questioning.'

'What for?'

'The deliberate poisoning of David Holland. I guess the charge will be either manslaughter or attempted murder, depends on the Procurator Fiscal, I believe.'

She looked at me. 'I see what you mean by your remark earlier.' She didn't sound very grateful that I'd volunteered my services to stand in for Ellie rather than let the whole service crash and burn.

There was a knock on the office door, then it opened; it was DS Bain.

'Hello Lorna,' he said, while nodded politely to me. 'Ms Hunter... Lorna, we need to speak to a member of your staff. If you could lead us down to the kitchen...'

Lorna nodded with resignation.

'Of course, Detective Sergeant.' She glanced at me. 'Mind if she comes too?'

Bain shook his head. 'No.'

We all formed an orderly queue in front of the door to the stairs. Lorna first, then the two detectives, then the two uniforms, then me bringing up the rear. We all trooped down the stairs, a pause while she punched in the code on the keypad to unlock the door, then into the kitchen.

On the other side of the pass was Ali, who stopped washing the pan he was holding and stared at the six of us with astonishment. At the stove was the tall, balding figure of MacPherson with his back to us; he hadn't heard us come in over the roar of the fans. There was no sign of Ellie.

Then the door to the walk-in fridge opened and she emerged. She stood momentarily in the metal doorway staring at us, her jaw slack.

Bain walked around the pass flanked by the two uniforms. 'Eleanor Smith?'

'Aye.' She scowled.

'I'm arresting you on suspicion of involvement in the death of David Holland... anything you do say...'

As he read out the caution and one of the officers hand-cuffed Ellie, she glared at me with pure hatred.

As she walked past me handcuffed to the officer she shot me another malevolent glance. 'You carroty bitch...'

I smiled sweetly at her. 'My kitchen now, I think.' I walked around to the business side of the pass and patted it proprietorially.

Ali and I grinned at each other. 'Welcome back, Chef,' he said.

'Thanks Ali.'

Then Paul MacPherson walked up to me with a bemused expression.

'I've seen a lot of things in kitchens in my time, but this...' he shook his head wonderingly, then said to us, 'Would somebody please tell me what the fuck is going on?'

Chapter Forty-Six

The Tuesday lunch and evening service had gone well. MacPherson was an exemplary chef.

'No hard feelings?' I had asked after I had given him a condensed version of events.

'No, not at all,' he replied. 'I hardly knew the girl. I was in Glasgow until last week when Ollie McDougall got in touch and asked my head chef to send someone over to run the kitchen in this hotel that they're acquiring. The head chef at Number Three said he could spare Ellie; this would have only been the second time I had worked with her.'

'What was she like?' I asked, curious.

'Honestly?' He grinned. 'She was shite, I'm glad to be shot of her. And when she wasn't cooking badly she was droning about how good she was and how she was going places.'

You learn a lot about your co-worker during a service.

'Well, she is now,' I said.

So we'd worked the Tuesday lunchtime and the evening service amicably together. After work I had found a message on my phone from Lorna asking me to join her in the bar.

'Well,' she said as she poured me a glass of wine from the bottle on her table, 'thank you for holding the fort... no hard feelings?'

I shook my head. 'No, none.'

'I don't mind telling you, this has all come as a bit of a shock, and now I don't really have much of a kitchen team left.' She looked hopefully at me.

I shook my head. 'I'll work until I said I'd leave, Lorna, but no longer.'

'But what am I going to do?' she asked, almost tearfully. 'Innes is unhappy, she's made that clear... she probably won't be back. Euan's in prison on remand, and you're leaving in a couple of weeks... I'm feeling kind of scunnered.'

'Call Innes,' I said. 'She'll come back now Ellie's gone, promote her to sous – she's good enough and she knows the menu. Keep Paul MacPherson on as Head Chef, I'm sure your friend Ollie will okay that...'

'How did you know?' she almost whispered, 'about me and Ollie?'

'I think all your staff probably know,' I said brutally.

'Any more ideas?'

'Give Martin a pay rise, a generous one, backdated to when I arrived. He'll help out until you get a new apprentice. Then you'll have a good enough team. You've got along without a sous until now, you can carry on without a junior sous. Innes is worth two Euans and then some.'

'Okay,' she said, quietly accepting my suggestions. Her

atypical humility showed me just how shell-shocked she was by all of this. I guess it was because it had happened outside her control. 'I'll do that.'

'Good. I'm going to bed now, it's been a tiring day.' I stood up. 'Oh, and Lorna, one thing...'

'Yes?'

'When you call Innes, don't just apologise... grovel, she deserves it.'

Chapter Forty-Seven

I dozed on the early morning Sunday flight to Heathrow. It was eight days before Christmas. The kitchen was running smoothly; Lorna had done as I had suggested and I had found time to do some leisurely Christmas shopping for my staff. I hadn't a clue what to get Andrea. Maybe I should make a gigantic, hollow Christmas pudding and burst out of it scantily clad.

Jess was there to meet me at Heathrow. She told me as we drove out of the airport towards the M4 that she was back until January. The Masters was going well but she was glad of the break from the rigours of eight-hour days doing whatever IT people do in their labs.

'How's Francis?' I asked

'Happy as a sandboy, as he would say.' Jess grinned. 'So excited for Christmas; have you got him a present?'

'Yes, I got him something in Edinburgh. A sweater and a boxed set of the Topaz novels.'

'Well,' Jess commented, 'the speed he reads, that'll keep him going for several years.'

'And I got tickets for Murdo for Cannibal Corpse, they're

playing the Oxford Playhouse. I got two, so Lucy could go.'

'Lucky Lucy, she'll really thank you for that,' she said sarcastically, followed by, 'Look at that tosser...' as a Volvo 4x4, an SUV on steroids, pushed its way in front of us.

I reflected she was probably right, but he'd find a friend who shared his musical tastes. I was feeling so elated, so pleased with myself that nothing could dent my good humour.

'Are you back for keeps?' Jess asked.

I shook my head. 'No, I'm going back for a few days just to make sure the new kitchen brigade is working okay.'

'You're too conscientious.'

I shrugged. 'Maybe, but I don't like leaving a mess.'

Later that day I went round to see Strickland at 11 o'clock. For the past week and a half my conversations with him had been terse to say the least. I had told him about the arrest of Ellie, but I hadn't told him that I'd found out about his financial schemes.

Strickland's restaurant, The King's Head, had been a spacious, Victorian-built pub. Now it was a luxury restaurant. The kitchen had been extended out at the back to fit everyone in. My kitchen staff were me, Murdo and Francis, when he wasn't washing up. Strickland had about fifteen chefs, a core of six or seven and then a number of trainees, stagiaires, who were interns and either worked for free, learning from the master, or were paid a pittance.

I knocked on the door and was let in by the maitre d', an affable young guy, quite posh, called Tristan.

'Charlie!' he cried, 'fantastic to see you!'

'Hi Tris.' We kissed. 'Is Anton Mosimann in?'

'You betcha…' He led me through into the restaurant where Strickland sat reading a copy of the *Hotel and Caterer* in print form. My restaurant is pretty, easy on the eye. If she were a girl she would be the sweet-natured and kind of attractive person you might find behind an upmarket bar or the counter of your local artisanal cheese shop (assuming you live somewhere posh). Strickland's was more that of a successful career woman going to a party attended by the King. For some reason I thought of Lorna. Starched linen, a couple of amazing floral arrangements, lighting to die for. One of the major backers of his restaurant was a prominent interior designer and it showed, but in a good way.

He greeted me and I sat down opposite him. Strickland's short dark hair was greying now but with his imperious gaze and rock-solid arrogance he had the magnetism of a rock star with the looks of a Roman emperor (not one of the crazy ones.)

'Charlie will have a double espresso,' he said to Tristan, 'and I'll have the same.' He yawned. 'Sorry… late night last night.'

'Partying, Graeme?' He did look tired, there were dark shadows under his eyes. He shook his head.

'We got spanked last night, very busy… there's a hole in the MEP list you could drive a bus through. I was making canapés and petits fours until two in the morning.

The maitre d' materialised beside him in that discreet way, like a ghost solidifying, that restaurant managers in exclusive places have. He reverentially placed our espressos down on the table.

'Hey, Tris.'

'Yes Graeme?'

'Go and get Charlie one of those salmon canapés I made last night.'

'Certainly.'

Tristan disappeared towards the kitchen and I told Strickland the news about what had lain behind the death of his friend. He shook his head sadly. 'Killed by a disgruntled employee. What a way to go... I remember when I was his apprentice at Chez Marie – she was the owner, this crazy French woman.' He laughed. 'He taught me how to cook, and Marie, she was quite old, she'd have been in her forties...' A dreamy look stole over his face, 'She taught me...'

'Thank you, Graeme,' I said icily. I had no wish to hear the other things Marie had taught him. 'There was one other thing I found out.'

'What was that?'

'That you're buying the place.'

'That's not true Charlie.' He put his coffee down and smiled at me.

'No?'

'No, I bought it yesterday.'

Chapter Forty-Eight

'Look, Charlie, I won't lie to you. I could have been more transparent but...'

'But you lied to me!' I protested.

'No. Dave was my first head chef and my friend. That man taught me so much. Sometimes we'd be up until four in the morning prepping, and sleep on the restaurant floor. The cleaners would hoover around us. Six-day weeks. I had Sundays off; God it was hard. But he didn't have a temper, never a tantrum or a hissy fit.'

He sighed. 'I genuinely thought you were a good fit as his sous, and you would have learned a lot. Yes, we were going to buy the place together, but now he's gone.' There was no room for sentimentality in Strickland's world. 'I bought his shares from his brother. Cobalt have been on board for a while. So you see, I didn't lie, I just didn't tell you the whole truth.'

Well, that was up there as an excuse with 'I didn't inhale'.

He was interrupted by Tristan bringing me the canapé. I almost gasped in wonder.

It was a transparent cup of jelly, about the size of a small fairy cake. Inside was a circular puck of orangey pink and balanced on top, like a little bunch of miniaturised black grapes, some caviar and a couple of strategically placed microgreens. It rested on a small circle of bright green foam.

'Oh my God, it's beautiful,' I breathed.

'Eat it,' he ordered.

I picked it up with my fingers. It was so light, the jelly cup that held the salmon mousse was so thin and delicate. I bit into it, the three textures, the cool gelatine flavoured with… 'What's the case flavoured with?' I asked.

'Dashi, gives it that umami kick.'

The creamy salmon mousse with flecks of flesh in it for texture and then the salt, fishy taste of the caviar and the wasabi hint from the foam.

'It was hard getting the wasabi foam right,' Strickland said, 'didn't want to overpower things.' He smiled complacently. 'I think I did it.'

It was the kind of food you might serve God if he rocked up at your restaurant.

'My word, Graeme…' I was speechless with awe, at the skill, the delicacy, the attention to detail and the culinary expertise that had gone into something so exquisitely small and ephemeral. It was miraculous.

'I know,' he said, smiling. He knew how good he was. 'You don't need to say anything.'

So I didn't. I drank my coffee and stood up. I looked at him. He was a bastard but he got away with it because he was a genius. And he knew it.

'Do you forgive me?'

308

I shook my head in exasperation. He knew I would.

'I'm finishing in a week, then you'll have Patrick back.'

He shook my hand formally. 'Thank you, Charlie.' He looked at his watch. I knew my time was up.

'See the lady out, Tris,' he commanded, smiled at me, nodded goodbye and disappeared into the kingdom of his kitchen. Soon to be joined by another, north of the border.

I walked back across the Common to my own restaurant. Inside my kitchen Murdo and Patrick were hard at it.

'I've just been talking to your boss.'

Patrick paused in his measuring out of ingredients for Yorkshire puddings. We had forty booked in for lunch, that was forty Yorkshires plus fifteen in case of YPD, Yorkshire Pudding Disaster, that is, the pudding not rising properly, burning, or sticking to the tray. Batter for fifty-five then, a lot of eggs.

'Oh, yeah? How is Napoleon?' I was pleased to see that it wasn't just me who thought he was like the egomaniacal Corsican tyrant, another crazed short-arse genius.

'Oh, he's in a relatively good mood. I found out who was responsible for his mate's death,' I said, somewhat immodestly.

'Good for you,' Murdo said. 'What about the other one, that reviewer, Mike Sinclair.'

Patrick paused in his weighing out the flour for the Yorkshires, turned and asked, 'Mike Sinclair, reviewer; did he work for the Brook-Schlager people?'

'Yes' I said. 'Why?'

'He was a piece of work,' Patrick said angrily. 'I was a

309

buffet chef at a luxury hotel in Devon when I was sixteen, he was down there reviewing it. He invited me up to his room, to talk about my future in catering. I was thrilled. I thought he was going to get me a job at the Ritz or something... bastard just wanted to have sex with me... started touching me up and got really nasty when I told him to eff off... said he'd get me sacked if I didn't, then he tried to grab me.'

'Really?'

'Oh yeah.'

'What happened?'

'I hit him, gave him a black eye. I reported him to the restaurant manager, but she didn't do anything; no one wants to upset Brook-Schlager. C'est la vie, my honour remained intact. Well, until I let the sommelier have his wicked way with me, but that was consensual... that batter look okay to you Chef?'

'Oh fine.'

But my mind was elsewhere. I knew who had killed Room 23 now, and why.

Chapter Forty-Nine

My walk from the West End where the airport tram had dropped me off towards the Moray Place Hotel found me in thoughtful mood. Part of me wanted to let sleeping dogs lie, but I knew that I couldn't. An innocent woman, Katriona, was going to stand trial for murder and I could stop it. It wasn't a job I had much stomach for, but I had no choice.

I walked off the main road into Randolph Crescent, an architectural amuse-bouche leading on to another square that led on to Moray Place itself where the hotel stood. I lingered at the entrance, looking at the elegant curve of the buildings, the Doric columns like an Athenian temple, their beige sandstone streaked with the accretion of soot and pollution, giving it a dark mottled effect.

I walked up the steps into the lobby of the hotel. Craig was on reception; he smiled at me warmly.

'Charlie, good to see you.'

I looked around, it was 3.50 and there was nobody about.

'Craig, can I have a quiet word with you?'

He looked up at me from behind the reception desk, his

gentle, androgynous face worried now. I don't blame him. Nobody ever wants a quiet word for a pleasant reason.

'Um, okay, please come in the back office.'

I walked through the hatch of the reception desk and we both went through into the back room. I sat down in the chair in front of the computer desk and waved a hand at the sofa. 'Have a seat.'

He did so, his slim hands with their long fingers nervously intertwining themselves. He looked at me with anguished eyes under long lashes. 'Is something the matter?'

'I know about Mike Sinclair, Craig,' I said, 'but I'd like to hear it in your words, please.'

He took a deep breath. 'I knew it would come out…' he whispered, and he tried for a devil may care laugh but it came out as a strangled sob.

'He tried to touch me…' he whispered.

'Mike Sinclair made a pass at you?'

He nodded. It was Patrick's story all over again. On Monday night Sinclair had called him for Room Service to have a drink delivered to his room. He had tried to kiss Craig. 'He was horrible, he was drunk, and old and he was high on something, he grabbed me… he was much stronger than me and he forced me down… he wanted me to… well, you can guess. I got free and I promised him if he let me go I would come to him on Tuesday but I wanted to be wearing nice clothes, look my best… the usual thing I guess' – he gave a wan smile, it was heart-breaking – 'and he accepted.'

On Tuesday he had tried to tell Lorna and she'd told him not to be such a cry-baby, that she'd had all sorts happen to her and she'd survived.

'She couldn't have been less sympathetic…' Craig said, sadly. 'Tuesday was horrible. I finished at midnight… he knew that. I saw him a few times during the day, he winked at me, blew me a wee kiss. I threw up twice… then midnight came and…'

'And you went up to meet your fate,' I said.

'No, he didn't,' a voice said from behind me. 'I did. I killed the bastard.'

Chapter Fifty

Donald sat down wearily beside Craig and said to him, 'You can go home now, Craig. Don't worry, nothing bad is going to happen, okay?'

Craig nodded and stood up. 'I'm sorry,' he said awkwardly, 'this is all my fault.'

'No, Craig,' I said, 'whoever's fault it is, it certainly isn't yours. Donald's right, go home and everything will look different in the morning, I'm sure.'

We both watched Craig as he left then Donald turned to me.

'I was listening outside the door,' he said to me apologetically. 'Poor Craig.'

'So, what exactly did happen, Donald?' I asked.

He smiled unhappily. 'Thirty years ago I was in Craig's position and I remember it like it was yesterday. Thing is, I've always had a lot of self-confidence whereas that poor wee mite doesn't.'

'That's true.'

'One of Craig's problems is he can never say no; he's a

people pleaser, he just wants everyone to like him. He can't stand up for himself. It's a terrible affliction to have. I knew something was up' – Donald sighed – 'I could see what was happening, how stressed he was, and I put two and two together. I heard him being sick in there,' he pointed to the door of the private bathroom they had in reception. 'I sat him down, he didn't want to tell me but…' he breathed out deeply, 'I can be forceful. I demanded he tell me what was going on and he did.'

'And he went to Lorna about it, I gather.'

'Only because I made him, but being Craig, he minimised everything. He said he was being sexually harassed but not the seriousness of it. I imagine she thought someone had stroked his bum or tried to feel him up, not semi-blackmail him into sex.'

'She should have done more,' I said.

He put his head on one side and looked at me doubtfully.

'You really think that she was going to upset Brook-Schlager? Would you have?' It was a very pertinent question. Would I? This place was her life. Would I have done anything different? I've fought off a lot of unwelcome sexual attention without any angst; would I have just told him to pull himself together and deal with it? Just like she had? Could I really throw the first stone?

'It's a good question,' I admitted.

'I went up to see Mike Sinclair myself… I told him that Craig was off limits but I wasn't. I took a bullet for the team, as they say.'

'Oh my God, Donald…' I gasped, 'how terrible for you!'

He smiled. 'It's not as bad as it sounds. I spent some

time on the meat rack as they say when I was a youngster. I didn't have to, but I had expensive tastes in those days. Anyway, put it this way, it certainly wasn't the first time I've had sex with someone I despised.' He frowned. 'Probably won't be the last either.'

'But what happened? Why did you kill him?'

Donald's face darkened. 'He showed me the review that he'd written, he was really out of it on the drugs that Katriona had sold him and booze... if he hadn't been popping Viagra on top I doubt he'd have got things up. Just before he passed out he called me an old, has-been queen. And I kind of boiled over.'

I didn't speak as he stared into space.

'When I saw that review I knew that my time was up here, and I love this hotel, Charlie. It's my life...' He added softly, 'Isn't that sad? But there's something about the Moray Place Hotel that gets under your skin. I don't want to leave. But with that review Lorna could use it as leverage with the other shareholders to sell the place to that consortium that owns Number Three and I'd be out. My face wouldn't fit. Neither would Craig's, or rather his attitude wouldn't. They're brash, he isn't.'

And so it had all been for nothing. Donald didn't know what I did – that he was about to acquire Graeme Strickland as a boss.

Another pause. 'So that old queen remark was the straw that broke this old queen's back.'

'But how did Katriona's hairs come to be in his bed?' I asked.

'Ellie is a nasty piece of work, as you've no doubt noticed.

Katriona's just as bad, she's very homophobic too. She left me alone, but she tormented Craig.'

I remembered the exchange that I'd overheard between the two of them when she'd reviled him as a batty boy.

Donald continued. 'Endless nasty remarks… and the other month she'd printed out a flyer from a hardcore gay S&M event at a members only club down in Brixton and put his name on it and left it on the reception desk for him to find. Several guests must have seen it before he noticed it. Nothing was said but he was sure someone would complain… she was horrible.'

'So you framed her?

'Yes.'

'How did you get her hair?' He bowed his head and addressed the carpet. I think he felt guilty about implicating her, but not about the killing.

'I went down into the waitresses' changing room just off the dining room. I know all the keypad combinations. I found a hairbrush in her locker… it was that easy.

'Then, after I'd put the hairs on him and in the bed, I went down in the dumb-waiter to the kitchen so I wouldn't be picked up on CCTV going down the stairs at one in the morning.'

The same method as Innes, I thought. He lifted his head and looked at me.

'So, now you know, what are you going to do, Charlie?'

Chapter Fifty-One

I had a message later that evening from Lorna. It asked me to meet her at eight the following morning.

I went down to her office at the appointed time. She was as immaculately turned out as ever, today in a black two-piece trouser suit, and a string of pearls around her neck. I wondered how she would react when I told her I knew who had killed Mike Sinclair.

'Thank you for coming, Charlie, and thank you for coming back to Edinburgh.'

'I don't tend to break contracts, Lorna, although I have been known to storm out.'

She smiled, somewhat bitterly. 'I know the feeling.'

She breathed deeply. 'I have had a shit weekend, Charlie. Ollie dumped me and the deal with Number Three is off the table.'

'How come?' I asked.

'Some member of staff at the Waldorf saw me with DS Bain and told Ollie. He was furious. Then he must have called the police and informed them of Bain and me. I'm guessing that, because Bain called me. He said he had been put on indefinite sick leave and that he was going back to his wife, that we were through and that he was going into rehab at Craiglockhart.'

'I'm sorry.' I wondered if it had been Ollie who had grassed the DS up, or if it had been someone else. I recalled my phone call to Carmichael; perhaps he was not as boyish as he looked.

'Oh, and then he told me Katriona was going to be released, on the murder charge that is. She still has to answer for the drugs but that's a separate issue. I gather there was not enough evidence for a strong case against her.'

I felt an overwhelming sense of relief.

'But you weren't really seeing Bain anyway,' I pointed out.

'No, but it's the principle of the thing. Dumped by two men in twenty-four hours and my business plans wrecked.'

I didn't need to ask which hurt the more. Both of those relationships had been business, not just pleasure.

'Well,' I said, 'the main thing is, you're still in control.'

I wasn't going to get involved with the Naphill Holdings story.

'That's true, and you're right – that is the main thing.'

But she was wrong about that.

The following day Graeme Strickland arrived.

Chapter Fifty-Two

On the Wednesday morning it was Strickland sitting opposite me at what had been Lorna's desk. He smiled in a kind of cruel, almost feline way at me as I walked in and sat down.

'So, you got what you wanted?' I said.

'Yeah.' He leaned back in the chair and stretched. 'Obviously I paid more than I wanted as I had to buy Dave's share as well, but maybe it's for the best. There's one captain now, not two running the ship.'

'Well, congratulations. Where's Lorna?'

'I gave her the day off, I think she's still in shock.'

'Are you keeping her on?'

He shrugged. 'May as well... she seems very efficient. Now, Charlie, what would your advice be, vis à vis the kitchen staff?'

'Paul MacPherson is good. Offer him the job here, give him a salary increase, he'll bite your hand off. He doesn't like where he is at the moment.'

'Mm, hmm, I see.'

'Next, promote Innes to sous chef. She'll be a fantastic

asset. Ali is great and Martin irreplaceable. Well, there you are. Paul, Innes, Martin and Ali, not to forget Rosa, it's a rock-solid kitchen team.'

'Okay, anything else?'

'Yeah,' I pointed a finger at him. 'You asked me to forgive your behaviour. I will, on one condition.'

He sat back in his chair and stuck his chin up in the air, Mussolini or Napoleon style.

'Name it.'

'Innes needs therapy,' I said. 'The help is available, but she can't afford it. The business can and the business needs Innes. You pay for that, for at least a year, and I'll forgive you.'

He must have been feeling guilty because he immediately said, 'Deal.' We both stood up and we shook hands.

'You've got a running kitchen team now, Graeme,' I said. 'I'll stay for a couple of days to oversee the transition and then I'll leave on Friday.'

'Thank you, Charlie.'

'I'll go down to the kitchen now... oh, one last thing; tell Donald and Craig their jobs are secure.' Now Katriona was free it would be up to Donald's conscience as to how he dealt with his crimes. I wasn't going to make it my call.

'You drive a hard bargain you know,' he grumbled.

'Yes, I do.'

I smiled and left his office. I was after all

Charlie Hunter
Bitch Boss from Hell
For all your catering needs

ABOUT THE AUTHOR

Photo credit © Alex Coombs

Alex Coombs was born in Lambeth in South London and studied Arabic at Oxford and Edinburgh Universities, and is a qualified chef. Alex lives in the Chilterns.

www.alexcoombs.co.uk